MY MISTRESS, HUMANITY

A Novel

ALSO BY CHUCK ROSENTHAL

Loop's Progress
Adventures With Life and Deaf
Loop's End
Elena of the Stars
Jack Kerouac's Avatar Angel: His Last Novel

MY MISTRESS, HUMANITY

A Novel

Chuck Rosenthal

Hollyridge Press
Venice, California

Hollyridge Press
P.O. Box 2872
Venice, California 90294

Cover Design and Drawings by Thomas Micchelli
Author photo by Gary Goldstein
Manufactured in the United States of America by Lightning Source

Publisher's Cataloging-in-Publication
(Provided by Quality Books, Inc.)

Rosenthal, Chuck, 1951-
   My mistress, Humanity : a novel / Chuck Rosenthal.--
1st ed.
   p. cm.
   LCCN 2002102738
   ISBN 0-9676003-5-9

1. Fantasy fiction.   I. Title.

PS3568.O8368M96 2002   813'.54
                        QBI02-701453

Softcover Original
11 10 09 08 07 06 05 04 03 02   10 9 8 7 6 5 4 3 2 1

For my father

For Gail

For Marlena

I opened my heart to the whole universe
and I found it was loving
and I saw the great blunder my teachers had made
scientific delirium madness.

—Roger McGuinn

My Mistress, Humanity

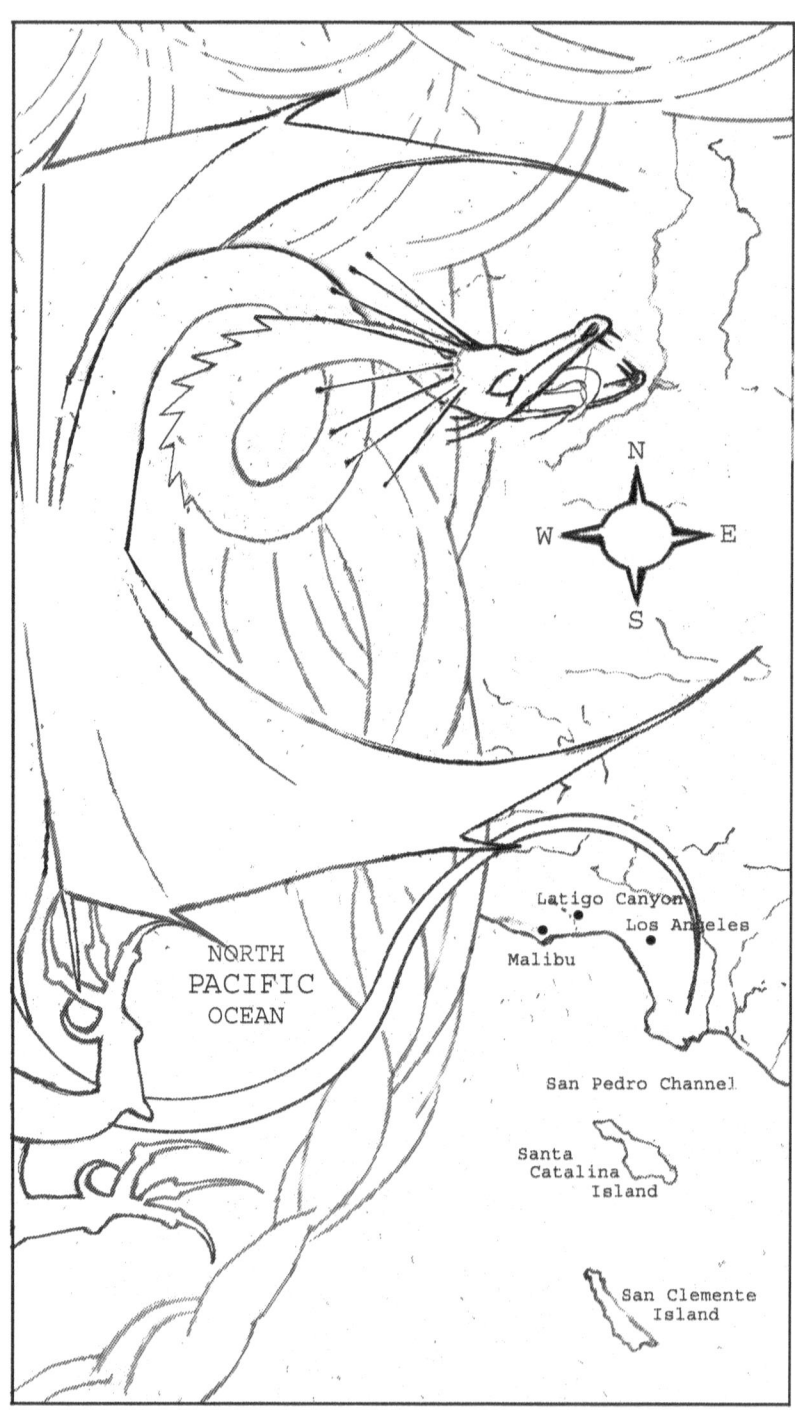

Hestor Zu

International Mars Exploration Laboratory
Amundsen-Scott, South Pole
Antarctica

October 8, 2015

Dear Charles:

For the longest time I felt a certain logic in living here at the end of the earth while I prepared, literally, to leave it. Now it appears absurd. Even as the Antarctic darkness begins to wane, there seems little sense now, even less hope. Yet those around me move forward with the routines of progress while the world, our world, crumbles under chaos. You do not know how badly I want to come home.

No one can leave, though supplies stopped arriving a month ago. Kevnev, the Commander here, says it barely matters. If we could survive on Mars, we can survive here. Antarctica is probably the safest place on earth. Yes, maybe the safest, but there is nothing here to live on but the animals we protect and raise in the bio-sphere satellite barns and what we produce in the greenhouses under artificial light. Besides, he is Russian and has both genetic and cultural dispositions for holding out in the snow and ice.

Our last recruits, who reached here in April, arrived for a mission already abandoned. Some brought old, portable, manual typewriters—Olympia, Smith-Corona—my new friend Paulo Clemente, an Italian glaciologist, brought an Olivetti—beautiful, hard, metal machines, almost ancient; their clicking and pounding in the night like the drums of some other, lost time. "For when it all goes," Paulo said. "You won't need manual typewriters when it all goes," I said to him. "You can write long hand." But if electronic mail is dead, we still have mail planes that can reach us from McMurdo. When there are no planes, we will have our power sledges, then boats and dog sleds. When it is all gone, we will rebuild.

We took our last Martian habitat training on the dry dunes just east of Ross Island over a year ago, so I marvel at these men and women who go about their daily training, preparing for weightlessness, plodding through the tasks of a bio-sphere, and traveling with manual typewriters for when it all goes. They won't be able to cart those things on board a ship to Mars. And there will be no ship to Mars.

You must let me know if you hear from El and Lisa. If a year ago, Los Angeles and New York were electronic suburbs, now they are three thousand five hundred miles apart. You, my love, are in LA, and our daughter and granddaughter are in New York. I am in Antarctica. I worry about them. And how I miss you.

This morning, in the first hint of gray spring, I dressed and walked to the hill above the compound and stared across the ice field, dreaming of California in October; the mist lying on the coast and drifting into the mountains, the dazzling spray of afternoon light spreading across the oaks and chaparral. I told myself, Charles, that if you had been prepared to give me this dream, this dream of Mars, and be alone for three years, then we would survive this, too, whatever its uncertainties. It is simply a matter of them remembering us down here, I told Kevnev. Then they will scrub the mission and let us return to what is left of our lives and our homes.

Is this the end, Charles? For so long we thought we might blow ourselves up, or that it might come from above, from beings who found us before we found them. We thought we might suck the air out of the sky with our folly, or that the oceans would rise, the mountains fall, that we might over-populate the earth, the solar system, or that a new plague would sweep over us. Who would have thought that the threat might be as enigmatic as our souls? That it would arise from mystery?

When Paulo Clemente arrived here, he said that his sister was in Rome when the Vatican burned. She told him that above the Basilica of St. Peter's a dark cloud formed in the sky, and before the lightning descended, for an instant the mist parted like black smoke and revealed an animal the size of a mountain hovering in the dawn. It breathed fire and fanned the flames with its wings.

"A dragon?" I said. "Your sister saw a dragon?"

My closest friend, the medical doctor, Adjoa Neri-Evans, said, "Your sister saw a dragon, son? She was there? And she lived to tell the tale?" We laughed.

"I wasn't there," he replied. "How can you explain what people see? Soon they'll be seeing Christ parting the good and the evil onto His right and left."

"Don't get His right confused with yours," Adjoa said. "It could be a big mistake."

"The biggest," he said and he laughed, too.

Has it come to this, Charles? Will we die at the hands of our fantasies? Our nightmares? Well, we are a species of story-tellers, of destroyers and creators, a forbidden planet of bickering little gods. Maybe a new god is coming after all.

Write me, Charles. Now, more than ever, your words are like psalms. I am yours, always.

My love, my love,
Hestor

Charles Borromeo
Latigo Canyon
Malibu, California

December 16, 2015

Dear Hestor:

I've just heard from El and Lisa, as well as you, which means that the mail is up and running again, for now, and you should hear from our daughter soon. Uri Wight is dead. I know you never cared for him, but if he was an atavism of manhood, at least he made a living at it, or posing at it, and he *was* El's husband, if however briefly, and Lisa's father. I'm making this point so as to anticipate your shock if you hear from El and find that she's grieving for him. She still uses his name, though Lisa is using yours, Lisa Piccolo Zu—Piccolo is an old, Japanese *anime* film character—well, what's in a name?

Uri Wight died in Miami with a hundred other poets. How any of them managed to travel there in these times is beyond me, but they'd gathered to raise their voices against the darkness and their hotel went up in flames.

There is no television anywhere that I know of. No electronic mail. All but the most local phone service, which we've jury-rigged here ourselves, is dead. Radio is still jammed and short wave communication sporadic. But we now receive a newspaper once a week and it said there that witnesses saw a black cloud in the shape of a heart darken and swell over the Miami hotel, then break into lightning or fire. Everyone, famous, infamous, and unknown, Uri among them, died.

No, darling, I never liked Uri Wight either. And you know that I've always been against artists gathering in large groups. These dark times make me laugh at the darkest things, but you might be pleased to know that I've moved all of my manuscripts—including my ill-conceived and poorly wrought poetry—out of the house. Maybe I shall burn it all. I don't need some monster to drop by and do it for me.

Believers, people who think there is something behind this collapse besides the weather, say the phenomenon has scorched universities' technological and animal research facilities yet left the libraries and dorms unscathed. It has rubbed out oil refineries, nuclear power plants, weapons labs, aircraft carriers, bombers, nuclear subs. Others say it attacks temples, mosques, and churches. And poets, I suppose. Much of that is rumor, yet there are times it feels like the hand of God, no? What other choices are left? Well, my love, I am neither scientist nor theist. Just an old polytheist willing to wait and see. And I seem to have little to fall back on these days but bad humor.

If it's the end of the world, who would have thought it would take so little and so long to end it? How long did it take the dinosaurs to die? A week? Ten years? A million? Anyway, in this corner of southern California we are still functioning. The sun shines and we collect the light. The wind blows and the new windmills run our generators. Rain is still rain. In our backyards, gardens grow all year: corn in the summer, lettuce and onions in the winter, wheat in the fall, rice in the wet spring. Like the Indians we're gathering acorns, cactus fruit, and grass seeds. That rifle of mine you always hated feeds me rabbit and venison, raccoon, squirrel, possum, pigeon, quail.

Against all of my inclinations, Hestor, I am a man of the community now. For us, gasoline is short and travel almost an absurdity. We've blockaded both ends of the canyon and we all do our time there, well armed. There is only so much room, so much land, so much game in these hills. It's at the blockade, near the ocean, where we receive our mail and news.

I don't know who possesses resources and who does not. The government, the military, must still have some. Though fuel is scarce here, we occasionally see planes, even commercial jets, in the sky. For us an automobile is worthless. A motorcycle is a chariot. Horses and bicycles are priceless. But if a bike ride to the ocean is all downhill, the ride home is hell, especially for a middle-aged man like me. It's easier, if longer, by horseback, and when I make the trip on Xena, the youngest mare, I camp overnight near our barricade on the coast.

Fish are plentiful and the fishing makes an excursion to the ocean well worth the trip. It's been a couple years now since the mechanized fishing fleets, among others, were scorched and sunk by those mysterious, quick-lightning storms that swept the oceans. Now the ocean shore is filled with fishing villages, the bay with oar boat apartments and sail boats, and yet there are more fish than ever. We have seals and otters in the kelp beds. Yes, now the Malibu coast has kelp beds.

The corporate farms are dead and people have carved the unde-fendable stretches of the San Joaquin Valley and Sacramento Delta into a million small farms. There's talk of organizing them around market villages and finding a way to get surpluses into the cities which are dark and violent. People have pushed into the suburbs where vegetable patches are guarded by walls and machine guns. In Los Angeles I've heard there is overwhelming sickness and death, and resilience.

I suppose you can't hop on one of those mail planes (already I can hear you responding, "That idiot! How much better off would I be as a fugitive in Tierra del Fuego!"). Okay, I'm not going any-where. I'll wait for you. But I can remember the days when I could not go an hour without your touch, a day without your body pressed to mine. If age has made me more tolerant, less driven, more accepting, my heart still aches. I miss you terribly, and worry.

Nonetheless, I think I will see my end before I see the end of everything. I am still a blessed man, by your love, by my daughter and granddaughter, by this blood and breath within me. But your dog, dear Hestor, doesn't understand, and listens at night for your car wheels on the dirt road.

My love, always,
Charles

Charles Borromeo
Latigo Canyon
Malibu, California

March 5, 2016

Dear Hestor:

You are probably as aware as anyone that the mail has been down again for months. Even here, for the longest time we only received rumors about what was happening in other places from itinerants and migrants who passed our post at the mouth of the canyon as they traveled up and down what was once the Pacific Coast Highway. But word reached me (was it rumor, too?) that your facility had been destroyed.

Over two weeks ago a message arrived from the National Guard notifying me that a U.N. expedition would begin the evacuation of the Mars Laboratory and the other Antarctic scientific facilities. There was no information about the destruction of the Mars Lab or any casualties. I was told I could leave a letter for you at the barricade in two days, but the messenger never returned. Yet I am writing to you because my heart has told me that you are alive.

I recently received a letter from El, dated in January, that said she had liquidated her last resources to join a group of people who had relatives at any number of scientific outposts, and that she and Lisa were boarding a ship out of New York and heading for Antarctica. If only I possessed the means I would join them. In lieu of that, I've sent this letter to them, by means of the present, haphazard courier system—some things never change—in the hope that they will receive it before they leave and bring it to you. It is, simply, all I can do.

Whatever has befallen the world, it lives by rumor and horror. We seem collectively unable to imagine our destruction as natural and impersonal, and must find a being who has brought it upon us. There is a story about cities who have bargained with the devil for electricity. That in Bismarck an emissary showed up at city hall and said the city could have electricity and natural gas if they sacrificed a boy, a virgin boy, to a dragon. They gave up the child and kept their light and heat for the winter. In Lincoln, Nebraska they refused and that night a quick-storm took out all of their facilities for electricity and natural gas. A beast, a dragon, was sighted inside the clouds. The population of Lincoln fled south or froze to death. There are dozens of these stories, one only needs to change the names of the cities.

There's a rumor that the United States sent troops to prevent the flow of immigrants into the plains of Texas. Now that there are apparently no more nuclear weapons, nor jet fighters and bombers, the Mexicans sent troops as well. The story follows the same line as its original, in that first war between India and Pakistan at the Kashmir. When the armies met at the Rio Bravo a dragon appeared and wreaked havoc over the battlefield. Now there is no longer a border, nor a war, between Mexico and the United States.

We live in the Middle Ages now, without the Church. Soon there will be only villages and farms, and cities held ransom by dragons. I've met no one who has seen the dragon, but I guess we have all felt its destruction. I suspect we are looking in the wrong places. Outside instead of in.

Hestor, I miss you so. And I wait for you. I worry for you, and for El and Lisa. If life is an unfinished lesson, a preparation for nothingness, then I have learned from this dark, new world that I am both more self-reliant and more helpless. But return to me, Hestor. Outside our door the green oaks and eucalyptus hiss in the ocean's salt wind. Red-tailed hawks soar. At night the coyotes still cry at a sky ever-filled with starlight. Last night I spotted Mars on the ecliptic, still angry and red, still a virgin. Return to me. We will give the dragon its due and move on.

Yours always, my love,
Charles

The Dragon Journal of Lisa Piccolo Zu

First of all, dragons don't use their wings to fly. A dragon's body is filled with light, honeycomb chambers that turn calcium and air into hydrogen. Helium might be more effective, but it's too hard to produce. Dragons puff up when they build up for flight. This is why they appear to be able to change size. Once filled up, they float, more or less, and learn to use their wings to accelerate upward and downward and to change directions. To land they must deflate, that is, expel the hydrogen which ignites when it passes through a calcium-based chemical mixture in their saliva glands. Dragons need to ingest so much calcium that sometimes they even chew on limestone. They don't really breathe fire, but they do exhale it. The hydrogen doesn't ignite until it's almost a foot out of their mouths. It turns out to be a good weapon, too, but too much fire breathing and they will fall out of the sky. Dragons existed. That's why people remember them. But there are no fossils of them because they were made out of such light stuff. Dragons still exist in our minds, though, in a deep, deep place where we go when we leave our first dreams and cross over from deep sleep into the other world of dreams. Not our first, falling-asleep dreams, but the dreams on the other side of deep sleep. That's a real place and dragons live there.

It's true that dragons hoarded gold, though not from greed. In fact it occurred quite by accident. Because dragons contain an almost toxic chemical reaction which gives them both flight and fire, they secrete an acidic liquid from their glands. When a dragon sits in its narrow cave, resting, or digesting its latest meal, the secretion from its glands will eventually erode its nest. Over the years, as they began to encounter and eat civilized humans, the gold and silver that their prey wore wasn't digested and came out in the dragon's fecal material. Gold was not only a soft metal, it decayed the least quickly under the dragon's acidic sweat. In time dragons lay on beds of gold and even began to seek it for the comfort of their lairs. This is why they attacked the rich, not the poor; ravaged castles, not farms; bargained with princes, not paupers. For gold.

Because of this, I'm sure many royal people were eaten by dragons. But dragons themselves had no reason to prefer eating rich people, though maybe they were more plump and easier to catch. And they do have gold. Dragons, like most predators, prefer an easy time of it. If you sacrifice a virgin, it's not going to turn you down. Dragons themselves had no preference for them, at least not at first. It's a human prejudice. Sacrificing virgins, particularly female ones, makes only too much sense if you look at our stupid, manly world. It's an idea a lot of men thought up, not dragons. I'm only fourteen but I've seen enough to know that a lot of dads would love to be able to threaten their teen-age daughters with a dragon.

Some people say this new dragon takes boy virgins. I'd like to see that.

Today El got a letter from New York City. We don't get many letters anymore. She hasn't said anything to me yet, but I think she's planning a trip to the South Pole to find Grandma Zu. El had to wait for the world to collapse before she decided to go to the South Pole. I guess you used to be able to get there pretty easily. But life is pretty boring here in the Adirondacks, especially in the winter. Next winter here, it will be summer down there. What else do I have to do?

Hestor Zu
International Mars Exploration Laboratory
Amundsen-Scott, South Pole
Antarctica

May 3, 2016

Dear Charles:

I know there has been an abyss of time since you've heard from me, but, in fact, the mail planes did stop coming. Even now I fear I write this into the abyss. We were pressed by an early autumn and seem in the throes of the cruelest winter. The last time we heard from McMurdo, a brief radio message in December, a Russian boat had made it through the floes on the Ross Sea and evacuated some of the Russians. The Russian boatmen said the world was in chaos. Cities had fallen. Nothing was left. In any case, no more boats will reach Ross Island until the summer; even so, that still leaves them 800 miles from us here at the pole. There's concern here that McMurdo is in jeopardy. Certainly if they were up and running some-one would have been sent along the emergency evacuation route on the Ross Ice Shelf during the summer to evacuate us over land.

Inexplicably, in February our nuclear generator and, consequently, our biospheres went down. Though there are still alternatives for survival. We have fuel enough for our gasoline generators, heaters, stoves, and limited use of tractors and snow mobiles, though not enough to travel. The livestock we lost is of course frozen. We have dry food stored, and yet have some capacity for an artificial greenhouse inside the geodesic dome. If we are prudent, efficient, and innovative, I think we can hold out through the winter.

Charles, my dearest love, why am I addressing this to you? But I am thinking now of explorers like Robert Falcon Scott, who at least left his letters and journals with him in his frozen grave. Is it so grim?

Late in our summer, near the end of March, I decided to get out of the compound one last time before the onset of winter. I tethered myself to an out-building in case of a fast rising storm. The katabatic winds here can reach a hundred-fifty kilometers an hour in an instant. During my walk to the hill beyond the compound, I saw the oddest of sights streaking across the desolation. At first I couldn't even really say it was there. It seemed only a shadow, a movement or play of light, as if some invisible thing had spread its wings over the ice and left only its blue-dark trace running across the glacial snow. But I could see nothing in the sky.

I stood mesmerized under the miracle of this dancing black ghost upon the snow, an almost joyful flickering of dark and light, before I saw in the distance a speck moving with linear determination across the landscape. As it grew larger I saw it was a human on a mobile sled, and as he approached the shadow seemed to quiet and darken on the snow. Then the air filled with light and I felt a hot wind, foul at first, as if sulfur laden, and then again, almost sweet. As the shadow darkened below, something flashed in the air above me and I heard the pounding of a huge heart beat. Or was it wings? Then it fled.

The man in the sled raced after it across the ice. A lone man, in the Antarctic twilight, pursuing a shadow. It was then I heard his shouting. His rage. And then his sled careened over a mogul in the ice. For a moment it ran forward, flying on its edge, one blade tilted in the air, before it rolled and sent him sprawling on the snow.

I ran for help and we gathered him up, with his things, and brought him to the compound. Among his equipment was a long, narrow lance, its tip like a pitch fork but that the middle prong was longer than the two outside ones, and each tip had three prongs. He was unconscious for two days and delirious for two more, madly raving about a hunt, or a haunt, it was difficult to tell; how he had lost his soul, how we must turn him loose to do what must be done, how he would save the world.

Kevnev, ever the pragmatist, was determined to grant the fugitive his wish.

"He's neither well nor sane," said our physician, my friend Adjoa Neri-Evans.

We stood at the foot of the man's infirmary bed, discussing his fate.

"Who is sane anymore?" Kevnev said.

"He's familiar," I said to Kevnev. "I've seen his face."

"A man with no identification, carrying a spear across the Antarctic, and you think you recognize him."

In that he was right. The fugitive's hair was over his shoulders and his beard thick and full, obscuring his brooding features. He was not a young man. He looked like those men, the older ones, who used to hang around behind the Fish Hut there on the border between Ventura County and Malibu, mingling with the surfers and bikers; homeless men living on handouts, cigarettes, beer and dreams. Remember Charles? When I turned forty I used to joke to you that they were the only ones who still made passes at me. But there was a look under this man's brow and in the gaze of his piercing brown eyes, a gaze that seemed to flee between fantasy and grim determination.

"He looks like Werther Fausten," I said.

"Yes," said Kevnev. "It's a common plight of Nobel scientists to end up wandering the Antarctic wastes with a spear. At home it happens all the time, only in the tundra instead, of course."

But one evening later my suspicions were confirmed. The man awoke and identified himself as Werther Fausten, the famous neuro-nuclear biologist who five years ago received the Nobel Prize for his work in reducing unconscious thoughts, particularly dreams, to subatomic reactions in the brain. As you know, Charles, many thought the work would unleash a cure for mental illness: schizophrenia, depression, even some criminal behavior, and the implication was that what couldn't be genetically controlled would be altered with the correct combination of laser stimulation and drugs. And there were the moral concerns: who would control whom to do what?—the marketing of devices to control fantasies and create dreams, and the concomitant hologram and cyber-technologies—worse than the horrors of Huxley's *Brave New World*. Yet some of Fausten's discoveries had already been used in the space program to adapt animals to space, and in humans to combat claustrophobia, poor responses to weight-lessness, space sickness, even boredom.

That night he was almost calm, his eyes steady and sober. He identified himself and asked me where he was. I explained that we were the International Mars Exploration Lab, that we found him when his sled crashed as he raced across the glacier.

"You won't be going to Mars now," he said.

"No," I said, "it's unlikely."

He coughed as he tried to sit up and I helped him by raising the back of his bed. "You can't use the button. You have to use the crank," I told him. "Our nuclear generator is down." The effort to sit up exhausted him. He still had an IV in his left arm which fed him a standard solution of sucrose and salt.

"You must release me or you face the destruction of what is left of your asylum," he whispered.

"You don't seem in a position to make threats," I said. I did not know how to take him, how to read him. In that regard, Kevnev was correct. Nobel Prize or not, he'd been wandering the Antarctic alone with little but an odd-shaped spear. And now, after two days and nights of raving, there was nothing to indicate that he was anything but apparently, momentarily, lucid.

"You are not Chinese," he said.

"American," I answered. "There are Chinese here."

He waved his hand faintly and turned his gaze to the ceiling. "Different dragons altogether." He tried to laugh and ended up coughing. "You must be the psycho-faunacologist. Zu," he said. "The 'woman who talks to animals.'"

"I mostly listen," I said.

"I was born in Switzerland. My mother was French, my father German."

"I probably know at least as much about you as you know about me."

"I came to the states as a boy and went to Harvard to study philosophy, to become the man who would shatter the mind-body problem, finally and for good. I fell in love with a young woman, Veronica DiSil, a Catholic girl who attended Boston College. Her parents owned a farm outside Albany, New York. She was an animal lover, like you."

"You should rest," I said, interrupting him. "You've been unconscious or delirious for four days. We can talk another time."

"No," said Fausten. "No, there isn't much time. And I am telling you important things." He breathed deeply. "I shall not be irrelevant. But while I am getting better I must tell you everything." His eyes became fierce again. "I am the man who has changed the world! I have brought it this devastation!" He raised his fist. "And I will end it!" That simple act tired him and his hand fell to the bed, his eyes rolled to the ceiling again and into his gaze of fantasy. "God made the devil," whispered Werther Fausten.

I have known many people over the years, mostly men, who believed their genius would change the world. Some were talented, some were not. Some were intelligent, others mad. Some dreamed of greatness and others fell from it, whether real or imagined. If I had studied Fausten's work and found some of it useful, I am not, as you know, Charles, a reductionist. If events occur simultaneously, I prefer to see them as causing each other. I find the proximity between one moment and the next too intimate, too full of future and intention, and too laden with the past, especially on the tiniest level of things. I see a world wound in wholeness, bound in a science of mutual co-arising. Not even one's soul is discreet. Nonetheless, Fausten's work was marvelous. It seemed, at times, that like Freud he'd plumbed the depths of the psyche, found the anxiety of the cell in the perturbations of the atom. And now I could see, that even so, it was the work of a different man, or a different part of a different man. Not this man. Not this man in front of me.

"I'll bring you a digital recorder," I said.

"I need your audience. Someone to speak to, a witness," murmured Werther.

"I yet have work to do here."

"Not for long," he said. "What I shall tell you is more important. Bring the recorder. I'll leave a record of what I have done, and what I must do. Just come some of the time. For me."

In the time since you last heard from me I have recorded his astounding story and transcribed it. I will send it to you, Charles, or bring it with me when I come home, or perhaps it shall go no farther than this, the mere transcription. Now it is part of what has happened here to all of us, so let that be enough, if nothing more than a remarkable footnote to this chapter of humanity's fragile dominion on our planet.

My love, my love,
Hestor

The Story of Werther Fausten

My parents were deeply religious folk. I was raised in the hills of eastern Pennsylvania, in a small town, Porterville, not so different from Germany. It's not surprising so many Germans settled there. My father, a Lutheran minister, and my mother, a minister's wife, taught me that my life was a prayer. To move is to pray. To think, to act, to breathe, these are the thoughts of God incarnate in the soul, the Word made flesh. But when God gave Adam dominion over the animals, and the duty to name them, He gave the mind language and with language came doubt. Doubt was the crack in the human heart that Satan transformed into the Valley of Death. My father believed very hard.

My father worked for his flock, his church, and my mother and I worked for him. But if my mother desired a life more open to the world, simple desires like shopping in Philadelphia or traveling someplace in Europe besides Germany, my father turned his eyes the other way. He admired the Amish and Mennonites who rejected technology and kept to the land, to their communities, to their families. If animals did not have souls, then neither did machines. In the end, it was his discomfort with computers and his refusal to use them for church finances which led to the fiscal ruin of his church and forced his retirement.

I was never a great athlete. I struggled as a second and third team participant in fringe sports like cross country, wrestling, and distance running in track and field, to keep me away from home after school, to keep me away from my father who, as I began to mature, I naturally began to hate. Before my puberty my mother sometimes let me stay home from school and we'd slip off in the afternoons for movie matinees followed by hot fudge sundaes. How little else I remember of her. How little we remember really.

Like most boys, my second life began at the moment of my first love, a girl named Dianna who had entered high school the year before me. She was dark, brooding, and thoughtful. Her mother was divorced and they lived on the edge of town, a mile from my home but not a difficult walk. Both of my parents opposed the coupling. Dianna's mother was a fallen Catholic. They thought me too young to date at all, let alone spend time with an older girl.

Dianna's mother was more tolerant and seemed to take tremendous pleasure in my presence. When I skipped athletic practice to meet Dianna after school, her mother often lent us her car or left us alone in the house. In these places I learned the pleasures of a different kind of word made flesh, and my life, day and night, fell back and forth between sinning hard and believing harder. Often, Dianna's mother left the house with a man, and not always the same man. Seeing the daughter in the mother, I became insanely jealous of Dianna. My love, my infatuation, became predatory, burdensome, and exacting.

It came to a disastrous end. Porterville was not a large town. It was only a matter of time before my parents were notified that I'd been skipping practices to spend time with Dianna. Yet my father wouldn't have had to drive to her mother's house to put an end to it. That day I'd spotted Dianna hand-in-hand with another boy. I found them there, in front of her home, parked outside, behind my father's car. I didn't need to go inside to hear the substance of his raving. I heard it through the door, through the windows and walls. He called Dianna's mother a Catholic whore. He called Dianna a whore. But the rage was even deeper. My father was livid. He screamed. He was enraged that Dianna's mother had permitted incest between her daughter who was also his daughter, and Dianna's half-brother, his son.

A less exceptional boy might have been marred for life by this, but instead I found my hatred for my father dwindle from that moment on. All of his battles now came into focus for me. My passion for Dianna turned to pity. And I developed a certain antipathy for my mother's life. Her quiet suffering, her loyalty to my father, whether from knowledge or ignorance, became for me an emblem of the human plight; our bondage to myth and the web of pathology by which we held together everyday life. In a moment my eyes were cleared of religion and all it offered. I saw how much better it was for me to have known and met the depth of my sexual transgression. How easy it had been and how sinless, how pleasurable; and yet, too, the discovery of my incest was painless and liberating, and the truth better, much better, than the burden of my innocent possessiveness and infatuation.

It became a passion for me to tear the scales from my eyes. Scales, yes, of justice, of measure, of music, of dragons. I do not use the cliché without irony or regret. In my last year of high school I allowed a part of myself to play out the final days. I lettered in my respective sports, attended my father's sermons on Sundays, went to school. But in my free time I began the study of religion. I closely read the *Bible*, the *Koran*, the *Upanishads*, the *Vedas*, the *Mahabarata*, the philosophies of Shankara and Nargajuna. I studied the life of Christ and the life of the Buddha, read the *Tao Te Ching*, Confucius, and then the Buddhist sutras. I studied Zoroasterism, mysticism, Sufism, Scholasticism and Protestantism. I even read the *Book of Mormon*. But in all of that I found nothing. From the utterly ridiculous to the deeply meta-phorical, it all required faith in something unknowable; there wasn't a single notion in any of it that one needed if one simply chose to live. My life and all that I could touch and see, smell and taste, think and hear remained absolutely unchanged and immutable to any and all layers of faith, apologetics, or theology. All of it, even the nihilism of Buddha, was mere haggling over the selfish myth of personal salvation, a quibbling over daydreams.

In the fall I left for Harvard and began the secular search for truth. Even there I found I was light years of sophistication ahead of my peers and found myself sitting in on graduate seminars in order to find a level of conversation and inquiry as passionate and informed as my own. I began reading the pre-Socratic philosophers and worked my way through the field of Western thought, from Plato and Aristotle through the Scholastics and Moderns, through Hegel and those in his wake. I read the psychoanalysts, Freud and Jung.

By my sophomore year I fell into the inevitable pit of European epistemology, the legacy of Kant. And then the labyrinth of semiology with its myriad paths of schools until I came to the monsters who guarded the nothingness at the center: Barthes, Wittgenstein, Derrida, Foucault, Lacan. Yes, I read them all and more in the original language. I was a passionate boy. I chased down their phantasmal roots until I fell in with everyone else, into the intellectual despair of the end of the Twentieth Century, the century of solipsism.

History offered me less. Life was meaningless and suffering served no purpose; the good guys didn't win; most explanations offered to explain the mess we were in were self-serving lies. Life wasn't clear, it was ambiguous; motives were many and mixed; values were complex, opposed, poisoned by hypocrisy, without any reasonable ground; most of passion's pageants were frauds, and human feelings had been faked for so long, no one knew what the genuine was; society, its institutions and advertised dreams, were simply superstitions that served a small set of people while keeping the remainder in miserable ignorance. What was noble about man? Where was love? We had been murdering each other since the beginning of recorded time with an ease that suggested we took pleasure in it. Our foresight did not exceed our greed.

As the species reached out with its technology to touch the stars, it seemed we would export a mentality more befitting of the Middle Ages. Intellectually, culturally, we lived in Medieval times. While the masses bred the species to the edge of self-extinction and plague, our intellectuals discussed how many concepts could fit on the head of a pin, our artists tried to illustrate the same. Serfs and kings paid vassalage to corporations. We tithed to AT&T. Our illiterate middle class was miseducated in new, secular mythologies by our worthless universities. Cell phones, wrist faxes, and the internet disseminated shared ignorance.

Remember, Dr. Zu, I was a young man, disillusioned, angry for truth. Yet if I had torn down heaven and hell to find the devil, then Satan often hid in the holiest places. The center of Eden. Despite my despair, I could not crack my everyday faith in my peculiar individuality, my identification with the world of thought, and the impulsive, nagging intuition that my genius was unique. If the miserable world had turned a trillion trillion times, might it not yet be saved by vision, by true science, by my own genius? But how?

Then a series of events changed everything for me. In the Commons at Harvard I met Veronica DiSil, a Catholic farm girl who laughed at my obsessions and lived in her own world where even animals had feelings and immortal souls. Once again I fell in love.

The Story of Werther Fausten

I loved her and she did not love me. I loved her and we argued. She baited me and I bit.

"Everything has a soul, Werther," she said. "Every living thing feels and thinks significantly."

"The soul is a wish, a daydream," I said to Veronica.

She laughed at me. "You need a pet," she said. She brought me a caged rat and put it in my room. "Here," she said. "Learn something." The little rodent, with its night-time racket and perpetual scampering, drove me mad. She took the creature back and claimed that within a week she'd housebroken it.

I raved to her over coffee, over beer, after movies which, like my mother, she loved. I showed her hundreds of behavioral studies, graphs and videos, an experiment where cats, confined together in small rooms, failed to pass on the slightest bit of information to each other. She found it all hilarious and absurd.

The more logical and empirical my arguments, the more laughable she found them. The ironies of my infatuation with her confounded me. When away from her I dreamed of her wide hips, her rough, work-worn hands, her soft, dark-red hair. Yet the more my passion grew, the more she seemed to toy with my emotions.

Sometimes, on weekends, we drove in Veronica's little truck, or my old Fiat, to Albany and her parents' farm. Her mother and father had been wealthy liberals. After Veronica's father died, her mother abandoned cultivating the land and now rented out the acreage to corporate farmers. She lived at the edge of the property, in a beautiful, Victorian farmhouse, but at the center of it all still kept a horse ranch with barns and stables, an enormous riding ring and dozens of riding paths which extended throughout the property and into the nearby woods.

Horses. Here was Veronica's passion, where she had spent her time as a girl and yet spent her summers, with these huge and recalcitrant, yet flighty vegetarians. She had begun to build a house there, at the center of the stables, working there in the summer and on the warmer autumn and spring weekends, sawing and hammering with her own hands, and recruiting help from local farm boys who were easily coaxed by their own infatuation with Veronica and a free six-pack of beer. The ranch and farmland was hers to inherit when her mother died and she planned to take back all of the rented land and live there, at the center of it, with her horses and other assorted domestic pets: cats, dogs, pigs, goats, chickens, turkeys, pigeons, ducks, geese, even a cow.

She believed that each of these creatures possessed a distinct personality, in fact that all sentient things did—she could not speak with certainty for rocks or vegetation, though she suspected there was something similarly recognizable in plants—and that all things evolved spiritually toward individuation and that the universe was becoming increasingly individuated. This made me laugh.

"And where does that lead?" I said to her.

"Where does anything lead?"

"How we differ from them is that we have hands and larger brains; we use tools, language, abstraction. Human animals write symphonies, theorize, build spaceships. It might only be a quantitative difference, but it's a big difference"

"How many humans write symphonies or build space ships?" she said.

"Enough to make a difference."

"So some of us can do some things better than them?" She said this as we walked to the barn. It was my first weekend at her farm and Veronica was fetching her bay mare for my first horseback ride. "How is that different from Descartes?"

I followed her. "Descartes attributes the distinction to the qualities of our immortal soul, our mind. He believes animals have no souls. They're organic machines."

She turned to me. "That's the stupidest thing I ever heard," she said. "Everything has a soul. Mortality is—well—it's *irrelevant*."

She began to lead the mare, but because I had not moved she stepped right into me. Till then, as intense as I'd been about her, I was still cautious and naive, and other than our friendship, and the ferocity of our arguments, we'd had little intimacy. I took her shoulders to steady her. Her emerald eyes met mine, for the first time seeming to reflect my own unease and passion. I let her go.

"We are all organic machines," I said.

"Well get on this one," said Veronica.

I remember the day so vividly. The sun was high and warm and the breeze sung in the leaves of the sycamores and maples, one of those eternal afternoons of youth when nature seems gentle and benevolent and the accidental cruelty of everything is hidden beneath the moment's pleasure. At the pasture Veronica had me climb the fence to mount the horse.

"No reins or saddle?" I asked.

"This is the best way to learn," she said. "This horse won't hurt you. Just hop on and grab onto her mane."

Of course when I did so the animal took off, loping at her own caprice as I bobbed along on top of her, bouncing upon her neck and then almost falling over backward, gripping for my life with my hands and legs.

"Don't do that!" yelled Veronica. "If you hold on with your legs it tells her to run!"

When I released my legs the creature broke into a wicked trot that bounced my privates into nausea. Veronica laughed so hard it didn't take me long to figure out that I'd fallen prey to a joke. As soon as I found what looked to be some soft dirt, I dropped off, miscalculating the animal's speed and landing hard on my butt.

Veronica ran up to me as I lay sprawled on the sand. She stared down, hands on her hips. "Undone by a stupid animal," she said.

But you see, I was falling in love. That evening we drank beer on the porch of her unfinished house, listening to the chorus of mating frogs in the nearby ponds and streams. Lazy dogs lay at our feet and cats prowled about. Veronica's favorite pig sat at the steps. Several of Veronica's volunteers dropped by and exchanged stories of frigid winters, late harvests, hot summers, tornadoes and floods; tricky horses, mean turkeys, amorous bulls, and cows giving birth. They eyed me and spoke to me with a specific cordiality and distance, as if I were some farm animal which, if they had not encountered me before individually, at least they were quite familiar with my breed.

I had never presumed nor clearly perceived where I would sleep that weekend, but at the end of the evening, when Veronica surprisingly took my hand and wished them all good night, one boy in particular lingered there on the porch with a look of forlorn longing, a look so mysterious and baffling to me that it surely expressed the mirror depth of my own desires. It is a moment I looked back on again and again in the coming years, because when I, myself, became as that boy, I vowed to find the roots of those desires and the means to conquer them.

We went inside, Veronica and I, to the one finished room in the house where Veronica kept her bed, and there, in the night and the morning, she made love to me. She rolled me on my back and placed her index finger on my lips. She placed me inside her. That was all.

In the next month we argued and fucked and fucked and argued. I found it gloriously eternal and in my mind constructed my future around Veronica. I'd learn carpentry and build an office in her farmhouse where I'd spend the days at my computer, turning the philosophical world topsy-turvy in ways that had not been done since Plato. At night, done with her horses, Veronica would return to me and make love. But it wasn't to last. Veronica's passion for me ended as abruptly as it began. One day at school she stopped calling and stopped returning my calls. That next weekend she left for Albany without me. Shattered and confused, I drove my old Fiat to her farm. I found her there working at the edge of the pasture with some of her boys, replacing a corner of the pipe fence.

She looked up and smiled. "Werther," she said. "We can use your help. Get some gloves."

I spent the afternoon digging holes and lugging pipe with the rest of the volunteers until, at dusk, we retired once again to the porch for our beer and stories. At bed time, when Veronica arose and I followed her, she met me inside the doorway, putting her open palm in my chest.

"I'm sorry, Werther," she said. "I don't want to sleep with you."

"But I've no place to stay," I said.

Her shoulders drooped and I followed her eyes to the door where, outside, the farm boys still hung on the porch. A man in love is a fool, but even so, I could not walk back out and face what I now knew would be their knowing, superior gazes.

"All right," she said, "you can sleep on the floor, but in the morning you have to go."

"What happened?" I said to her. "What's the matter?"

"Werther," said Veronica, "I don't have to sleep with you. Or anyone."

"I love you," I gasped to her. "Don't you love me?"

"Leave it to you, of all people," said Veronica, "to talk about love."

She did not have to lecture me. I understood what she was saying. We'd slept together. We'd had our fun. And she'd had fun with many others, among them, the young men who gathered outside her door. But you cannot deny that I was, objectively, different from them. I could engage her intelligence. I could change her life. She was young then, but how long could she hold court on her little ranch outside Albany with her bevy of local swoons.

I did not stay. I did not sleep on the floor at the foot of her bed. I ran from her house, bursting through the screen door like a monster and running past her entourage, through the pasture and into the woods. I wandered there for the longest time, beneath the dark trees, the starlight flickering through the wind-tilted leaves and the sound of the night-time woods filling me insatiably. What to do with this desire? This love? This firing of cells within cells, and beneath them the microcosmic matter of my being, no different, no less and no more than the automatic fire within the distant, twinkling stars?

I spent the night there in the woods, huddled against the trunk of a tree, until the dawn came alive and the stars went out behind the light. The mating birds whistled and chattered from the branches and the squirrels chased each other across the floor of the woods. Had I not asked for no more than that?

But as much as I understood the idiocy of my plight, I was still a very young man and yet determined to show Veronica her mistake, to win her love with my intelligence, my creativity, my persistence. Then, when it was done, when I became the flint which ignited her frailty and she came to me to contain her fire, then I would walk away. Having shown her the science of emotion, I would leave her with a mysterious ache in her heart, an ache I had known and understood too well. I longed for the knowledge then, the chemistry of emotion which would free me, which would free the species of its self-victimization. But at that moment, I was a helpless philosopher and a boy in love. I did not recognize that in this sea of dreams lay the prescient isle of my destiny.

In the coming year I studied plumbing and electrical contracting, carpentry, roofing, drywalling, auto mechanics, and animal training, particularly with horses. I showed up on occasional weekends at Veronica's farm, offering my casual assistance to whatever project in which she happened to be engaged, then leaving in the late afternoon, before she gathered her minions around her in the dusk. Sometimes I spotted her at the coffee shops or bars in Boston or Cambridge and inquired about her ranch, and hearing about one problem or another, gave her my advice or agreed to come by on the weekend to see what I could do. I fixed a nagging leak on her roof, engineered a drainage system for her pasture, helped wire her house, even tamed a horse for her who would not be saddled, simply by chasing the creature around a small a bull pen until he tired, and then only letting him rest when he came to me, and the saddle, which I placed next to me in the center of the ring.

But whatever gratitude my time and help engendered, it did not rekindle her desire. One weekend, I drove to her farm on Friday evening and worked through the night building a horse teeter-totter in her pasture. Before she arrived on Saturday morning, I had her favorite gelding and mare out there, standing on either end, bouncing each other up and down like a couple of kindergartners. I stood there with her short whip in my hand as she arrived in her truck and got out, awe struck. She came into the pasture and approached me.

"Werther," she said.

"Yes, Veronica," I said to her.

"Werther," said Veronica. "You're nuts."

I laughed, and finally she did, too. I put my hand out to her.

"No, Werther," she said. "You're crazy. I don't want you to come here anymore."

I wish I'd been quicker on my feet, because it was a moment—looking back now, through everything, I see it—a moment in which her apparent aversion was clearly a denial of the depth of her need for me, a need which would one day be her joy, and on another future day, sadly, her ruin.

"I stopped here on my way to Utica to see a friend," I told her. "But I had car trouble. I only did this to kill the time while waiting for you, to get permission to leave the car."

She eyed me skeptically.

"It stopped running, so I'll have to come back at least once more to repair it."

It earned me a ride to the bus station, where she shook my hand, but her leaving before I bought my bus ticket saved me a worthless trip to Utica. In the coming months, using my skills as an auto mechanic, I purchased another old Fiat from a junk yard, put it in running order and drove it to Veronica's ranch in the middle of the week, when I knew she wouldn't be at home, and abandoned it there. When I didn't hear from her, I did it again. In the next ten months I abandoned eight Fiats in her yard, but she never picked up the phone.

Admittedly, it was an idiosyncratic strategy, but it was a kind of poetry, as well, far more metaphorical than candy or roses, or poetry itself. Finally frustrated, I broke my silence and drove my ninth Fiat to her ranch on a weekend. There, one of her sullen boys, left to mind the farm in her absence, told me that Veronica had left, months ago, for California.

Taking solace in her flight, I left Harvard and pursued her, beginning in Crescent City and meandering down the California coast, inquiring through postal services, real estate offices, and phone directories until, after two months search I found her outside Cambria, a small ocean village south of Big Sur, rebuilding an old fishing shack, and living with a half-dozen cats and her oldest, favorite dog.

"Werther," she said when she saw me at her door. "My God. Werther."

I kissed her cheek. "Did you have any doubt that I would come?" I said.

And that night she took me in and we made love again, though in the morning she asked me to leave her for good.

"I will stay here outside your door," I told her. "Until you realize my love for you, I will never leave."

"Werther," Veronica said to me, "your love is irrelevant. I don't and can't love you!"

It was then that she told me that her father had abused her when she was a girl. It had made sex a cruel and unsatisfying experiment for her, something she must always pursue and never enjoy; that inside her constant shame she saw herself as a shameless whore and needed the attention of men, all men, and that none of them could find the place inside her which would replace the horror of her father's transgressions. She could not love, nor could she stop pursuing love. Everywhere she sought admiration and intimacy, and everywhere she found it, it produced antipathy.

"All men are my father, Werther," she said to me, "my father who did not love me and who would not leave me alone."

"But I *do* love you," I said.

"Werther," she said, "hundreds of men have."

It was then that I began my vigil, camping in my sleeping bag outside her door. In the mornings she worked on her Master's thesis, an essay on the image of horses in Victorian novels by women. Then she walked to the beach where a colony of northern elephant seals lay sprawled for a mile across the shore, honking their sexuality and pressing upon each other for dominance. Like any sensitive mind, I saw the world of sentient existence play itself out in front of me in their ferocious dalliance. I flirted with our absent God's glory amid the crabs scuttling over the reefs, the anemone suckling in the tide pools, the gulls and terns who dipped with capricious avarice into the ocean, plucking life to death for life. I cracked mussel shells from the rocks and fed the meat to a colony of Moray eels who slithered to me like dragons from the black rocks. I counted the grains of sand and numbered the stars in the sky, the hairs upon my head.

Some days Veronica ignored me. Others she came outside in the morning and shared coffee or at night opened a bottle of wine. Yet other days she screamed at me to leave her alone and go away. Once she called the police who came and arrested me. But when they released me and I returned to her, she accepted it quietly. It settled then into a quiet acceptance and I was convinced that it was only a matter of time before she understood that I was the opposite of her fears, that I loved *her* and wanted *her*, and the sex be damned. But it was not to be. My father, who I'd kept in touch with by mail, sent a letter. Veronica came out on the porch that evening as the red sun hung for a moment over the ocean. She handed me the envelope, watching as I opened it and read my father's words. My mother had brain cancer and had been given only a year to live. My father asked that I return home.

My mother took her illness bitterly and abandoned religion, cursing God and His angels and His ministers, which included my father who spent less and less time with his own duties and more and more time at my mother's side. As the doctors prodded them onward with vague hope, inflicting their paralyzing surgery, their debilitating cures of radiation and chemotherapy, each step prolonging my mother's misery, disabling her further into her miserable death, my mother, in her last days of wretched pain, eventually returned to her original faith and to my father's love.

My father's pastorage came to ruin as the man appointed to assist him usurped his authority, exposed him, ironically, not for his sexual transgressions, but for years of anachronistic finance which had left the church in debt. Before my mother could die and be buried, my father's assistant replaced him as minister of his church. Such are the human lessons of holiness. Unblinking, my father, the adulterer, nursed my mother, feeding her, cleaning her, turning her to prevent bed sores, removing her waste.

Upon my arrival from California I had, as my parents requested, returned to Harvard. My father had not opposed my study of philosophy, seeing it as a logical preliminary to theology school at Yale. But now, as I came home at every opportunity to help him with my mother's care, I became more and more disillusioned with philosophy and its abstract concerns. If it had proven a worthless hindrance in my pursuit of love, a phantasmic, futile pursuit, it became frivolous in the face of death. As I watched my mother die, her life, her spirit, her thoughts, draining into madness, then lethargy, then coma with the mechanistic degeneration of her cells, I perceived the monolithic, absolute dominion of blatant, physical reality. I watched my mother, the organism, degenerate and die. I saw her mind die as her body died. I saw the emptiness with which each of us lived our days, the void that each of us dared, in reasonless hope, to call mind or soul. Now, with certainty, I knew there was no such thing.

My father's struggle opened up to me and I understood his misdirected life; how deep in his insistence on belief lay his infidelity, how his faith in humanity turned its back on human nature, how his unacceptable desire for a simple life led him to his sullen perch atop this chaos. More than anything, those days cemented my bond to him. In those last weeks my mother never spoke again and I found my father at night curled up beside her, his breath on her cold cheek, my mother's vacant eyes always half open and gray, devoid of both wakefulness and sleep. When she died, my father held his last ministry in the shell that was once his church and buried my mother. And there, too, I buried the last of my illusions.

The Dragon Journal of Lisa Piccolo Zu

Dragons were never as big as people have imagined. Figure it out. Even if they were only the size of elephants, how would they get into the air? They'd need a wing span the length of a football field even if their bones were light like birds. Also, if we're to believe that anyone ever truly slew one, then it's pretty far fetched to think that a knight, no matter how skilled, could take on a fire breathing creature the size of a house with only a spear or a sword. Because, in fact, there were dragon slayers. St. George was one. And if you look at any of the paintings depicting his battles (these were painted a little more closely to the actual time of dragons than the fantasy stuff we see now) you'll see that the dragon is only a little bigger than the combined size of the mounted knight and the horse.

This brings up a couple things. Back then people had already begun to associate dragons with the devil. This is just a silly Christian thing. Bad thing = evil = the devil. Kind of a natural response given the times, but pretty simple and pretty dumb. A dragon is a creature. It would be like calling a mountain lion or a tornado the devil. Right now we could all go to church and say the rosary a hundred times and our current situation would still be here. I mean, we could *try* it. Just because it hasn't worked in the last six thousand crises is no reason it won't work this time. Some people want to say the Phenomenon that's taking the world apart is the devil and some people want to say it's the weather. It's none of the above.

Dragons are not in competition with Jesus. They don't think like we do. They're dragons. They do think with purpose. That's what we have to find out about the dragon in the world today. What it wants.

But first, dragon slayers and sacrificing girl virgins. Now you don't give a guy a sword and a spear, dress him in some armor and put him on a horse, then send him out to fight a dragon and *not* call that a sacrifice. Give me a break! How many of those guys do you think came back? Though there were some knights, like St. George, who knew how to do it. Next, many women did successfully slay dragons, if you can call persuasion a form of slaying. That is, there were better methods than fighting. But given how the world works, these women threatened male power so they were called witches. And we know what happened to them.

It wasn't long before the power these women possessed to persuade dragons to leave became something to be feared. Soon women weren't being used to fight dragons but were accused of being in cahoots with dragons. So one day you're in your kitchen mixing up some herbs and the next thing you know somebody accuses you of being a witch and you're dragon food. Maybe your husband was having an affair and wanted to move on, or maybe you were the one he was having an affair with. Now you can see how this virgin thing evolved—like everything else, out of its opposite—originally you were sacrificed for *not* being a virgin, except, of course, it was to hide some wrong that some man was doing. Next, like the Sultan in *A Thousand Nights and One Night*, you sacrifice women out of jealousy, so nobody else can have them after you do. After that you just cut the whole process short and sacrifice them before they can even think about doing anything.

A lot of men who went out or got sent out to fight dragons were criminals or errant knights, not heroes. Remember, dragons tended to sit on a lot of gold. So as you see, dragons took the rap for dealing with a lot of human problems. If Jesus were around back then, he would have been dragon fodder.

When dragons passed from reality into people's imaginations they grew as large and as frightening as the very real threat they once were. Look how big Godzilla is. In fact, a big, bull dragon was about the size of two horses. Females ranged from about the size of a big basketball player to the size of a horse. They were snake-like, had talons on each foot, and were four-legged with large, thin heads. Their wings were an outgrowth of their rib cages, not an adaptation of their forelimbs like birds, and they tucked them tightly against their backs. Chinese dragons, though, were wingless.

Dragons could easily stand upright. When inflated and reared up, wings spread, a bull dragon could appear the size of an African elephant. Deflated, with wings folded, an upright female could appear almost human. This, along with their ability to mesmerize their victims, accounts for the wide variety of descriptions of dragons, along with the fact that dragons, like other animals, cats for instance, came in any number of sizes and species. This often accounts for different interpretations from various geographical regions and cultures, India, China, Europe, and Mexico for example.

There's a lot more to say abut dragons, including arguments about whether or not female dragons could fly and if dragons could talk, but I'm done writing about dragons for today. Yesterday El told me that Uri Wight died. Uri Wight was my dad, though I don't remember him. Wight is still my mom's name. El said he lived with us when I was little and once, when I was three, I said to her, "El, remember that guy who used to stay with us all the time?" But now I don't even remember saying that. So I really don't have a lot of opinions about Uri Wight or a lot of sadness about him. He was a poet and died in a fire with a lot of other artists. Some people say the dragon killed them. That would be a very unusual thing for a dragon to do and if I ever meet the dragon I'll ask her about it. Personally, I think a poet being killed by a dragon is very ironic.

The Dragon Journal of Lisa Piccolo Zu

Many leading authorities on dragons contend that female dragons did not have wings. They argue that the females didn't need them because they lived by ponds or small lakes where they bred. Males, after fighting it out for domination in the sky, descended and mated with the waiting female who, after depositing her fertilized eggs, left them, without maternal care, to develop, hatch, and then feed in the confines of the warm, fauna-filled pond. The smaller, female young were generally eaten by the bigger, cannibalistic males, thus there tended to be a lot of males flying the skies and fighting it out in the domination hierarchy, sometimes, during mating season, many at once. Their spiral battles, filled with fire, were supposedly something of great splendor. Only enough females survived to occupy one per pond.

This is what my grandma, Hestor, would call "one of the many vestiges of patriarchal zoology." If you look at most existing species: among insects, arachnids, birds, herd mammals and mammalian carnivores, even reptiles and what we know of the dinosaurs, we see they are dominated by matriarchies. Among ants and bees, females work and fight, males are drones. Among lions, females hunt, rule, and communally raise the young. Even the myths about reptiles failing to care for their young after birth have been destroyed by observing the motherly protection of pythons and, most notably, crocodilians.

So why wouldn't female dragons fly? No reason at all. Especially since they probably evolved around the time of dinosaurs and like them, predecessors of birds, not reptiles, they had to hunt to feed their young. This would also explain why so many dragons have been mysteriously portrayed as feathered. If you look at a species like the orangutan, it's the mature males who grow too big to live in the forest canopy and must abandon the tree tops for the forest floor. Most likely, this would be the case with dragon flight, as well. It was probably male dragons who grew too large and old to fly and ended up spending the last of their days on the ground in lairs.

As in most species, it is not the male, the bull, who chooses the female to mate. Males fight for the right to be chosen by the female of the herd. You can see this in sheep, horses, seals, komoto dragons, a hundred different species. The male is tolerated as long as he's needed to mate, then he's gone and the females get back to the business of keeping the species going. In dragons, it's unlikely, to my mind, that the top bull descended from the heavens, like Zeus, to lay upon the mud-dwelling female. I much prefer the image of the male and female dragons dancing in a dome of light, then locked in flight like eagles, their fire billowing out as they fell from the sky. This is probably the explanation for a number of documents which claim that male and female dragons were found together, expired on the ground, a time, as any good dragon hunter knew, when they were very vulnerable. But what do I know, I'm only fourteen.

Male dragons were often horned. Females crested. They did not mate for life. Males did not help rear the young. Except for some exceptions among fish, that's a later evolutionary development. That males fought each other is believable enough. That's what males do. For territory and sex. That dragons were cannibals is another reptilian myth, derived from the days when people thought that alligators ate their young when they were, in fact, protecting them or transporting them. Cannibalism, as anybody knows, only serves to self-limit the most proliferate species like insects or fish, sometimes urban rodents. Dragons were pretty big animals and pretty private. They weren't communal like birds, but like birds, they had egg clutches of a limited size because you can only feed so many young dragons.

I am one of the few people in the world whose grandmother is an astronaut, though now, for quite a while, there aren't going to be any astronauts. I really don't remember the world before it was like it is now, a world without constant disasters where people went wherever they wanted and did what they pleased. Though I remember the television and radio and cell phones, fax machines, washing machines, stereos. And computer games. Some kids still have the little ones which are okay if you can afford batteries. El says that some time soon there'll be lots of batteries again. I'm not so sure. I'm not so sure that the world isn't going to become a better place. One without human beings. Or at least without very many.

It's funny that up until about ten years ago there was a world which had been modern for a very long time, where everything was scientific and people had machines to do everything. Where nothing mythical existed. But in my life, there has never been a world without dragons. In my life, science, and machines that do everything, are myths.

Tomorrow, El and I are leaving for New York to get on a boat. It's one of the new boats with an electric engine powered by a battery that collects energy from the sun and wind, but like the first schooner-steamships, it has sails, too. El says a disaster like the Phenomenon won't strike that kind of boat.

"What kind of boats does the disaster strike?" I asked her.

"Big boats," she said. "Not little boats. But not really even because they were big boats. There were just a lot of boats and a lot of storms. Now there are fewer boats and fewer storms. Besides, it's 'disast*ers*,'" she says, "*not* 'The Disaster.'"

"Nuclear boats and gas boats," I told her. "Aircraft carriers, submarines, battle ships, oil tankers, big whaling and fishing fleets."

"I know your theory," she says. "Everybody has a theory. Some even make sense. But there was a lot of human activity on the planet," says El. "A lot of humans doing a lot of human things. When big things get destroyed, they get reported."

"So little things get destroyed and go unreported," I said.

"Lisa," she said to me. She wanted to tell me that I was getting too old to believe in myths like dragons. She wanted to tell me that I was a pain in the ass. But she just said, "Lisa."

"People have seen her," I said.

To this, my Mom, El, said nothing. El got a Ph.D. once upon a time and taught filmmaking at NYU, though she never made any movies. El studied movies, she didn't make them. You don't see many movies around anymore. Now El says, "Good riddance." But after I came along, and then Uri Wight left us, El inherited a lot of money when her aunt died. That was a pretty good joke on Uri Wight. El quit teaching to become a sculptor. She learned welding and wood carving. She got kind of famous for a welder and we lived most of the time in our cottage in the Adirondack Mountains, which she inherited from her aunt, too. That's where we are now and that's where El has her studio. We had an apartment in New York, but I think that's gone now that the power went out there. We haven't been there since. Grandpa Charles writes and says we'd probably be surprised by all the gardens and wind mills that are atop the apartment complexes, how people are probably filling the vacant lots with vegetables and tearing up cement to plant food; how well people are managing, really. I would be surprised. But I guess in a few days I'm going to find out.

People think El is beautiful. She has dark hair and blue eyes and she does what she wants no matter what. When I was little I didn't want to be like her. I didn't want to look like her or be with her. Everybody said I looked like Uri Wight back then, and though I barely knew him, I wanted to be with him, not El. But as I got a little older and started figuring things out, I started admiring El more and more, and I started to look like her, too. I think that's kind of amazing, how when your insides change, your outside changes. I think that's how a lot of things work.

"We're going to go down and get Mom," El said.

"I know. I know," I said. "Grandma Hestor Zu at the South Pole."

"Do you have something better to do?" said El. "I want to be in Dunedin, New Zealand when the ice starts to break."

But I am ready to go. There is something in my heart that tells me that I will see the dragon and when the time comes I will have to say something to her. All dragons want something. What can I tell her? What can I give her when she comes?

The Story of Werther Fausten

Back at Harvard I turned to the sciences. I took the introduction courses in math, biology, chemistry, physics. In my vain pursuit of Veronica I had lost a semester and my transfer into the sciences left me a year behind, but in another year-and-a-half I'd qualified for pre-med. In medical school I graduated at the top of my class, moved from my internship to graduate work in surgery, specializing on the brain. It wasn't long before I abandoned surgery for pure research.

At the end of the century, most medical research concentrated around efforts to find cures: cell research for cancer; viral experiments spurred by the HIV plague and the fears of African super-viruses; the search for new, powerful antibiotics to meet the mutating ultra-germs; nerve regeneration and microchip robotology to deal with paralysis or the loss of limbs; and cloning and gene mutation, which in theory offered technologies for disease prevention, but more often than not led to organ farming and gerontology improvements for the rich.

But the rich can always afford their myths, however briefly, including the myths of immortality and perpetual youth. It was the poor of the world who suffered under centuries of false beliefs and illusions, who in fact were fed them as the staple of oppression. What a man my father would have been without religion.

I envisioned a world where our technology synthesized science and Tao, where every human could play the fabric of his own brain like a computer, like a symphony; where each child danced in the rhythm of her cells and, like a magician, played tricks upon reality. It was simply an issue of understanding the brain. Of ending the faith in the mind, in consciousness, and giving over to the matter of existence.

Some wished to call me a reductionist, but it was never true. I was never interested in asserting the reduction of two, or even more, concepts into one. I was finished with the old debates of mind versus body, energy and matter. In truth, before I was done, I had shattered those metaphors with the discovery of a micro-biological model deeper than DNA, deeper still than atoms, electrons, quarks, strings.

It is, of course, unexplainable to you. It would be like trying to explain Relativity Theory to a child. What comes closest is to say that I unlocked the bio-*prana* of dreams, but not dreams as personal, psychological moments of consciousness, but dreams as they reside in space. In the recesses of empty awareness, beyond the *place*, and I mean that almost literally, beyond the place of dead sleep, I discovered the biological realm of non-being. Here, in the depth of everything, everything existed. All time. All phenomena. A place north of north and south of south, a place outside the universe and at the center of each individual; a pool of being that made space-time irrelevant, the subtle substance of Brahman/no-Brahman. But it was neither spirit nor energy, consciousness nor matter. It was, more than anything, fluid psyche, and trans-neocortical *location*.

These absurd metaphors are what it takes to crack the paradigms that hold a civilization at bay. I had no adherents. My colleagues thought me mad. But one must invest in one's own genius. Certainly there are a hundred million fools in each generation who think that they can save the world, but there are those, too, Newton, Freud, Einstein, Mozart, who if they did not believe the call of their own certain genius would have left the world bereft.

I began with experiments on myself. Of course, there were always simple, chemical combinations, organic and inorganic, which could alter emotion, attitude, even thought. But as you know, I found that in the right combination with physical and mental exercises, mostly for the eyes, that with sounds and non-visible light I could create a laser of dimensionality within the brain's synapses on which I could travel, psychically, and change or even create emotions or consciousness, but more essentially, unconscious thoughts and images.

Quite literally, I found myself in the center of Freud's DreamWork, behind the censor's back, in a realm of absolute certainty.

Do not misunderstand. I could enter no one else's location. This was not spiritual possession. Certainly, as well, there are commonalties among all human beings. It was these "generals" or archetypes, as Jung or Plato would have it, which allowed my early breakthroughs in treating pathologies and phobias, some of which even NASA has used to deal with the exigencies of long-term space habitation. Even you, Dr. Zu, whose approach to psycho-faunacology is so pluralistic, have used my principles to ready domestic species for life in space. There, I came to agree with you, and Veronica as well. The classic distinctions between human and non-human animals are specious.

But as I began to work with others I found it necessary, as did Freud, to learn so much about each individual, both medically and psychoanalytically, it often took months of inductive experimentation to find the predictable combinations to help them. More and more I became convinced that my essential mission lay within my own genius, and as I progressed I found myself beyond the land of dreams, in a region of pre-perception. In time, though I had told no one, I was opening the mysteries of sages and yogins, but without the spiritual shenanigans and ontological hoopla. I was on the verge of a science of telekinesis and telepathy.

From what little was understood of my work, I was misinterpreted as a reductionist, a man who could make the brain dance with shots and pills, but as you see, that would be like accusing me of calling every-thing in the ocean a fish. Others accused me of being a virtual reality trickster, of hiding some advanced means of manipulating a microchip probe, with the hook-up simply occurring within the brain instead of an interface with a machine. Of course, I used computers in my analysis and simulations, but in the end there is still no comparison between machine and brain, though obviously I believe that there is a fine line between quantity and quality, deduction and intuition, and that the line between electronics and biology is far from ineffable. Yet what I had discovered was real, not virtual, an actual, infinite, individual real. A biological, not a technological, nexus.

But of course, I would be misunderstood. I had, as Kuhn suggested, changed the paradigm. But I had not just changed the most recent, scientific paradigm. I had changed the ontological paradigm of all human thinking. I had broken open the universe. I had changed the world forever. Who, in my time, would understand that?

And yet I continued, not drawn by fame, for certainly, at the time, I received as much infamy. No, not for myself, not even for the pursuit of truth. But for the good, the *common good* of mankind. Think of the possibilities when each individual possessed the potential to change their world; not just their psychic world, though such a boon would be gift enough, but their material world. Envision the end of illness. Visualize the end of individual wealth for a world of ubiquitous wealth, the end of hunger, greed, jealousy, lust, even violence because they would have become useless and irrelevant. Think of a pure world in which much of our life-wasting technology was no longer needed. I perched on the cusp of bringing this to my world, to everyone.

It was during this time, just after the turn of the millennium, when all of the bugaboo had come to nothing and the apocalyptic religious movements were in retreat—re-calculating their magical numerology and coming up with new prophetic revisions, a never-ending task that could go on till the end of humanity, until someone, finally, was right, and even then they would be right for all the wrong reasons—that I attended a conference at the State University of New York, Albany. There, after I gave a short, keynote lecture, one which no one, not even the most discerning doctors and scientists came close to comprehending, Veronica approached me from the audience.

It had been years since I had seen her. Her hands were still rough and wrinkled, her eyes yet deep and lively, though around them now the almost imperceptible wrinkles of early middle-age had begun to fold the corners. Her auburn hair hung down loosely at her shoulders and she wore a long, flowing skirt. At this point I had the power not only to control how I saw what was in front of me, but how I felt about it, as well, yet I was surprised, as she took my hand, how much passion spontaneously arose inside me, almost as if it had sprung from my heart.

"Werther," she said softly. "It's good. It's so very good."

I left the conference with her and had dinner in town. Over wine I discovered that she'd attained her Ph.D. in literature from the University of Southern California, then returned home where she took a job there at SUNY-Albany. She still lived on her farm. In fact, she'd briefly married one of her farm boys.

"I thought I might mother my way into love," she said. "But I couldn't love my way into mothering him. It was a disaster."

"I'm sorry," I said.

She smiled. "My own mother is dead. I own it all now. And my biological clock is ticking."

I raised my eyes directly to hers. I had paid my years of purgatory to her love and it was she, and no one else, who had made me a solitary man. However impassioned I had become in my work, my failure to win her love had spurred me as deeply as my own mother's death. Now, after a decade, Veronica sat in front of me again.

"You want a child," I said.

"If possible," said Veronica, "yours."

I am not a man easily stunned, but I found, that with half of my dreams laid in my lap, my first instinct was to evade her.

"It was you who told me that immortality was irrelevant," I said.

And she laughed. "You're such a knucklehead it's enough to endear me," she said. "I'm talking simply of wanting love. Motherhood. What any woman wants. I'm not thinking of death now, my own or anyone else's, but life, life, purely and simply."

"Do you love me?" I blurted. "Can you?"

"Werther," said Veronica. "I want to love you. Make me love you."

"You can't do it yourself?"

She sat back. She lay her fingers at the stem of her wine glass and let them caress it, as if at play in front of her own eyes. She did not look up. "Once," she said, "all you asked for was me, under any terms. I'm saying take me. I've followed your career. I have everything I need. I'm not here because I need your money or what your fame can give me. If I could choose a man to love, Werther, I would love you. Though I cannot love. But the one man who I want to love can make me love him."

"I shall not experiment on you," I whispered.

"Not to experiment on me, Werther. To love me. To marry me and share a child. And together to pursue your dreams, of changing the world, of changing me. What have you to lose?"

"To look at you everyday," I said, "and wonder."

"To look at me everyday," said Veronica. "To sleep with me. To make love to me."

She began to cry as I gazed across the small table and dared to take her hand. I had the power to walk away. I'd done so before. And now, even more so, it took only a brief moment of concentration to place myself in my ego-less location of power and be unaffected. But I found myself locked, Buddha-like, in the paradox of selfless sympathy. How could I go forward to change the world, to save it from itself, and yet deny Veronica whom I once loved so deeply? To what point? And should I deny myself the pleasures of love, the simple hopes of a simple man, because of this burden, my genius? I tell you, this was no Pandora's box. I sought not power, not fame, not to quell my curiosity. I did not even seek love. It was not even my desire for love which brought this demon, this dragon, to haunt the earth and threaten the end of everything. I did it from love and out of love. From beyond the desire to help everyone, from the simple embryo of human impulse to reach out, to be kind, to help the person next to me. That love was involved makes it all the more ironic. That which makes us destroys us. Within the knowledge to heal the world lies the knowledge to lay it asunder.

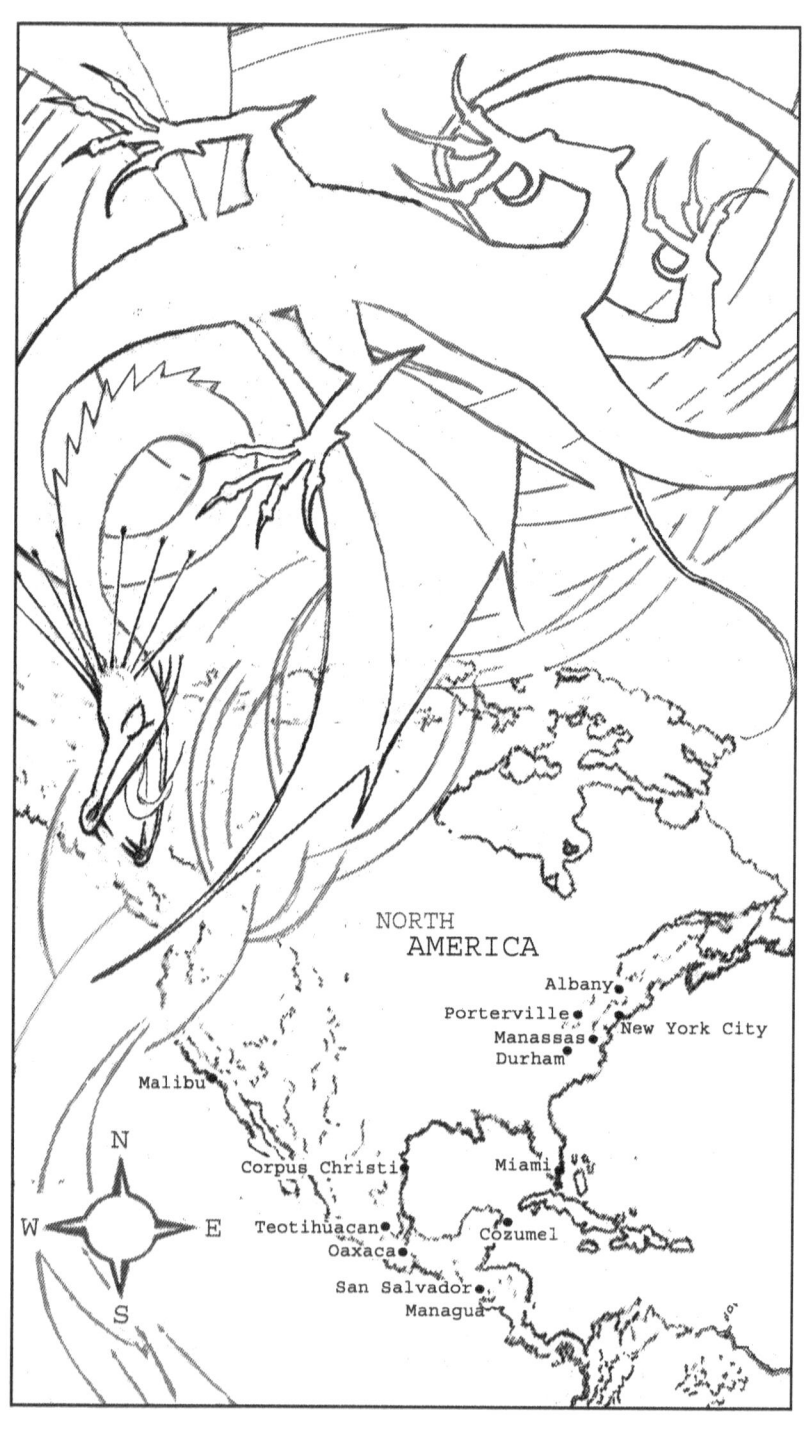

NORTH
AMERICA

Albany
Porterville
Manassas New York City
Durham

Malibu

N

Corpus Christi Miami

W E

Teotihuacan
Oaxaca Cozumel

San Salvador
Managua

S

The Dragon Journal of Lisa Piccolo Zu

Dragons did not fly like bats or birds either. Their wings did not take the place of their forearms. They weren't extensions of their fingers. Like I said before, dragon wings grew from their rib cages, and the ribs of their wings, more like cartilage than bone, were made of the same, light, honey-comb material which protected their organs and around which their muscles and nerves grew. Like birds, their bones were light, maybe even a little hollow. They were not lizards, but like the dinosaurs, reptiles with scales, so it's difficult to say whether they were warm- or cold-blooded, though it's probably a mistake to try to classify them in that way. For one, the combination of their size and their ability to stand upright creates problems in explaining how their blood pressure would stay up if they were cold-blooded. Paleontologists have this problem now when they try to envision the same things in the sauropods, the long-necked, vegetarian dinos. You need an efficient blood pushing system, and probably a big heart. It seems that dragons were more omnivorous than sauropods, and had bigger heads, as well. A lot of those big vegetarian dinosaurs ate stones, just like birds, to help them digest their food, and it's possible that early on, when dragons were evolving from dinosaurs, that's how dragons first consumed the limestone which created their first, fiery burps, something which turned out to be an evolutionary advantage in terms of defense, as well as flight. This could explain why it became possible for them to seek out and consume silver and gold, too, even if by accident at first. Eventually it became habitual for them to pursue and eat limestone to fuel their fires, not their digestion, and gold and silver to lie on in their lairs.

Like some of the Deinonychus, dinosaurs which some people started calling Velociraptors late in the last century because of a silly movie, some dragons even sported feathers, though more for ornamentation than for flight. Like dragons, Deinonychids ate eggs and meat. Dragon wings were stretched skin, like a bat's, but of course not the same, more like the wings of a huge dragonfly, but a kind of translucent leather. Both their front and back feet had talons.

Because of drawings that artists made after the extinction of dragons, lots of people write about the strength of these talons, the dragons' whip-like powerful tails, and their huge, ferocious heads. Of course, none of this makes too much sense if you want to get them in the air. Even in the late Twentieth Century, when all the talk about the end of the world got people talking about dragons again, and when interest in dragons was renewed, some of the new writers (EI would call them "revisionists"), who figured out the chemistry of dragon flight, still pictured dragons with thick legs and big heads. Before that, people who thought about it, and not a lot of people did, thought that dragons were kind of like pteradons or pteradactyls which, if you know anything about it, didn't fly so good anyways.

These revisionists argued, pretty logically, that dragons couldn't really have been practically invulnerable—otherwise how did they get wiped out—they thought the big heads were for holding big eyes that like a cobra mesmerized the dragons' foes. This explained why people sometimes thought that dragons spoke to them. Some of the few, lucky men who survived an encounter with a dragon often came away pretty befuddled, their heads full of gibberish and riddles. But the problem with that is that big heads mean big skulls. Big skulls mean no flight. The dragon head was large enough to hold its over-sized eyes and carnivorous teeth, but it tended to be light-weight and thin, too.

I want to spend some time writing about dragons and riddles and mesmerizing, communication with dragons and persuading, but for now it's enough to realize that whatever they did, they didn't do it with gigantic heads. Nor, in fighting, were their weapons mainly their tails and claws and teeth, though they could use them. Like any predator their greatest weapon was surprise. Then, for them, fire, and if faced with a head-on confrontation, an ability, like a cobra, to hold an opponent's gaze. I agree with the revisionists on the gaze, but not the head. I need to talk about invulnerability, too.

A dragon's arms were slender, her head thin, almost human looking when she placed her chin on her chest. In the black, reptilian slits of a dragon's irises, you could fall into eternity and forever lose your dreams.

Just before we left home, El got a letter from Grandpa Charles to give to Grandma Zu. I wish he could have come with us. He's smart and funny. He taught me how to ride a horse. But I guess we were lucky just to get a letter. It took eight weeks to get here from California and we had to give the courier fifty dollars.

Tonight we are in New York City. El was really prepared. I think she'd been getting ready a long time. She had sleeping bags and winter gear, dry-pack food and some water, back packs. Though we'd been doing some hunting and farming for a while, we didn't take rifles. El gave me a buck knife to wear at my waist and a .22 pistol that I wore in a holster under my clothes. El said a .22 was small and in the end did the most damage close range.

"Okay, El," I said. "That's good to know."

She didn't take it as funny. "I don't know what it's going to be like, really," said El very seriously. "I just want to be safe."

I also saw that she had a ton of cash. Some people have said that there are only city-states anymore, that there are no more states, and really not even any more countries. But it's not true. People are trying. The bus driver took our money.

We walked down the mountain and all the way to the old Interstate 87. The hike took eight hours. Then we camped by the road for almost two days before the propane bus showed up. Nothing else drove by in all that time, though a man from the local commune farm came by to check us out after our first night by the road and he assured El that the thing existed.

The bus was painted green and had a little fly wheel motor that ran on propane and charged a big battery that ran the engine. And it wasn't really a bus but just a long van. It came through every-other-week from Montreal to Burlington to Albany to New York. The bus driver said he made the route all the time. He wasn't afraid of bandits.

It wasn't like *Road Warrior*. There were people almost everywhere and few people traveled. Everybody knew their neighbors. There was almost nothing to steal and besides, most of his passengers were well armed. He pulled out something that looked like an assault rifle. He was big. He wore one of those wool tammies colored dark green, red, yellow, and brown over long dreadlocks, but he didn't have a Rasta accent.

There was another passenger. There'd be a full bus, the driver said, coming out of Albany. The other passenger was a man who actually wore a business suit. El, who never used to like men in suits, found this comforting. He was going to New York on business. "The business of America is still business, you know," he said. El and the bus driver laughed, but the man didn't.

Like Grandpa Charles had said, now, everything was farms, either small ones or collectives. El said there was a tradition of farming collectives in upstate New York, all the way back to Nathaniel Hawthorne's times and through the Hippies. There were a lot of windmills, even a few tractors.

"Maybe the worst is over," whispered El.

"Notice," said the bus driver. He waived his arm toward a cluster of wooden buildings in the center of a patchwork of farm fields. I saw corn and wheat growing, and smaller patches of vegetables, an apple orchard. "No churches," he said. "They say the dragon doesn't like churches."

The man in the suit raised an eyebrow and I poked El who just took a quick breath and held it, then released it slowly.

"Or fossil fuel technology," I said.

The driver made contact with my eyes in the mirror. "Or nuclear," he said. "They say that if you try to clear away forest to farm, the dragon will appear and burn your village."

"The dragon is an eco-terrorist," I said.

"That's right, kiddo," the driver said.

"Then why would he destroy churches?" said El. As much as she tried to resist engaging, something always got to her when I started up the dragon talk.

"Not, he," I said. "She. Male dragons are just interested in eating and mating, and marking territory. This is a nesting pattern. This isn't attack, it's self-preservation."

El started getting that apologetic look on her face that said, "My kid, the pre-adolescent. In a year she'll start puberty. All this fantasy will disappear when she starts thinking about boys."

"Besides," I said, "dragons communicate in riddles. What's she trying to tell us?"

"Why don't we just gather up all of our weapons," said the business man, "and threaten to do some nasty thing like chop down a forest to build a church? When the dragon shows up we'll just blow him—I mean *her*—away."

"Duh!" I said.

"Lisa!" said El.

"I'm sorry," said the driver to El. "I was just having some fun. Bus talk. You hear lots of stuff on the bus. I didn't know your kid was so serious about it."

"Little girl," the business man said to me. I hate it when anybody refers to me as *little girl*. "Where did this dragon come from? Monster Island? The Dragon Planet? Doesn't it take dragons to make dragons?"

"Let me explain that," I said.

"No," said El.

"Just let me explain."

"Lisa!" said El.

"I'm sorry," said the bus driver.

"I am, too," said the business man to El, though not to me. "Really."

It got quiet. I waited a long time, even till after Albany when the bus got pretty crowded. We didn't go into Albany itself, but picked up in a ghost town suburb outside a big, dead shopping mall. All around it was like retail death, just big, dead, empty K-Marts and Rite-Aids, seas of asphalt with rusting automobiles strewn across like the carcasses of a rubbed-out buffalo herd. There was a lot more devastation, with little farms popping up in-between, as we got closer to New York. That's when I finally spoke to El, though she ignored me. I held her arm and spoke into her ear. I said, "Who even said it was just one fucking dragon."

We got off old I-87 and drove down along the Hudson River on the New Jersey side. There were still rusty signs along the road that said Palisades Interstate Parkway. Down there we went slow because the road was in pretty bad shape and there were still lots of abandoned cars. Sometimes they were piled up so high they were like a wall, like a junkyard maze instead of a road, and you couldn't even see any of New Jersey on the one side, or the river and New York on the other. We'd moved up to the front of the van before it got packed. I sat next to the driver and El sat behind me. The driver told us that people used cars to make fences now, to block off neighborhoods in the city, or patchwork farms in New Jersey or on Long Island.

Lots of people were gone or dead. Maybe half. Maybe more. Though there were some buildings with wind mills and battery generators, like Grandpa Charles said there'd be, there just hadn't been enough eco-technology to go around. A lot of the survivors in Manhattan, the driver said, lived like Medieval lords and vassals, the wealthy holed up in the tops of well-guarded, well-armed skyscrapers and apartment buildings, though they had to use the stairs; there were few elevators working.

"No TV or radio yet," said the business man from the middle seat. "No tele-communication. How did the dragon manage that?"

"But there are still markets and bakeries and banks," said the driver. He caught the business man's eye in his rear view mirror. "By the way, what do you do?"

"I'm in the insurance business," the man said.

Everybody was quiet for a while after that.

When we crossed into New York through the Holland Tunnel the driver spoke again. "You can still get clothes, you know," he said. "Shoes, food. It didn't turn into chaos. It wasn't like that. People tried to help each other."

"It wasn't violent?" said El. "What about the poor?"

"Were you poor?" the driver said. "Me neither. Not too many wars were ever started by the poor, even if they had to fight them. I have a doctorate in social history."

"Mom's a Ph.D., too," I said.

The driver shrugged. "There are still hospitals," he said. "Plenty of work for nurses and doctors. It's not the end of the world. Things are just a whole lot different."

The bus stopped in Greenwich Village near a subway stop on Houston.

"Pack up," El said to me, "it's a bit of a walk to the pier."

"Just take the 1 Train right to the end," the driver said to her. He winked at me. "The dragon left the subways running."

Grandpa Charles says that human beings are not evil, they're just short-sighted and self-centered. For supposedly abstract animals, they don't do much thinking ahead unless they're confronted with a problem which keeps them from getting what they want. He says a lot of people think they're special because they're human, because humans have written symphonies and built space ships, but none of those people ever stop to think that they couldn't write a symphony or build a space ship. Most people can't even play a musical instrument, or don't know how their car worked. Most people were just animals who learned how to run the simple machines that were around them. He says that people think they're special because they have feelings, and because they feel their individuality very deeply, but that all animals have feelings, that even things have feelings and that every sentient thing strives, defines, dominates, emphatically expresses its individuality. "Isn't that amazing?" says Grandpa Charles. "I find that so puzzling."

"Why?" I said.

"Because he wants to be a Buddhist, but really he's an American bourgeoisie," Grandma Hestor Zu said. "It's the bourgeois conception of the universe."

"That wouldn't change the facts if it were true," said Grandpa Charles. "And I'd watch your politics if you want to go to Mars." Grandpa Charles says that most people really aren't very special.

"Which is absolutely irrelevant," said Grandma Zu. "There's no value to being special, whatever the hell it means. Being smarter or more unique or more sensitive doesn't entitle you to more life, to more of the planet."

"It doesn't?" said Grandpa Charles.

"Are you special, Grandpa Charles?" I said to him.

"As special as a chimpanzee," he said.

"They're pretty special, there aren't many left," I said.

"Precisely," said Grandpa Charles. "Unlike human beings."

"We should get rid of human beings," I said to him.

"Oh Lisa," said Grandma Zu, "now you sound like him."

"Who should?" he said. "How would you do that? Who would do it?"

"We'll do it to ourselves." Everybody thinks that if we destroy the world it will be the end of everything, but it won't. It will just be the end of human beings. Even if we destroy most of the eco-system, the earth will still be here and eventually animals will be back. Maybe the next dominant species will be better than us.

Anyway, I was pretty little when we had that conversation. It was before everything really came apart.

"Would you have us all dead?" said Grandma Zu.

"You can live on Mars, Grandma Zu."

"I'll be up there ruining Mars," she said.

"What about you?" said Grandpa Charles. "Are you going to die for the other animals, so they can have the planet back? If every-body's dead, that means me and El, and even you."

"Yes," I said to him. "Yes, I would." If that's the price, then even me.

The Story of Werther Fausten

I married Veronica in Porterville. My father conducted the wedding ceremony. He had attached himself to a moderate Mennonite community and retired, a man of the land. He worked an apple orchard and a peach orchard and traded his produce within the community for goods and services, or sold it at the farmers' markets, sometimes as far west as Harrisburg, transporting his fruit by horse and wagon. He heated his home with wood and lit it with candles. Kept a cow for milk, geese as watch dogs, chickens for eggs and pigs for meat. He learned from others, shared with others.

He was still young enough to have helped build several barns. He no longer smoked his pipe, but he did drink wine, tea, and coffee in moderation. He had nothing against dancing, either, and these habits kept him a moderate. But he was a man broken into sainthood like a wild horse. When questions of faith flared up inside him, he simply lowered his head and turned away. It was enough to make your bread, to pull your weight, to help your friends and, if need be, help your enemies. He lived and he forgave.

He forgave Dianna's mother, who'd died of pneumonia and alcoholism. And he forgave his daughter and my half-sister, Dianna, who came to my wedding with her two children, ages three and one, the first from her husband who was now long gone and the second, it was rumored, from the man for whom she left him, however briefly. Dianna had that tired look of a single mother. She'd been a heroin addict, my father said, and with the cut-backs on welfare she'd fallen into prostitution. It was then that my father found her during a Mennonite community visitation to the county jail. He paid her bail and negotiated the release of her children from foster homes. The

Mennonites had since taken her into their own half-way house. She'd begun work as a secretary for a Chevy dealer—a connection from the most liberal edge of the community—while the Mennonites day-cared, educated, and indoctrinated her kids.

Yes, my father had forgiven her. He'd forgiven me. He'd forgiven himself, too. And whatever trials had taken us on these paths of opposition—leading him deeper into religion and the way of simplicity and denial, leading me to the light beyond the cave, to science, affirmation, and action—they had become irrelevant to us. I loved him and respected him deeply.

"The self is an abyss," he said to me the night before I was wed, "the ego a construct of foolishness, a contract with the Devil. Ninety-nine percent of what most everyone holds dear, God finds irrelevant. Search inside forever, you will not find Him. Perpetuate the earth. Harmless survival and good works to others, that is all there is to paradise."

I did not say to him that he had not become a Mennonite. That he was still a Lutheran. That he'd barely wandered a degree from salvation through faith alone. That his solutions were depressing and Medieval. Or that he'd borne a son who would change the world. Of course, I have lived to see my vision transformed ironically, but as I speak to you now, Dr. Zu, I await the return of my health so that I may transform the world yet again.

When I met Dianna at the reception I took her hand, staring into her dark eyes while my father held her one-year-old and her three-year-old clung to his leg. In a moment, inside the tunnel of our mutual gaze, I fell into the eternity of the self, my memories of Dianna flashing in sequence, the confusion of my love for her and for Veronica raging volcanically beneath me, indistinguishably.

"I'm so happy for you, Werther," she said. "Veronica is so beautiful. I'm so glad I got to see you, I've been so busy."

She kissed my cheek and I hers. I said to her, softly, "I'm glad you came," while taking the meditative steps to seal off the foolish lava of my desire. As much as I loved and admired my father and the success of his journey, I saw in that moment, again, how clearly my work could foreshorten the labyrinthine anachronisms of charity, religion, penance and reform.

"She still smokes cigarettes and pot, and drinks too much," my father said gently, without condemnation, after we had walked away. "We're trying to get her to stop drinking."

A detailed introduction was impossible but Veronica, a brilliant woman, noted, as we stepped away, the similarity of our brown black eyes and brooding brow, my father's sharp chin.

I hadn't planned on seeing Dianna, so the next day, after visiting my mother's grave and wishing my father good-bye, as Veronica and I took our honeymoon, making the long drive through the center of Pennsylvania into western New York, to Buffalo and then Niagara Falls, I told her the story of my ill-fated first affair with my own half-sister.

I am a man of poetic sensibility, so the metaphor of our sojourn did not elude me. We left my father standing in the Lutheran cemetery outside his old church, his horse and buggy parked behind him. We left the grave of my mother, the womb, now dead, from which I was given life, and drove into the darkest of woods, the virgin Allegheny Forest. We emerged at the greatest waterfall in the world to consummate our odd contract, and on the way I told my wife of my first love, a girl, now my father's ward, who was his daughter and my bastard half-sister, the drug-worn single mother whom she met at our wedding.

"You will help her someday, Werther," said Veronica.

"Do you think?"

"Your father wears his infidelity around his neck," she said.

"There," I said, "you see? I was thinking of the poetry of our circumstance and yet failed to see it in my father's."

"You see it in the things around you," Veronica said. "I needed Coleridge. The poet loves, the critic loves the way the poet loves. But I want to learn to see things with my own eyes."

"Nonsense," I said. "You think of others while I think of myself, and then the world at large."

"Is that your albatross, Werther?" Veronica said to me. "The world at large?"

"I'm afraid I shall be yours," I said.

"Impossible," she said, kissing my cheek as I drove. We went on for a while in silence.

"Did you like my father?" I said.

"I didn't expect eastern Pennsylvania to still be so German," said Veronica. "People like your father, so full of determination and sadness, driven by ideas."

"He is not driven so much as romanced by them," I said. "And when you are in love you see only the thing, the idea, the person beloved, and fail to really see them at all. My father has taken a circuitous path to his bedeviled enlightenment."

"Is that so?" Veronica said. "So what lies must I tell you to have you see me truly?"

"And how would I know that?" I asked. "Coleridge simply misread Kant, you know. If you're going to go on seeing things through other's eyes, one's own are biased enough."

"Emerson misread Coleridge," said Veronica. "Kant misread the world and we have probably misread them all. So here we are, back to this horrible, modern place." She paused. We drove on a narrow, black highway, its double yellow lines winding through a tunnel of maple trees, their green leaves blind with brief life. "You love your father, Werther," said Veronica. "Don't you?"

"Yes," I said.

"Then you understand one simple thing."

"No," I said, "I feel one, simple thing. That is far from under-standing it."

"Well then," she said, "we'll make an interesting pair searching for it."

We made an interesting pair as it was. I preferred the slightly run-down American side of the Falls, with its simple railings and lawns, its asphalt paths wandering through the oaks and sycamores. Veronica loved the Canadian side with all of its tacky souvenir shops and cheap hotels. She had us rent a room with a hot tub and a heart-shaped waterbed. We shopped incessantly, visited the flower clock, rode the Maid of the Mist beneath the Horse Shoe Falls. "All this water!" Veronica said to me as we circled into the curve of the waterfall. She reached beneath my rain coat and held me to her as the blinding white water pounded the surface and the roar deafened all other sound. She kissed me then. "Werther!" she yelled. "Look! All this water!"

The Story of Werther Fausten

I loved Veronica so deeply that her acquiescence became its own burden and in it I saw my mother and her life time of silence under my father's infidelity. And if so, then who was my mistress? Humanity?

I'd recently gained research facilities at Duke University and money from any number of private and public institutions, one of them, Dr. Zu, your own, beloved NASA, as well as the European Space Agency, though I received even more money from the Russians who have always been forward thinking in terms of experimenting in what, under American scientific classification, was considered the paranormal. How strange to find myself at odds with the mainstream when I had given my life to it.

The thrust of my work, of course, was to manage the psychology of genetically altered domestic animals, some for farm production, others for the companionship of space colonists. I'm familiar, Dr. Zu, with your pioneering work in the field of psycho-faunacology, which has proven the deeply beneficial relationship between humans and animals in space—that the presence of a cat on board a space ship can make it easier for humans to exercise, decrease boredom and irritability, reduce conflicts, improve attitude, actually even reduce the decay of calcium in human bone—the act of caring, not just caring for, but caring about, is so essentially human; you have clearly established it. Even more remarkably, enhancing the capacity of the animal to care and bond with humans increases the creature's survival potential, as well, and then exponentially the chances of human survival. Animals are now indispensable to our colonization of the stars.

So if we were to alter living desert forms: plants, insects, lizards, and birds enough so that they could live in the carbon dioxide rich, early terraforming of Mars, so we must alter hens, pigs, sheep, cows, cats, dogs, even horses to withstand the rigors of hibernation, confinement, and low gravity in space, and then in greenhouse farms on the planet. Think of the benefits, psychologically and economically, of the genetically altered Martian horse. Even Veronica was intrigued. So I have wandered only slightly. I'm coming to the dragon or I suppose I should say the dragon is coming to me. I became the wizard of caring. The man assigned to find and release it in the mammalian brain.

The psycho-biological matrix, or placement, of caring, allowed my diversion into the realm of emotions and the deep link between the psychic and physical, a relationship which I could best describe as dialectical, if only you might hold the constant movement of all the shifting terms in a calm, ever-presence, almost as if I were trying to describe one's awareness in the depth of unconscious, deep sleep. This was my territory. Here lay the ghosts of the archetypes, the ghostly bodies of the seeds of thought, the wispy spirits of neurons. I was yet on the verge of finding the neural passageways to release this place into cyber-imagery, so it could be viewed on a computer monitor, or better, allow me, on computer, to hook into the cyber-space, metaphoric world of another subject's psyche. I was still my own subject, my own experiment, but I could dance in the world of my dreams while fully conscious and unlock my fears, my urges, my longings, my jealousies in the free-living sentience of my psyche.

I was stunned, oh, how I was stunned by the palpability and freedom of this animal-like world! What lives inside us! The chaos! If William James could speak of the consciousness of every cell, he had not thought, then, of its accompanying unconsciousness, its drive, its will, the psychic depth of its individuation. I walked deeper and deeper into this forest of beings in search of love, lured by the most docile and seductive forms which inhabited hate, greed, cowardice, fear. Kindness and sympathy were like worms—it is so hard to explain!— oh, the inept human heart! And worse, it seemed as if the most essential human emotion was the only one I could not find. I almost despaired at this mystery, that our goodness was so ugly, that our essence, myth.

I walked with Veronica in the hills of North Carolina's blue mountains, the scent of pine filling the breeze, a hint of snow in the air.

"It is a place," I said to her, intrigued, frustrated, self-absorbed. "As if the psyche were not personal, but a dimension, a shared, timeless history of the human unconscious that absorbed past and future into its moment."

"Then do we see the future in our dreams?" she said.

"Yes," I said. "Yes, but not the future as we think of it."

"Do you see me loving you?"

"I fear love is the ugliest thing inside me," I said.

She took my hand and led me back to our home, our bedroom, where she undressed me and then herself. I fell inside her beauty once again, forgetting everything, raging over her, absorbing her, loving her beyond passion, my voice singing out my love as we strained inside each other. I felt her quiver beneath me and I came within her with all of my being, falling upon her breasts in exhaustion and joy. You cannot know the despair I felt when I heard her sobbing, her throat releasing a deep, painful, reptilian groan, and I rose from her bosom to see her weeping under a waterfall of tears.

I lay beside her until she slept, then rose in the night to go back to my work, entering the plain of dreams. I must speak now in absolute metaphor or I cannot speak at all, but I must speak, because my words are the only path you will have to trace my life which I must give to the world to save it.

Beyond the first, rolling plain of fantasy, occupied by wish fields vaster than Midwestern wheat fields or fields of corn, lies the forest of emotion. It takes a month in this timeless place to pass to the edge of these woods populated by sentient dreams. On the other side is a desert of immeasurable proportions. In the year it takes to cross it you will dream a thousand times that you have found water and you will drink insatiably, yet you will always remain unsatisfied. To return to the forest you need only turn around, but to reach the other side of the desert you must walk interminably in the heat of the sun with a feeling of hopelessness and dread, fearing that there are unseen predators that will fall from the sky or rise from the sand. In fact, they do. There, fanged mouths open upon you filling you with horror, descending from the sky, rising at your feet, but at the moment of death, when you lie upon their slimy tongues and see the pit of their red throats, they disappear. Though it happens again and again, your fear never changes, in fact it expands.

On the other side of the desert is a mountain range, its height so despairing that time becomes irrelevant. Each crest you climb leaves another yet higher crest above you. The air is thin and you never get a full breath. The atmosphere becomes thinner and thinner and you dream of breathing while you suffocate on these reaches above the world. Suddenly a cave opens before you. If you enter, you must relive all of your dreams until you reach, again, the edge of the forest of emotion and sentient dreams. Here, the circle of despair is complete. You know with all the certainty of your existence that there is nothing to do but turn back.

Instead I took one, tentative step forward, my leg sluggish, my foot a hammer, my muscles as if they were a ton of soft clay. Then, faintly, almost indiscernibly, like the last fading murmur of a retreating plane or train, like a hint of breath upon my cheek, I felt a voice. I did not hear it. It was not in my ear.

"Werther," it said. Yet it was threatening, not inviting. In that whisper I felt death. "Werther." It was everywhere and nowhere. More than sound. In one way, palpable, in another, as non-existent as a presence you might feel when you wake in the middle of the night.

"Who are you?" I said, stepping forward again.

"Come no further, Werther." And then, unmistakably, as un-mistakable as it could be for something I neither saw nor heard at all, came a laugh. "A rhyme!" it said.

I stepped again and fell into pitch darkness. Now came a dance of images, like when you shut your eyes hard and face a bright light. I peered into the blackness. I stepped forward. I could not see, except now, like the sound I'd heard, like the feeling on my cheek, the darkness intimated the faintest of forms. I stepped forward again, absurdly walking in the spaceless black air. This time, the voice emerged more clearly, though I did not hear it with my ears but felt it in my soul.

"Do not come here," it said. "Do not come."

I went forward. I had come too far to turn back. What could be left? Unless this was the realm of endless coma, that place from where the dying emerge, if only for a moment, just before death, their eyes open with unimaginable clarity and life. You have seen it, have you not? Even as a doctor who has seen it a thousand times, I've felt, in that moment, that the patient had returned to life, that there lives inside of us something eternal. As recurrent as my fear in the desert of dread, where the mouths fell from the sky and erupted from the sand, so too, in that real moment in front of a dying woman or man, I am filled again with hope. Then the patient dies.

A figure emerged. An ancient crone. Her features so old and ugly, her skin, lizard-like, green-gray and wrinkled. Her nose was long and her huge, yellow eyes split with vertical, black slits. She was bald. An odd, skin-like cape descended from behind her head, as if growing from the raised haunches of her shoulder blades; cupping it from the inside she pulled it around her; it fell to the floor, covered her feet, disguised her wretched hands, covered her head. There was a smell of phosphorescence about her, and as she breathed, her breath slipped from her nostrils like illumined vapor, sometimes yellow, sometimes blue.

"Who are you?" I said again.

Her head swayed slightly on her shoulders, her left brow dipping forward, and her gaze, her gaze mesmerized me, held me like a rodent before a cobra. "Does everything need a name?" she said, though her lips barely moved, in fact I heard only a dreadful hissing and felt heat from the puff of flame that rose from her breath. No, I did not hear her but I felt her thoughts take shape inside me, a smell, a pinch, an acrid taste, and then the words, falling from these sensations like hieroglyphs. In that moment, I suddenly knew, and *feared*, that she knew more of me than I knew of my self.

"Who am I?" I said, before I had even conceived what I would say. I listened to my question as if it were, like her language, something that had fallen, like over-ripe fruit, from my heart.

Then she laughed again, and again I could not see an expression cross her face, though her mouth opened in a yawn exposing an array of inhuman teeth. Her laugh froze me, literally cold-frozen and still.

"Now," she said, "in the old days, it would be time to eat you."

It came to me then, that I was not before her, but sitting in my lab, conscious, confronting her as if I could move with a separate body in an astral plane. I was not hers, but she, mine.

"Oh no," she said, hissing her fiery breath. "No, Werther, you are mine."

I steeled myself. "These riddles aside," I said, "I must know what you guard. If love is what stands behind you, then you must let me pass."

"There is nothing behind me," she said, "what'ss behind you?"

For a moment, I understood that she was the beast beneath us all. There stood the battle I must fight, the sacrifice I must make, and that the irony of love lay within her. I must split her breast to set it free. Or did she guard it? Or was she my guardian? I was dazed.

"Sslay?" she whispered inside me. "Sslay me?"

She stood slightly more erect, as if she had expanded with an intake of breath and, miraculously, now gazed down upon me.

"Leave, Werther," she hissed. "Leave and do not return. Or you will never be rid of me."

"I seek caring," I said to her.

"Then care."

"And love."

"Then love."

"Do not mock me!"

"Impossible?" she hissed.

I fell back, as if riddled literally by her questioning. "I will know," I said to her. "I *will* know."

"You will know devasstation," said the crone. "Go back now, or to keep you from desstroying my world, I will be forced to desstroy yours."

She raised her narrow head and something rose from her throat like lightning. A light flashed and I turned away to guard my eyes, but that momentary turning was all it took to transport me back. I lay on the floor of my work room, caked in the dry, salty residue of what had been a heavy sweat. My face felt scorched and when I looked in the mirror I saw the burn on my forehead, cheek, and neck where they had been exposed to the creature's fire as I turned from her breath. It was almost dawn. I had been at work for over four hours. Returning to the bedroom, I sat and stared at Veronica, still asleep in our bed. The gray winter light fell upon her cheek and began to illumine her auburn hair. If she could only feel for me what I felt then. If I could but unlock my unrelinquishing love. If I could do it for Veronica, I could do it for every human being and the world would be irrevocably changed.

The Story of Werther Fausten

Spring came to the foothills of the Blue Ridge Mountains. Crocuses sprouted from the crisp ground, the leaves hinted at budding and the first daffodils burst gold into the sunlight, even through the last, white dusting of new, spring snow. Veronica, on leave from her university, pointed out each change of the season. The rise of Cancer and Leo in the east after sunset, Orion's headlong dive toward the western hills. But I was filled with the self absorption of a man on the brink of the world.

Who was this creature at the edge and center of my being? Inevitably, because she was female and a crone, I went back to Jung. Certainly she was no shadow of my ego. Could she be archetype, anima? For so long I had considered Jungian theory simply as metaphor, and certainly much of my research didn't seem to confirm the dualisms or myth archetypes so prevalent in the Collective Unconscious. More so, as my work had proved a thousand times, psychoanalysis was imprisoned by the metaphor of the mind, limiting, subjective, caught in the labyrinth of the division between matter and consciousness. I said all this to Veronica as we walked in the woods, in the twilight.

My work with animals, which I was completing with rote facility during those weeks after my encounter, had indicated that they shared with us an initial level of dream impressions which were most often recapitulations of one's day. An image, a conversation, a run with the pack. Next came the accompanying emotions, simple wishes, desires, excitements, fears, which are capable, particularly in the other animals, depending on their sophistication, of hatching lust, desire, even loyalty, and it is here, Dr. Zu, where my work with the dream life of animals has improved their capacity to interact with humanity, producing animals that are hard-wired for the super-domestic and consequently adapted for space colonization.

On the edge of these kinds of animal emotions lies the emotions affiliated with the human ego structure, that is, survival emotions like fear and lust which attach themselves to the process of perpetuating human identity. However social-psychologically constructed, this self, once formed, both employs and victimizes itself with the same emotional intensity as any organism, and the images which accompany these in the unconscious occupy an intersubjective zone, quite socialized, quite individual, tempered and nurtured by culture and experience, but reducible to the classic mind body parallelisms, right down to the sub-neural levels—this feeling is accompanied by such and such chemical reaction—are they the same? Different? Two sides of the same coin? Is the relationship causal? Do they co-arise? And on and on. Here is where science and philosophy have lost themselves almost from the beginning. In fact, these enigmatic dualisms, much like the wave and particle attributes of light, are expressions of a more essential metaphor, a more fundamental reality. They are emanations of the Depth Unconscious, that dimension upon which our very own dimensionality lies like skin over muscle and nerve.

There is a dark space then, like the River Lethe, which one crosses to attain a shared world, not a world of inter-subjectively shared images, but an actual place. Like Plato's world of forms, it infuses the initial dream world. If there are non-human animals who can pass into it, I do not doubt it, but then, too, there are humans who seldom reach it, or after they do, simply awaken and forget. These are the lands I passed through on the way to the crone's cave. Yogins, even psychics, can travel here and even meet. This accounts for many stories of astral travel and prescience, even meetings with the recently dead. But those few who have traveled to this place, some by accident and others by training, are in a sense victims of it, watchful pawns in its workings, and often incapable of discerning anything meaningful in the collapse of time and imagery into impression. Though I could. In time I would have opened up all of it.

At the end, in a way almost Emersonian, at the depth of the individual lies utter objectivity, as if the psyche, like a galaxy, swirled around a black hole, which, if one could pass through it, would lead to another dimension, and if one could return, unlock the human heart. The crone that guarded that passage was as old as the first sentient feeling in the universe, alive and real as the first moment of time, the first particle emergent from the Big Bang. Yes, she guarded love. She guarded everything.

I stood before Veronica, sweating from exhaustion. "I had not really understood it, until this moment, speaking to you," I said to her.

She raised an eyebrow, this woman who held me so deeply, so totally, who, for the pursuit of her love, had taken me to the edge of millennial knowledge.

"It doesn't sound much like science, Werther," she said. She turned from me and walked away a step.

"If you read Einstein or Hawking, you see them struggling with metaphors, like poetry," I said to her back. "If your poets have killed poetry, it survives in cosmology and physics. It lives in the unfolding theories of the universe."

She turned to me, then paused, the first hint of the cold, spring night curling in darkness around the white steam of her breath. "I have to go home," she said. "I have a lot to think about and I need to think about it where I'm myself, where I have my horses and my land, my work, my job, my teaching, my own research, however superfluous it is to the world."

"I am on the brink," I said.

"Then come to me when you're done, when you are over the brink, when for a moment—" she paused. "Werther," she said, "I'm confused."

"Do not leave me," I said.

"I'm just going away. Going home. Going somewhere where there is someone besides you and your genius. Where I can walk inside my own genius."

"You will run away again," I said.

"Werther," said Veronica, "it is you who has run away."

"I'm here with you everyday. Every night."

"I'll be in Albany, on my farm. Come along if you want, Werther. Walk away from this. You've finished your animal research. Come with me."

"I've done this for you," I said to her. "To make you love. To make you whole. I've done this for the world."

"I no longer need it, Werther," she said. "Come to Albany. Leave the world alone."

"I love you," I said to her.

"Do you?" Veronica said. "Really?"

"At night, after we have made love, you weep."

"I married you," she said.

"I hold you in my arms and know there is a place behind your eyes where you are hiding."

"Werther," she said. She came to me and touched my cheek. "I'm leaving. I'm not running away. I am your spouse. I will be at my home. When you're ready, come."

I watched, forlorn, as she packed that night. I couldn't bear it. I'd taken such pleasure in her presence and the presence of her clothes, her possessions. I mourned the passing of her delicate under-clothes, how she hung them to dry over the bathroom stall, the smell of them in her drawer or hamper. I helped her with her suitcases to the car.

"When will you be back?" I whispered when she went to her car door.

She exhaled heavily. I saw in her eyes something I hadn't seen before, both depth and presence, that somehow, in her leaving, she stood before me totally and completely, completely herself, completely mine, for a moment, for the very first time.

Upon Veronica's departure I prepared myself for my greatest experiment. I would need to descend again to the edge of that final land and meet the crone who guarded the first moment of time and the center of the human heart. I did not remember if the bones of any other sojourners lay at her feet, but if no one had yet met the likes of her and convinced her to open up her secrets, then, so too, she had never met the likes of me. I was not a dead man nor a dreaming man, not a man caught unaware by her presence and dazzled by her riddles. I was a scientist, a man fully conscious, ready and armed.

I knew, if need be, I would end her life and open the world to the last of things and the dawning of a new human age. If I were wrong, then what of it? Whose life was lost besides my own? But where would the world have been without the warriors and geniuses who had stood up to evil, who had been willing to sacrifice themselves, their reputations, their livelihood, their lives, for the advancement of humankind. I did it for all this, and for Veronica, for her love.

That night, in my lab, I prepared my equipment and re-entered the world of dreams, this time with more certainty and clarity than ever before, as if my very awareness shortened my journey. Beyond the plain of pleasure and desire, at the edge of the forest of emotions, a warm wind slithered through the sentience and I heard the crone's visceral call echo inside me. "Woo-ertherr," it whispered in my blood. "Woo-ertherr." My nerves felt her. My bones. Yet if it was a timeless world where seconds passed like years, so too, the months of my journey ticked away like the smooth, rolling second hand of a Swiss clock. Through the desert of fears and beyond the mountains of faith and doubt, hope and despair, to the abyss, and through the history of all my dreams, I advanced to the edge of the depthless cave. I didn't hesitate for a moment, but walked in. I flew. Then came to land on floorless space, floating in pitch darkness. I waited. Ready. I waited there without sound or touch, without smell or taste, without the slightest hint of form or color before me.

For a moment I thought my journey was complete. That I had defeated my enemy simply by mounting my courage to meet her, and that by encountering my fear, by both stepping forward to meet it and stepping back to study it, I had destroyed it. I would walk now into the infinite, into the bottom and top of everything, and return with all its knowledge. I stepped forward, but encountered resistance. I tried to move, but could not. I was locked in nothingness. Suddenly, I felt the deepest, deepest fear and dread, and then, worse, the most vacuous, loveless emptiness, the loss of all and everything. I felt it everywhere, painfully, eternally. Surely, it was hell.

But if I could not move forward, neither could I turn away. My bones ached with emptiness. I disintegrated into a million trillion particles of pain. The deepest, empathic fire and ache, the pain of all things. With every cell I wept pitifully. It went on and on and on. It lasted forever. I felt that the very nature of existence was suffering and that suffering was all that one being and another could share. Then, in the moment that I thought that all was lost, that this emptiness would be my eternal existence, the sound of my name came to me, and as deeply and as hurtfully as it pierced every cell of my being, it equally kept me on the edge of an end; I felt now, in every particle of my disintegrated being the visceral intimation of caring. "Whoo-ertherr," it sang in long, soft syllables. The world was filled with it. "Wer-ther."

I felt love so terrifying, so destructive, I thought I would explode, and live on, exploded. To this moment, I tell you, the feeling was maddening, impossible, inexplicable. I cried out, but could not utter a sound. Soon I found that I could not even think, but only feel, feel this love rising inside me like a thundercloud. I felt my own lightning swell and I burst apart yet again, this time in an explosion of zagged light. Before me stood the crone.

"Werther," she hissed into my soul. "Werther." Her gaseous breath slipped out in a hint of flame. "Did you find what you came for?"

"Let me pass," I said.

"Into what?" She spoke slowly, listlessly, the feeling of her meaning slipping from her like a leak from a gas stove, a sissing that was not even a sound but more of a smell.

"Into what is behind you," I said.

"I am what is behind me," she said. "And now, as well, I am what is behind you."

"Let me see."

"You have already seen." She stepped aside. I saw myself beyond her. I saw my back. I saw her. I turned and she was there.

"I have failed," I whispered.

"Miserably," she said.

It was then that I realized that all was not lost, that if the secrets did not lay beyond her, they might, as I originally suspected at our first meeting, lay inside her. I envisioned the reality of my father's faith and became viscerally aware of the reality of evil, of the devil, of hell. Yet this being in front of me was neither spirit nor ghost, and the realm she guarded spread both behind me and before me. I struggled with the riddle, its answer on the edge of my consciousness like a forgotten name which leaps away from memory when you are on the verge of pronouncing it. Then it came to me in a rush, an understanding, a quest, a commandment, an answer. It came to me in that moment as clearly as it yet stands before me now. I must slay her.

But before I could even put my realization to words inside my mind, the creature lurched forward, her head leaping from her shoulders as if on a spring. I could see then that she had folded her long, narrow chin against her chest. Her ears, once pinned to her head, sprung erect as her tongue lashed out from her narrow jaws. The cape that once hid her hands now spread from her shoulder blades and back. They spread out in an enormous span; black, leathery wings, triple her height, though her size now doubled, too, as she leapt erect from a crouch and stood on her powerful hind legs, her feet and hands opening to expose her talons.

Her head hung before me, her gaze bewitching me. "*Ss*aint George," her mind hissed. "Adam. Jesu*ss*. Hitler." She turned her back yet kept her gaze upon me, her head twisting to lie on her shoulder. "Shake*ss*peare?" she said and laughed. "I have been happy here, Werther. I have been happy here. It was not me who came for you, but you who came for me. How I love men who *ss*peak and act for all humanity." She turned her scaled chest to me again. She backed away. Her body expanded, almost doubling again, and she seemed to lift off magically, without the slightest motion from her wings. Then she spread them, holding herself impossibly in the motionless air like a horrendous balloon. "You came to *ss*ave the world?" she hissed. Her mouth yawned and a ball of flame rolled in her throat. "What would you give to *ss*ave the world, Werther, be*ss*ide*ss* *my* life? Would you give *your* life? Give me your life, Werther, and I promi*ss*e to *ss*ave the world."

I didn't need to speak. She could read my mistrust as it crossed my face.

"Oh," she said, her head turning on that wretched neck. "You don't believe me. You came looking for love, Werther. Give me your love then. Love me, Werther, and I will leave your world un*ss*cathed."

"I cannot love evil," I said.

"Is that what'*ss* at the bottom of everything then, is it? Evil?" She exhaled fire and descended, standing again before me. "Well then, how did the poet *ss*ay it? 'Let u*ss* go then, you and I.' Let'*ss* *ss*ee what havoc we might wreak."

If I could have but given my life to her then, or taken hers, I would have done so, if ever I might have known that I could bargain with her faithfully on her terms. Yet on what could I base my trust? You must understand, that at that moment I had no answers, only riddles, questions, insanity. I could think of nothing but to flee, and in doing so, I would at the very least leave this creature, this beast, be she the heart of humanity or my own evil twin, leave her where I found her, beyond the river of forgetfulness, in the darkness behind the fire of Plato's cave.

I turned from her, and finding, suddenly, that I could move, ran from that spaceless dark. But unlike the last time, I did not immediately return to the edge of dreams but had to fight sluggishly through the blackness as if it were tar. I felt her hot breath behind me even as I emerged from her cave and broke into the cold mountain air; even as I cowered behind the rocks I felt her voice everywhere now, calling me, her phosphorus breath at my ear, the slow beat of her wings pushing hot air at my back, yet each time I turned to run, her image slipped from the corner of my eye; I heard her cackle and felt her disappear.

This is how I ran back to consciousness, reliving the horrors of my first passage in reverse, yet this time with a monster at my back whose fire threatened to end my life, if not the life of the world. And this is how I was driven onward to complete my escape. In that timeless time I cannot estimate how many months passed in my running, how many years, as I crossed again the parched terrors of my fears, the jungle of emotions, the plain of wish fulfillment. At the edge of consciousness, beaten down, drawn to exhaustion, from this dreamland, as if staring from inside a bubble, I saw myself in my laboratory, wired to my equipment, my eyes moving with both fear and clarity, my head turning to see myself. In that moment, I was both beings, seeing and feeling the same things as we stared infinitely back and forth at each other through the mirrors of conscious and unconscious worlds.

I pressed against the bubble of my dream reality and it gave way like thin, polyurethane. I walked into it, but it would not release me. I wept, both inside and outside this field, on both sides reaching for myself. Behind me then, only my dream self heard the dragon's call, slow and withering. "*Ss*tay. *Ss*tay, Werther. To return now is to open your world to me." But I didn't, couldn't listen. I strained and burst through. I tore myself from my equipment and stood, gaunt and sweating in the dawn. There, in the corner, diminutive now, herself weeping, stood the crone.

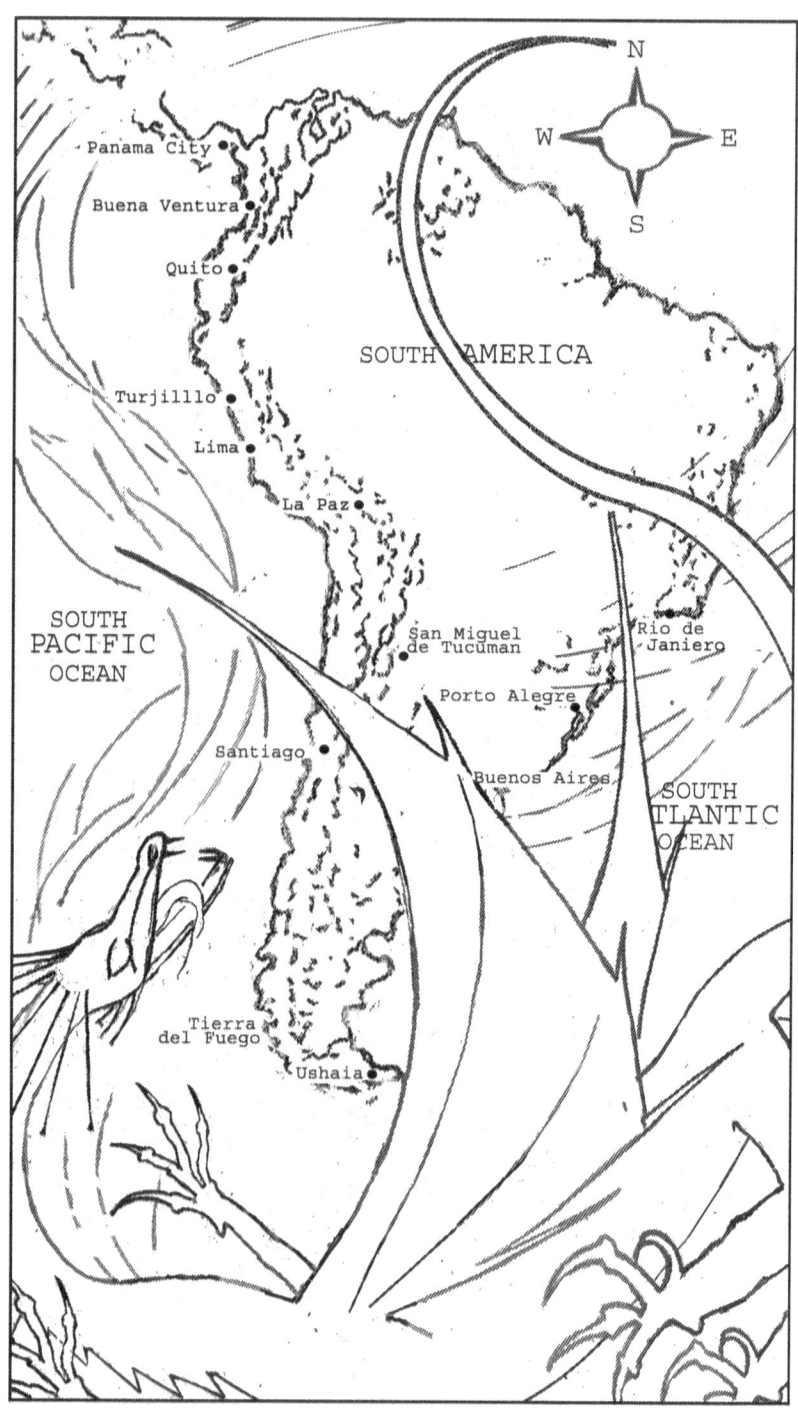

The Story of Werther Fausten

Again I turned and ran, into the forest, into the bursting day. I ran senselessly and endlessly in the sunlight, a man insane with the precious fullness of life as the world awoke around me. I remember little but that my own raving rang in my ears and echoed back upon me until, at noon, I saw my home again and went back inside, staggering to my lab where I found nothing but my own blinking instrumentation and the cords of wires that I'd torn from my flesh at dawn. I stumbled to my bedroom and fell into a deep, dreamless sleep, awaking in the morning of the next day and realizing at that very moment the depth of my failure.

Whatever I had found, I could not control. As the day wore on, it became increasingly clear to me that in all likelihood I had, unaware, succumbed to sleep and fallen prey to my dreams. All that I'd seen was imaginary, a product of my own desires, whether or not they were meager or great, altruistic or selfish, whether the product of vision and light or the corona or my megalomania. Whether or not I strived greatly, I had nonetheless failed.

I packed my things and by late afternoon left for Albany, arriving in the early morning, catching Veronica in bed, waking her with kisses on her eyelids.

"Werther," she said, smiling, as I brushed the sleep from her eyes. "You came. I dreamed of you."

"I've come to release you from our contract," I said to her. Even as I said it I could barely dare think of losing her, my heart breaking at the thought of our inevitable parting. "I have failed. Completely and miserably, I have failed."

She sat up in bed, her hair falling on her shoulders in thick waves. She took my face in her hands. "But Werther," she said to me. "You haven't failed. I'm so glad you came because I love you, Werther. I love you."

The Dragon Journal of Lisa Piccolo Zu

It's been a long time since I've written, but so much has happened. El and I got off the 1 Train down where people used to catch the Staten Island Ferry. It was a strange kind of fantasy world there, crowded with tents and huts, giant, rusting ghost freighters and war ships where people now made their homes. Booths lined the narrow walkways where people put out wares like old pots and knives and leather, even some small electronic stuff (I saw a really old Nintendo Game Boy—it had a tiny screen—pre-hologram), but mostly food, usually dried fish and different preparations of kelp, though there were people selling cooked rats and insects, too. The whole place was pretty stinky, but it was an animal stink, an ocean stink, a life stink, not the kind of stink it used to be, of car exhaust and chemical disinfectant laid over other chemical smells.

At the water's edge were thousands of oar boats and sail boats, all equipped with fishing tackle. El held my hand as we made our way to the pier to find our boat. She stopped and looked around, the street full of pedestrians and bicyclists. Like always, New Yorkers weren't friendly or unfriendly, just busy. I wondered where all the people who used to race around in mid-town wearing skirts and panty hose and coats and ties had gone. What were they doing now? Were some of them selling fish? I looked into the water which was different now, too, as blue as it was green and clear enough so you could even see into it a little.

"Where do you think they're putting all the poop now?" I said to El.

El just kind of looked down and lowered her eyelids a little, like she does when she's acting like I'm asking an absurd question, but really she just doesn't know the answer.

"Poop was never the problem," said a voice behind me. "Where do you think the fish poop?" It was a boy, older than me, already a teen-ager. He was cute. He wore baggies and his hair, dyed jet-black, was long and spiked out, Japan Style. Like us, he wore a big back-pack. "You looking for the eco-boat?" he said.

"Yes," said El.

"Poop recycles," he said to me. "It was the other stuff that was killing everything."

El wasn't uncomfortable around kids. She usually tried to treat them like people.

"It's through the old ferry station, isn't it?" said El. She looked around again. "Right or left?"

"There's a sign," I said. It was an old Staten Island Ferry sign. It pointed one way, while an arrow for the Statue of Liberty boat pointed the other.

"Left," said El.

"I'm surprised it hasn't been taken down and used for something," said our new friend.

"New Yorkers have their pride," said El.

So we found our way to the boat. It was kind of big, but not really so big that you'd want to live on the ocean in it, like we were going to. The Captain, Rayford Evans, had been an eco-engineer before the big collapse. He met with everybody that night on deck, at the back of the boat. The bow and hull were thin and made of a composite pioneered for space travel. It was hard enough to crack ice. But because battery technology was still poor the ship couldn't be that big and it had to be light. The boat was named "Adjoa," after his wife who was with the Mars Lab like Grandma Zu.

We had two masts with big sails, and though you didn't want to be completely reliant on wind, there were windmills set up front and back, bow and stern, and the sails were lined with a kind of luminescent fiber that captured solar energy as well as transferred wind energy to the batteries. There were solar panels everywhere it was flat and where you couldn't walk, and a propane generator that ran a flywheel, too, just like the prop-bus. But we needed as much of that stuff as possible because of the batteries. And we'd still need plenty of wind and plenty of sun.

The boat, adapted from a sailing yacht, was twenty-five meters long. There were about twenty of us passengers, though we'd all have to pitch in and help with everything. Besides the captain there was another man, Nigel, the first mate, and two women, Angie and AJ, who stood with their arms around each other's shoulders.

"They're lesbians," whispered our new friend whose name was Hunter.

"Me, too," I said.

"Yeah, right," he said.

"Yeah, right," I said. But I really liked him okay. You can pretty much tell right away with boys how much attitude you're going to get, whether they're going to be mean or sexy or both, or just nice.

Captain Evans, who was getting bald and had a short beard like a regular sea captain, said he wasn't too worried about the "meteorological phenomenon," because we were a small boat. Lots of people liked to call the dragon some kind of phenomenon, people used "meteorological phenomenon" because of the storms and lightning that came along with her attacks. That's something I can explain later. But the captain talked about how after the nuclear facilities and oil production facilities were destroyed, lots of nations like the U.S., Russia, England, France, and China still had plenty of fission material and gasoline stored up for their war fleets. Those boats attracted the phenomenon, which seemed to be drawn to energy, starting with the nuclear aircraft carriers and working on down. There might probably still be a few nuclear subs out there, but not too many. Later the big, automated fishing boats started drawing the storms. But now there hadn't been a sea occurrence for a long time. The Captain liked to use words like "occurrence" and "phenomenon" to refer to things.

"So we're safe?" somebody said.

"We still have an engine," the Captain said. "But without one the ocean can be a rough place. It's a rough place anyway." He gave us our route. We were heading down the coast, then through the Caribbean. We had our first pick-up in the Yucatan. Then we were dropping off Hunter when we passed through the Panama Canal.

After that, it was the marine station in the Galapagos Islands, then Santiago, Chile, and then the long run to New Zealand for our final supplies before sailing to McMurdo Station on Ross Island, just off the Ross Ice Shelf in Antarctica.

We'd sail near the coasts. He hoped we could find supplies on the way, but he didn't know what the economic situation would be the farther we got south. Word was, though, that the less technological the society, the less things had changed. We could fish, of course, but we'd need fresh water.

"It will be dangerous," he said. "But those of you here have chosen to pass your time searching instead of waiting, battling instead of just surviving. Remember, this isn't a democracy. We'll discuss things, but in the end this is my boat and my word goes."

He looked real hard at me and Hunter.

"Aye, aye!" I said. He laughed.

On that trip down the east coast, Hunter and I spent a lot of our free time playing cards. What we liked best was to watch each other play solitaire. First he'd play a game and then I'd play. We let each other cheat. When the sea wasn't completely rough, we'd put on life jackets and go out on the bow where the dolphins swam beneath us for miles. Once, while we were sailing along through a huge pod, the Captain yelled out "Look! At ten o'clock!" and off to our left, like a gigantic wing, a thousand dolphins spread out across the water and rushed toward us, leaping and calling. When they reached the boat, gliding beneath us, it was as if we were sailing on their silver backs, some of them huge, almost twelve feet long, and so many mother's swimming in perfect harmony with their babies.

"See that?" El said to me. "See!"

I knew what she meant. She always did that mother and baby thing with me, how we lived in sync for so long.

"That's how it should be!" she yelled. "That's how it should always be."

"She's a Motherist," I said to Hunter one night after we'd eaten. We were out on the deck in the warm night, summer stars and the Milky Way bright across the sky. Angie and AJ were out there, too. Angie played the mouth harp and AJ played the guitar and sometimes they played love songs and sang to each other. It was loving and cute.

"You're lucky," Hunter said to me. He was from D.C. His mother had died of breast cancer about five years ago. His father joined the Naval Reserve right after that, though now he'd been activated and he was living with someone else near Norfolk, Virginia, starting a new family with his new wife. Hunter hated them. He was heading to Panama to meet his mother's parents who were Scots born in Guatemala, his grandfather to missionaries and his grandmother to diplomats. They'd gone back to Guatemala to live when everything started.

"Good move," I said.

"It's my choice to go," Hunter said. "I want to go." He said he could remember when he was little, things were different. His father was a mechanical engineer and didn't join the Navy until after his mother's death, though Hunter's parents weren't getting it on long before that. They fought all the time. His father stopped spending time at home, working during the week and on the weekend going out on his boat. He lost the boat early on, when survivors from the city took the marinas. It was a motor boat anyway, completely worthless. His father started seeing this other woman before Hunter's mom was even dead. When things got really bad, the military, the Navy, still took care of its own.

"Not much of a navy now," I said to him.

"They're working on boats like this one. Only stealth boats. They'll be smaller, but they'll carry tactical nuclears. They propel using lasers and they have fins, so they can cruise through the air or even submerge like subs. And they won't have radar signatures or energy signatures, so they'll avoid enemy detection and the phenomenon, too. Once they get the satellites back up using laser power, it won't be like *the past* anymore, it'll be *the future*, big time." He looked at me. He knew what I thought about things. "If it's a dragon," he said, "they'll kill it."

"It's not the dragon's fault your mother is dead," I said to him. Sometimes you just have to cut to the quick with boys, because they're always expecting you to be nice and, especially, to listen to what they have to say. He stood up quickly and looked down at me, so I looked away. "Sit back down, please," I said.

"Dragons are just old fucking myths," he said. "You're just a child."

"The future is an old fucking myth," I said.

He sat back down again. I wasn't expecting him to. I really thought that he'd leave, start hanging out with the youngest men if they'd let him, but Hunter had a good heart. He was just really confused. "Sometimes I want to blow everything up," said Hunter.

"That's why I said what I said. But the dragon beat you to it, so you want to blow *her* up. It doesn't matter what your reasons are, that's what boys and men do. They blow everything up. But that's over now. You're not going to get to blow stuff up anymore. There's not going to be any stealth boats either, Hunter."

He reached in his pocket. "Do you want to share a cigarette?" he said.

"Yes."

He had a lighter. It was his father's. But he still didn't light a cigarette so good, given the wind. It was a Lucky Strike. He took a pretty deep drag on it and exhaled, then he offered it to me. He said, "I have pot, too."

"Great."

I smoked the cigarette. I knew how to smoke. The kids from the families up in the mountains got together all the time. People were growing everything in the fields now, tobacco, pot, not just food. It didn't take anything to pick a few leaves, dry them out and roll them up. But you didn't see too many manufactured cigarettes. I figured that if his dad was in the Navy, that explained it.

"You can smoke," he said. He was surprised.

"That's right. I'm working on breathing fire."

He took the cigarette back. "You're funny."

"That's right. Smart, too."

He held the cigarette deep in the crotch between his index finger and the middle one. He smoked like that, with his hand covering the bottom half of his face. "There'll be stealth boats," he said, exhaling. "There'll be stealth boats. In three years I'll enlist. I'll drive one." He made his hand move in the air. Holding the cigarette, it made a trace of light like a sparkler and left a trail of smoke. He handed me the cigarette again. "I'll fly it right down your dragon's throat," he said, but he made his eyebrows go up and he laughed. One second he was sharing his cigarette with me and the next he was treating me like a kid. But like I said, he couldn't control it. He was fucked up, but he was still nice. Like El always said, that's men. You just have to find one that's trainable. I guess not like Uri Wight. Because when Hunter was trying to be a man, a hero, a stealth ship captain, he didn't even realize what a little kid he was acting like. And he wanted to be like his father, who was a jerk and cheated on his mom, when really that's not what he wanted. He wanted his mother. That's what I think. It made me wonder about boys and their dreams.

"Finish that," said Hunter, "and then I'll show you something."

We went down to his room. We had to knock because there were four Chilean men who used it, too. They were going to Santiago. The room was like mine and El's, only a little bigger, with bunk beds around a low table that you could sit around on cushions. The men were there in T-shirts and sweat pants, two playing backgammon and sipping whisky and two others playing soccer in that little space with a ball of trash. The beds, like ours, had pull-down blinds so you could get a little privacy, and that's where we went, onto Hunter's top bunk and pulled down the shade. Like all the bunks, it was your little apartment, hung with bags where you could keep your things, like an Indian teepee. Hunter turned on his flashlight and pulled a deck of cards from under his pillow. It was *Dragon-Fire*, a famous Japanimation card game.

"This was raging before everything went down," Hunter whispered. "Kids all over the world played, but adults, too; college kids, even professors. A deck like this was worth hundreds of dollars, even then."

"See," I said, "you like dragons."

"It's a warrior game," he said. "The dragon's only important because you have to take possession of its eggs."

"*Her* eggs."

"The eggs elevate your power, until you get them all."

"And rule the world!" I said, laughing.

"Yes!" he said. He didn't get it.

It was a complicated game, really, that you played with sixty cards in two groups of thirty. Then there were lots of power quadrants, like electricity or water or magic, though only four could be used in any game, and there were cards that empowered some cards and not others, and ways to evolve your power. Each card had strengths and weakness, different mystical and battle powers and defenses, and ways it could combine with other cards to accentuate them. And there were limitations for the ways a card could evolve, depending. The other thing was, you were supposed to announce your major attack quadrant and expose all your cards, too, so your opponent knew everything about you, like chess. It was all in how you maneuvered your field of play. You didn't just buy a deck, either. In the old days, when everyone was playing, there were thousands of different cards that you collected and organized into different power decks. You could present a deck for tournament, but you couldn't exchange cards between decks once you started a game. The weirdest thing was that there was no dragon.

"How does it sound?" Hunter said.

"Capitalist," I said.

"Duh!" said Hunter.

Anyway, it was a game. When I left he walked me out of his cabin.

"We'll play sometime," he said.

"And I'll teach you about dragons."

"There'll be stealth boats," said Hunter. Then he took my hand. It was cute. So I gave him a hug. He let me. When I held him, I could feel his lips press the hair just behind my forehead.

The Dragon Journal of Lisa Piccolo Zu

Dragons were not invulnerable. I don't know who started that one up. I guess the old story was that their scales were like steel and layered over each other like mail. But they shed their skins, too, and supposedly if you found them while they were shedding, you might be able to pierce a spot on their underside while they were still soft. That accounted for the pictures of knights carrying those pointy tridents instead of swords.

But if dragons had steel-like scales they'd be a bit heavy for flying, wouldn't they? In fact, dragons were quite fragile. The reason you couldn't just whack at them with a broad sword was because it was hard to get near them. For one, they could fly. For another, they could mesmerize their victims with a stare. Held in a dragon's gaze you were a goner. The few people who escaped after that were so addled that they came away babbling and that accounts for the stories of the dragons presenting riddles to their prey. A really savvy dragon could steal your dreams, too, and leave you a kind of superficial simpleton. So if dragons communicated at all, it was through your unconscious.

Even if you could get close enough to whack a dragon with your sword, they were kind of flimsy and diaphanous (that's probably the wrong word, but it sounds great!). It would be like hitting a somewhat deflated balloon. So the reason that dragon slayers carried those pointy tridents was because you could *pierce* a dragon with it if you caught her straight on.

Dragons possessed great stealth, too. Their caves were narrow, but for their lairs deep inside, and they always faced out, toward their narrow entryway, so no one could approach them unawares, or more importantly, without avoiding their gaze, and their fire.

Though a dragon might sometimes attack in full display, most often they traveled within their own cloud of vaporous smoke, almost as if disguising themselves as a fast moving cloud. Sometimes you still see Chinese dragons perched on mountain tops portrayed that way. When they appeared in the sky above, billowing into an ever-larger thunderhead of vapor and fire, and when they hovered, suspending themselves in the air, their tails dangling and the smoke billowing around their wings, it often appeared as if the cloud took the shape of a huge, fiery heart. Then the fire split from its center, as if the heart had cracked open to emit lightning. The light could be so bright at that moment that you might turn your head away and think, as Captain Evans did, that you'd encountered a "meteorological phenomena." But if you don't turn away, as the fire wanes you will see the dragon emerge at the center of the cloud before fleeing behind her veil of smoke.

It's difficult to know why or when dragons acquired these evasive tactics. For my part, if there's a difference between male and female dragons, I kind of think that evasion, and by that I mean intelligence, is the difference. Females of lots of different species, mammals as well as reptiles, tend to be more intelligent about hunting, memorizing geography, protection, and evasion because they're often smaller and have more responsibilities, that is, bearing, raising, feeding and protecting their young, if not, like in a lot of cat species, feeding the male, too. Smoke clouds were probably used at first to escape the big bull dragons whose sexual readiness extended beyond the time of female sexual receptivity. Later it came in handy as humans developed more sophisticated weaponry, like long bows and cross bows.

Of course, with the present dragon a lot of this might go out the window. It depends on how she came about. She might be the hatchling of a long, lost egg, but then again, she might have hatched from our universal unconscious. A lot of monsters that plagued the earth from time to time might have arisen this way, and this explains why there were more accounts of them in the past, when humans were more in touch with their dreams and unconscious minds. It makes sense in a lot of other ways, too, like how people used to be a lot more spiritual than they are today and why a lot of non-technological cultures don't draw such distinct lines between the living and the dead, heaven and earth. Homo-technologico fell out of touch. It was only a matter of time before something like this emerged.

Anyway, if that's the case, then it's difficult to determine what laws of time and space this dragon is subject to. It would be like a dream existing in our world, experiencing our world the way we move around and experience the dream world. I told all of this to poor, fucked-up Hunter.

"You're living in a fantasy world," he said to me. "You're a child."

"Thank you, Mr. Stealth Boat," I said. "Given the alternatives, that's a really nice compliment."

We were playing his dragon game. I'd just cornered him by feigning an evolution to a different power quadrant. I'd done it earlier and let him hit me from behind. This time, I was waiting for him with full power. I took all his male power cards: his emperor, his sorcerer, his warrior.

"Jesus fucking Buddha," he said. "What's left?"

"Acceptance," I said to him. "Love."

He put his hands in his hair and then he grinned or grimaced, it was hard to tell.

"You're smart," Hunter said. "You set me up from the start. But next time I'll be ready."

"There will be no next time," I said. I rolled my hands in each other. "Next time it will all be different. Wooa-ha-ha-ha!"

He laughed. He could do it. He had a good heart. You just couldn't fill it is all. It was too empty.

The Story of Werther Fausten

In the next month we found that Veronica was pregnant and we planned a vacation to Italy. We hoped to time it between the end of her morning sickness and before carrying our child became too uncomfortable for her. Despite her pregnancy, Veronica was still vibrant and active and as we planned our trip we rode horseback everyday, taking long, romantic rides in the blooming hills outside Albany, stopping at streams to picnic and sit in the infrequent sun.

Before leaving for Europe, we visited my father in Porterville, Pennsylvania. Dianna, who had recovered from her addictions, had left the half-way house and now she and her two children, a daughter aged four and a son two years old, lived with him in his cottage, though they were preparing to leave. She'd found a small house of her own, rented to her from the Mennonite community, and we caught them all in the joy and sadness of her departure, along with the bitter-sweet news of Veronica's pregnancy; my father, aging, his progeny, by direction and misdirection, expanding onto the ever-more-populated earth.

"Don't think I'm so religious or too simple to understand all of the ironies," he said to me that night after Veronica had deftly retired to give us a moment alone. "I look at you, your intelligence, the good things you've done, the things you've overcome, and think, I should have had more, a dozen. What does a man have in the end? What does he leave? What marks his life as not having been a waste of time? And what better way to pass one's time than with children, caring for them, loving them." He walked to the screen door and went outside, leaving me alone. I followed him onto the dark porch, under a faint crescent moon in a bejeweled sky.

He looked at the stars. "Be fruitful and multiply," he whispered. "And where will we all live?"

"You're getting philosophical," I said to him.

"You're finally noticing," he said. "I've spent my life searching for God."

"A lot of people have."

"You don't find God," said my father. "God finds you."

"Has He found you?" I said.

"When I'm not looking."

"And who is He?"

"Who am I?" said my father. "Who are you?"

In that moment, both so laden and so spare, a chill ran through me. Something haunting in my father's rejoinders, his riddles, that recalled the crone of my dream world. In the last months I'd had restful, dreamless nights and felt more peace in my life than ever before. Now I stood before my father, his first legitimate grandchild in my wife's womb, and found him prodding, disturbing.

"Are you unhappy, Father?" I asked him.

"Why have we been created such cowards, Werther?" he said to me.

"You have never been a coward," I said.

"My *life* has been cowardice," he said. "I've thought at times that we were created because God failed with the angels. No revolt this time. All humility and cowardice down here this time! Pain, greed, foolishness, cruelty, illness, death. Enough to keep us humble, you'd think Have you ever mused that perfection might lie in simplicity, Werther? But that God loves complexity, and everyday the world grows more complex and God desires it more, and everyday it rejects God more. Consider that metaphor as the dialectic of creation."

"You can still visit Dianna and her children," I said to him. "Better, when Veronica and I return from Europe, come live with us."

My father turned to me. He placed his hand on my shoulder and smiled. "Solutions," he said. "Solutions. Who said I wanted solutions?"

Oh, that last peaceful night. I walked the porch after my father retired. The fantastic night spread wide across the eternal sky as if the stars were alive and each held a secret. How the constellations danced! How the world, the universe, flickered its infinity in the mind of one man! Was it coincidence then that I turned my gaze to the polar star, to the anchor of the night? The great bear above the small one, drawn back in fright, and the small one flying in front of the dragon's teeth? Great Draco between them, spreading itself like wings of light? No? Call it a dream then. Then call this whole, horrible end of all things a dream.

The Story of Werther Fausten

Of all the countries, Veronica most loved Italy. More than verdant Ireland, or the arid depth of Spain. Rome, full of sex and ancient slaughter, its monumental decay and enfolded architecture. The hills of Tuscany and the jewel of Florence. But most of all, magical Venice, if ever more magical in that it existed at all. At night, the whir of its underground pumps, spilling the ocean back onto itself to save the fragile island, the oceans beaten back with international money, American technology, and Chinese materials to save Atlantis. No matter that one needed reservations and tickets to enter, as if it were Disneyland, Veronica marveled among the haunts of Hemingway, Keats, Shelley, Byron, Marco Polo and Thomas Mann, the exotic shops, the marvelous waterways. We whiled away afternoons at Florian's, listening to the concerts in St. Mark's square and feeding the thousands of pigeons, each of which, she pointed out, were distinct individuals, the centers of their worlds.

"I find that more an indictment than anything else," I said.

"Yes," she laughed, "you would."

Then we returned to Albany to await the birth of our child. The birth was difficult. Veronica labored for almost a day. But our son, Michael Werther, emerged eventually, beautifully and miraculously, as all children do, though none so beautifully and miraculously as one's own. We returned to Porterville to allow my father to perform the christening, Veronica dispelling my negativity and doubts with a gentle smile. "It's simply a ritual, Werther," she said.

To my father, after the ceremony, I said, "Is this a solution?"

"No," he responded, ever gentle and quick, "an absolution."

Dianna came with her children, her life in order and taking shape. If she looked a bit tired, so too, she looked vibrant and clear-eyed. "I owe so much to your father," she told me, as her children, now almost five and three, tugged and tagged around my father's legs, my father separating them, tickling them, holding out his fists to have them guess which one held candy.

I did not say to Dianna, *your father, as well*, and wondered, then, of what would be if my mother still lived. How much of my father's heart was opened by her death and the death of Dianna's mother, his paramour? How far would my mother's heart have come? "You look so good," I said to Dianna. "Healthy. Happy."

"Lucky," she said. "Very lucky."

Back in Albany, free from my work, in fact, more free than I had ever been, I spent my days minding Michael's infancy. And the lives of my father and mother, and Dianna, as well, opened up before me in quick understanding, in empathy beyond the comprehension of a childless man. How I would sacrifice my life for my son, thoughtlessly, without hesitation. My mind reeled with a hundred scenarios which could threaten Veronica and Michael: kidnappings, lightning storms, fires, murderous burglars in the night, and how I would leap between the threat and my family's safety. But if this was the paranoia spawned by idleness, then equally it nurtured in me the bliss of a man fulfilled by simple purpose.

"Another," I said to Veronica as she nursed our son.

"Overpopulation, Werther?" she said.

"Only two. It's within moral limits."

"One at a time," she replied.

The bitter irony now, to look back on that time, when I gazed on my love and my progeny and saw their lives stretching eternally beyond me, beyond all of my concerns, political, moral, scientific, beyond, even, the grave. It only takes love and soon a man, fearful of its loss, contemplates, longs for, immortality, for himself and for those he loves. My child grew. My love for Veronica grew. I forgot about my research and the madness it had spawned. Dreams, forgotten dreams, some the wishes of the day and others the desires of the night, but dreams all. I neither watched television nor read the paper. I forgot about the world. Months passed. It was a golden time.

But not long after Michael began to sit up and take solid food, I got a letter from my father. He wrote periodically and, of course, he loathed electronic mail. Neither did he use the phone. He wrote:

Dear Werther:

My son, I have the most horrible news. Dianna's children are dead. She had left them unattended in her home, which burned down while she was away. A fire started, it seems, while one of the children was playing with an electrical receptacle. Worse, enough evidence has been gathered by the police to implicate Dianna beyond negligence. She has been arrested for murder.

I cannot express my sadness and dread. I have not been permitted to see her, to hear her explanation, but if I find the deaths of the children unbelievable, then I find Dianna's implication unimaginable. I am sorry to bring you this sadness. I am suffering the most horrible grief. Please come.

Your loving father

The Story of Werther Fausten

If I knew the best and the worst of what Dianna could be, then I knew she could not have murdered her children, by malice nor negligence. It took time, but assuming responsibility for her legal counsel, I obtained a good defense lawyer and within days acquired the forensic evidence of the fire. If at first it had been presumed that Dianna had left her children at home unattended, later evidence from witnesses indicated that she'd fled her home after the fire began. Yet from everything I could surmise from the way the house burned, though the children were scorched beyond recognition, in fact, burned far worse than the remnants of the room around them, it was as if they had been slain by fire and the house burned down around them afterward. For even if they had started the fire near the receptacle, were they yet too young to walk to the door only a few feet away? What evidence could indicate that Dianna was capable, physically or psychologically, of carrying out such an absurd execution of her offspring?

The prosecuting attorneys mocked my reasoning. One could conclude Dianna's malice from the facts, as well as from her checkered past. However unlikely her mechanics, the facts were unassailable.

When I was finally able to see Dianna in the jail, she was hysterical.

"Werther!" she cried. "Werther! You don't believe it, do you? My children! My children!"

"Dianna," I said. "What happened? What could have happened?"

She was delirious and told me an unbelievable tale, one, she said, that she was afraid to tell the police. One morning, about several months ago, before Dianna left for work, an old woman had stopped by the house. She'd been homeless, with no food, no place to stay, and Dianna had taken to packing her a lunch, then packing her a bag of food for her supper, too. The woman had an utterly amazing subtlety and prescience, becoming intimate with Dianna so quickly, so easily, it was as if she were privy to her dreams. In no time the woman had befriended the children, as well, and sometimes played with them in the yard when Dianna stepped out for groceries.

For Dianna, of course, the situation suggested the ideal. She'd been spending a good portion of her small income on child care. Suddenly an angel, a friend, who delighted in her children, had become a willing partner in their education and care. She'd been the wife of a scientist, she said, at the University of Pennsylvania, an archeologist affiliated with their famous museum, before he had left her, in her fifties, for a graduate student during the final excavation of the courtyard near the Temple of Quetzacoatl in Teotihuacan.

"Do you know that excavation, Werther?" said Dianna.

"Yes," I whispered. "Quetzacoatl. The feathered serpent. The Wind."

"You see?" she cried." Do you see? How could I make that up?"

"I don't understand."

"The divorce destroyed her," Dianna explained. "She fell into alcoholism, drug abuse, like me. She lost her children. Ended up homeless. In the streets."

"You brought her into your home," I said.

"Yes, Werther, like your father did for me. She was kind, Werther. She was good to them." She broke down then, sobbing. "Oh, Werther. You won't believe me. No one can believe me!"

"Tell me," I said.

"That night, that night Werther, when I came home from work, I found my children motionless at her feet. When I looked at her, her eyes seemed to expand. They looked twice as large, and deadly, with black, vertical slits at their center. 'My children!' I screamed, but she held me in her gaze. Oh my God, Werther, at her back, she sprouted wings! I thought, the devil! The devil! And I ran to them, Werther, I ran to children, but only in my mind because I couldn't move! She breathed fire on them, Werther. She consumed them in fire! And as the room burst into flames I fled. My God, Werther! My God! I did not kill my own children!"

She fell into hysteria again as I held her, my bastard half-sister, and yet, too, my first love, accused now of murdering her own children.

Who could believe her story, unless you believed that nightmares stalked the earth. I left her and wandered into Porterville, afraid to leave the town, afraid of everyone around me and yet afraid to be left alone. What could I conclude? Was there a strain of madness that plagued my father's blood? And so, then, his ambiguous religious fervor, and my passionate search to link hard science and the mystical. Were Dianna's children the victims of that same kind of torn self, one that, because she was less educated, less disciplined, found her swinging, inevitably, like a pendulum, first to promiscuous sex, then to motherhood, then to alcohol and drugs, then to humility and conformity, and finally, in reaction, back again to madness and murder? Were Dianna's children murdered by my dreams? What could I tell a judge, a jury, a courtroom? That I dreamt one night that a monster escaped from my soul and now it had murdered Dianna's children? What else could I conclude but that she was mad and that her insanity was the only escape left for her if she were to plea for her own life.

I went to my father that night and stayed with him. I called Veronica on my cell phone and assured her that I was okay, but that I would stay until the indictment and then, if need be, return until the end.

"Is it possible, Werther?" she said. "How is it possible?"

"It is impossible," I told her. "And true."

I'd stopped at a liquor store on the way to my father's and bought a pack of cigarettes, a foolish, nervous self-indulgence to get me through the minutes, and a bottle of wine, as well. I opened the wine and got out two, small, juice glasses. My father took the glass and we quietly sat and drank, the window shades open to the full moon which fell from the sky and threw its light, its shadows, into his unlit study.

Finally late in the night, the moon gone, the false dawn black-gray in the windows, my father stood and muttered, then walked to his room.

I left him to stand and smoke on the porch, the flame of the match, as it touched the end of the cigarette, a sizzling, primitive illumination in the air which had suddenly turned so cold that my breath was visible without the smoke. It was as if I could see the end of the world in the flaming head of a match. My lungs burning, my head dizzy with cigarette smoke, I exhaled onto the flame which danced for a moment in the gray cloud of my breath as if it were the center of some greater fire.

Dianna was indicted on two counts of first degree murder the next day. Though I was not permitted to see her, I spoke to her lawyer who had failed to convince her to plead guilty to negligence and involuntary manslaughter. He surmised that she could not avoid conviction and the death penalty. To plead insanity was her only hope.

I spent the day in hapless pondering. How could I step forward? What could I tell the court? That there might, in fact, be a monster loose? A monster who arose from my dreams? I would have to be insane, and yet felt even more insane to consider that Dianna's story might be true, though I knew in my heart that she could not have killed her children. At my father's home, I stared into the dense woods surrounding his garden and farm, the verdant foliage quiet with a million tiny lives each preying upon each other for their momentary survival. How could we evolve into such beings who transgressed even this simple code, who murdered each other, our own species, our own children?

I was hopeful of seeing Dianna again the next day, and then returning to Veronica in Albany until the trial, but all of that was cut short. That afternoon Dianna, her children not yet even buried, committed suicide by hanging herself in her cell.

My father prevailed and succeeded in preventing the family from being cremated and paid to have them buried together in a single plot near my mother's and his own grave. As he said, in the end, what did it matter? The graveyard is a land of sad stories ending sadly.

My father presided at the funeral, attended only by me, the funeral director, and a few public officials. He did not read the Bible over the graves, but Shakespeare.

Let's talk of graves and worms and epitaphs,
Make dust our paper, and with rainy eyes
Write sorrow on the bosom of the earth.

King Richard's soliloquy in *Richard II*, Dr. Zu, you can read it for yourself.

"On the death of kings?" I said to him as we turned from the graves.

"And their lives, too," he said. "There is so little on queens."

It wasn't far from the cemetery to his house and in the horrible brightness of the day we walked to his home, over the highway and through a cornfield, finally through the woods that surrounded his small farm. We had been silent for so long, and I so lost in thought, that I did not notice his weeping. For the first time in my life, I held him. Then we turned for his home again.

"I'm thinking of mission work," he said.

"For whom?

"Does it matter?"

"Maybe," I said. "Maybe it does."

"No," he said. "It doesn't."

"Father, take some time," I said to him. "Protect yourself. Come live with us."

"No," he said. "I'm tired of thinking of myself."

"The world is meaningless," I whispered, "but for what we bring to it ourselves. Life is capricious and cruel."

He stopped and turned to me again. He put his hand on my shoulder. "That is why we need God so much."

And so ended a tragic digression of my father's life, and mine. A thousand ironies buried under the earth's skin. I sat with him again that night, but that night he took no wine and I finished the bottle myself as I packed and prepared for my long drive home in the morning. When he had gone to bed I went out again to the porch and smoked my last cigarettes, obscuring the starlight with my smoky breath. What would my father do now? I did not know. I knew only that after all of this, I loved him even more, a man whose wisdom stretched beyond his means to be wise, whose meager sins met with severe punishment, whose life I did not understand nor know. He had loved two women in his life. Today they lay buried at his feet with his illegitimate daughter and her children. And what were their sins?

I looked to the sky, the great dipper shining above and the small one reaching to it from the horizon. I knew something else should be there, something stretching out between them, but my mind went blank and suddenly the air was filled with a palpable presence. My spine tingled and the hair on my arms rose in fear like the back of a dog. I felt as if the woods suddenly obscured something horrible and threatening and then, then, as if the air itself were speaking I heard that dreadful call. "Werther." It came as if on a whisper of faint breath through the thick, still air. "Werther."

It came to me in fear beyond fear, in depth beyond belief. Can you understand how much I wish to disbelieve what I am telling you? I do not want this burden, but it is mine. "Werther," it called in the silence. "Werther, you must come to me."

And as if I were back in my lab, I stepped from the porch into blackness. There, at the edge of the woods, a form took shape, first in the body of the crone, but then expanding into a creature of myth, its thin head extended on its scaled neck, its spaded tail whipping the air, the diamonds of its huge eyes vertical and black with infinity. In that moment I knew the truth and walked across the void to the monster as its huge wings stretched out before me, blackening the woods, the sky, its eyes holding mine, its eyes holding everything, its wings surrounding me in darkness.

The Dragon Journal of Lisa Piccolo Zu

One night Hunter got some wine from the men in his room. They liked him okay and called him *chilito*, which kind of meant "little penis," though Hunter didn't know it and I didn't tell him. We went out on the bow of the boat after supper and smoked pot, then went back down to his bunk and rolled the curtain down. We played the dragon game and sipped the wine. I didn't like it. It was too sour, but Hunter said that adults liked sour wine.

"It's called *dry*," I said. "But it's still sour."

"Because you're still just a kid," he laughed. Okay, at least he laughed. I beat him again at the game and he took it pretty well. He collected his cards.

"Stay with me tonight," he said.

"That's crazy," I said. "Even if I wanted to."

"There are no rules," he said. "No one can do anything to us. What could they do?"

"Then what?" I said to him. "You get off in Panama. I have to stay on the ship."

"Exactly," he said. "Anyway, get off in Panama."

"I'm a little young to run away with a man," I said. "A boy."

"It doesn't matter," Hunter said to me. "It doesn't matter anyway. Nothing does. It's the end of the world."

"But it's never the end of the world," I said. "It's always going to be the end of the world, but it never is. What about the laser stealth boats?"

Hunter put his cards away and took my hands in his. He looked right at me and whispered. "I feel like I'm going to die. Do you ever feel like that? Like you're going to die any minute?"

"No," I said. "El says that's something men feel, because they think they're so important. You're probably just going through puberty."

"What do you know about puberty?"

"Plenty," I said. Because I was old enough. It's not something you go around talking about, but I was old enough.

"So stay with me."

"I'm not going to stay with you, Hunter," I said. "I'm not even going to be your fucking friend if you keep it up."

"If I stay a virgin I'm going to die," he said.

"Virgin or not, everyone eventually dies."

"I mean soon. Right away."

"And I'm supposed to save you."

He looked down and away. "Just kiss me," he said.

"I have to go, Hunter."

But he held my arm hard. "Just kiss me."

"And then I can go."

"Yes."

So I gave him his kiss. He tried to make it sloppy, but I pulled away. Then he grabbed me and I punched him in the throat. It almost made him cry a little, but he tried to act tough while he caught his breath and I crawled out. One of the Chilean men, Jorge, was in the middle of the room and he looked at me kind of strange. He shook his head.

That night I talked to El. El liked it when I talked to her because, well, I didn't really like talking to her that much anymore. In the end, she was my mom. We didn't have that much in common. I told her Hunter was talking about dying or killing himself or something, I couldn't tell.

"Did he ask you to have sex?" she said.

"Maybe."

"Maybe?"

"It was like the dying. It was hard to tell."

"He's just a boy, darling," said El. She turned the battery light up a bit in our little cabin. Below us, I could hear the whir of the engine, which we were using now because there'd been so little wind. "Do you have a crush on him?" she said.

"He's a friend," I said.

"Well, sometimes girls think that, when they're young, before they realize it's something else."

"You think I'm flirting with Hunter?" I said.

"No," said El. "He's a boy. A teenager. And you're friends. But it isn't always so simple. Boys, young men, are always threatening to kill themselves when they can't get what they want. Women are somehow held responsible for men's emotions." She hesitated, you know, that parental thing about knowing more than they can tell. "If I begin to talk about why, you'll think this is a lecture."

"It is already," I said. "So if I nod at you, it means I understand."

"I won't repeat myself," said El. For an adult, she was pretty well trained.

"I kissed him," I said. "So he'd stop."

El's eyes kind of danced. She smirked. "Did he stop?"

"No," I said. "I had to leave."

We sat there for a while before El said, "Well honey, it's a small boat."

"I punched him in the throat," I said. "I still have my gun."

"Not on you, I hope."

I didn't really want to start crying, but I did cry a little. It's one thing when the world is too big and too frightening, when everything seems to be falling apart, but another when your own, simple little world seems a wreck, too. Then what?

"In ten days Hunter will be gone," whispered El. "We'll go through the canal and be in the Galapagos. There will be new things, new problems."

But you never know what those problems will be.

I wrote that before anything happened. I didn't know. You don't have to be a child to have worries that make sense one day and the next make you feel like a fool, but you might be a child. You might be me.

Next morning, the next day, in the dead air, the boat sluicing over the flat water under the push of our engine, Hunter found me on deck, port side, near the bow. The air was thick, as if it hung wet on nothingness, the sky almost yellow and the ocean green. The sun sat in front of us to the south and it was a hot, depressing, lousy day.

"I'm sorry," he said.

"Me too."

He looked at the water and then straight out, toward the bow. "I suppose you'll be happy to forget all about me."

"You're just fucked up, is all," I said. "But I don't care. You're my friend. Don't you get it?"

"No."

"Let's just go back," I said. "Let's just be innocent friends. Then you can go to Panama and have your life."

He didn't say anything back to me and for a moment I thought maybe he was thinking about it, thinking about what I'd said, until I followed his eyes out the side of the boat toward the eastern horizon.

"What's that?" he said.

There was a wisp out there. At least it looked that way at first, like a wispy cloud, except it was moving toward us and it wasn't still enough to be a cloud really, but looked more like clouds did in those old, time-lapse weather movies, kind of growing and shrinking and swirling.

"Is it smoke?" Hunter said.

"Smoke from what?"

I was hoping that it would just move off. That it wouldn't keep coming. All this time I'd been wishing and hoping that I'd see the dragon and now I knew that I didn't want to see her. Not then. It wasn't the right time, the right situation.

I ran aft, leaving Hunter, and found Angie, one of the women sailors, working the wheel. I wished it were AJ, who liked me better.

"Where's the Captain?" I said. Angie gave me an odd look. It's not like we were friends. I was still a kid to her and she'd never had a kid and didn't want a kid. I pointed over the port side.

"A cloud," she said. "Maybe we'll get some wind."

"It's not a cloud. We should turn off the engine."

Angie lowered her eyelids halfway down and raised her chin a little. So I ran to the ladder that led below, to the Captain's cabin. I was going to pound on the door, but I composed myself. I didn't want to just be an hysterical kid, then nobody would listen, or if they did and I was wrong, they'd never listen again. Maybe I *was* wrong. Now I was scared. I ran back above to the port side of the ship again. The cloud formation was darker now, not large, maybe the size of my fist if I put out my arm, but closer. But it wasn't a cloud. It wasn't quiet like a cloud. I wished El was around, but I didn't see her. I looked aft again and saw Angie watching me like I'd get in trouble for sure for panicking everybody if I started anything. I went back down below, walked up to the Captain's cabin and knocked. It took a few seconds but eventually Nigel's voice asked, "Who is it?" through the door.

"Lisa Piccolo Zu," I said.

He opened the door a crack. I could see an eye and bit of his beard.

"I think there's something someone should see," I said.

"Someone?"

"Yes," I said. "Someone in authority."

"We're having a meeting just now," he said. "And lunch."

"Something is coming at the boat."

"Another boat?"

"I don't know what it is. It's on the horizon now, but I think it might get here before lunch is over."

"Isn't Angie up there?"

"It's like a moving cloud," I said.

"A cloud?" he said.

"It's not exactly like a cloud. I think someone should see it."

"Nigel," said the captain from behind the door. "Take two minutes and look at the damn thing."

Nigel breathed out of his nose and opened the door and came out. I just turned around and he followed me. I took him to where I'd been standing with Hunter. Nigel looked out toward the swirling mist. He looked for a while. "Stay here," he said, and then he came back with binoculars and peered out again.

"Is it like a sea devil or a water tornado?" I said. I didn't believe that, but that's what I hoped, and I was getting scared and in a hurry. I was trying to help him eliminate his choices.

He pulled down the binoculars and looked at me, then put them up again. After a while, again he said, "Wait here."

Nigel looked around to see if anyone was watching us, but really there wasn't anyone but Angie paying attention, though now she was paying real close attention. Nigel winked at me and said, "Don't worry," which was really the last thing you'd say if there was nothing to worry about. In a few minutes both Captain Evans and Nigel came up the ladder and walked over to me with a kind of exaggerated calm. Everything felt like it was moving so slow. The captain looked out the binoculars and then pulled them down.

"Cut the engines," he said to Nigel. He looked down at me and tried to offer a reassuring smile.

"The phenomenon," I said to him.

"Just a precaution," he said. "We'll just take every precaution."

We had two kinds of life boat drills on the ship. One was for if the ship was sinking and the other was for what the captain called "the eventuality of the phenomenon." If the meteorological phenomenon occurred, we were to abandon ship before it struck. I knew he had to think about that now. About when to alert everybody. When to give the order.

Evans rubbed his forehead and then looked through the binoculars again. Even to the naked eye, the cloud was twice as big now, purple-gray and billowing upon itself. It was coming toward us. Then the engine cut out and it was one of those strange moments when the silence is more disruptive than the noise. As the boat slowed and began to bob on the gentle swells, people came up to the deck. Nigel came back again. "Let everyone know," the Captain said to him quietly. "Go on alert. Evacuation readiness." He turned to me. "Find your mother," he said. "Get your evacuation gear."

El got real calm when I found her. I remembered her like this once before, when we had to evacuate the cabin one summer during a fire. On the boat we had to be already prepared for this kind of thing, so we had backpacks in our cabins with life jackets, flash-lights, knives, blankets and clothes. The lifeboats were even equipped with sails and fishing tackle. "We'll be all right," she said. "We're not far from Bermuda, a few days. Besides, it's probably nothing."

I gave her a hug and we went up top. Everyone was gathered at the rail on the port side now, though I didn't see Hunter. The cloud was coming. People knew it. They could see it. A solitary bustle of smoke piling over itself in the blue sky. Captain Evans now had his electronic binoculars. "Two miles out," he said. "If it comes in another mile, we'll deploy the lifeboats." He turned to all of us then. "Go to your designated boats now," he said. He was calm but loud. "Keep your composure."

As we went to the lifeboats it suddenly felt as if something had taken a breath, as if the air had been sucked out of the air and there wasn't enough left to breathe. The ocean went still and everything became silent. Even when people tried to speak, it was as if there weren't enough molecules to carry the sound. There were just people with their mouths moving, feet shuffling, gasping, even the racket of preparing the boats fell dead. And then came the first, hot breeze, the smell of something both sweet and rotten on its edge. Angie was with us near the lifeboat, and her friend, AJ. There were about fifteen of us. Angie turned toward the east when that hot breeze swept the deck. "Holy Christ," she whispered.

Now we could see the blue-black smoke a mile away, the curling mist bursting forward and then falling in at the middle, as if it were being pushed forward by something and then sucked in, as if the cloud were breathing. The hot breeze picked up to a gust and the water began to ripple, then rise around the boat. The captain, who'd held his hand in the air, dropped it to his side and Nigel ran for the other boat.

"I'm staying till the last minute!" Evans yelled. "Don't worry, if we're hit, I'll jump. You can pick me up!"

Angie and AJ lowered the lifeboat from the center of the deck and positioned it over the side and we all piled in, then the two women sailors followed, using pulleys to lower us down from the heaving side of the ship. The waves slapped and knocked the lifeboat against the hull. Above us, we could see the cloud racing south as if to pass beyond the bow. "Maybe it will go past us," El said.

And I said, "No." That's when I looked around again for Hunter. In the rush and panic I'd forgotten about him. "Hunter," I said.

El looked around and said, "He must be on the other boat."

We couldn't raise the sail there, near the ship, so two men aboard pushed us away with the oars and spun the lifeboat so we could take up a position a safe distance away from the ship's stern. Now the ocean slapped at us under the hot bursts descending from the imploding cloud which held itself in the distant sky above the bow. We saw the other lifeboat well behind the stern and I began calling out, "Hunter! Hunter!" but as we approached them I saw he wasn't aboard.

"El!" I shouted, "he's not there!"

"There's a boy missing!" El yelled to Angie, who sat at the back of the lifeboat yelling to the rowers to put the ship between us and the seething cloud.

"The Captain will find him!" shouted Angie.

But not if he didn't want to be found. The wind pushed against us in gusts that rocked the boat, almost as if, instead of gusting and letting up, it felt as if we were buffeted by a rhythmic blowing and sucking, like a pair of giant lungs. It never quieted, but ripped our ears, first whooshing out, then whistling in. The cloud grew, blocking out the sun; the air turned gray, the water black. From the center of the smoking thing, light began to burst and the air inside it sizzled and cracked, the top of the storm rising into two large humps in the sky. Our lifeboat began to pitch and roll over the huge ocean swells that had grown so tall and so deep that from the bottom of the swells we couldn't even see the ship.

El grabbed me. Everybody grabbed something or somebody. The oars were useless. Some men began to pray. There was a flash and a blinding light, a loud crack from the sky and then, when we rolled to the top of a swelling wave, I saw Hunter standing on the bow of the ship.

"Hunter!" I screamed. "Hunter!" But of course he couldn't hear me. I screamed to El, "Hunter's on the ship!" though she'd ducked her head from the flashing light. The sides of the cloud began to fold and flap like a pair of tremendous, dark wings, its top rising into huge humps and the bottom narrowing. I saw the captain then, scrambling across the deck of the heaving ship, trying to run to the bow where Hunter stood gripping the top of the bow rail. The boat rocked against the hot head wind and Hunter fell to his knees, barely holding on, his feet sliding away from him. Evans fell, too, sliding across the deck, managing to stay aboard by throwing an arm over the gunwale and locking his armpit over a rail post. Then our lifeboat rolled into a swell and the air flashed again. The sky roared, but not like thunder, like a howl, like a deep throated scream. When we rose up again, Hunter stood, and there she hung, above him.

I couldn't see the captain anywhere, but inside the cloud which now beat like a heart, the dragon screamed, her neck extending toward the bow of the boat, toward Hunter, who threw out his arms toward her, falling on his chest as the boat pitched forward; then he got up again. "The dragon!" I screamed. "The dragon!" But her light flashed so brightly, her throaty, hissing roar cracked my ears. Around me, everyone, even El, ducked away as our boat began to dip into the next huge swell and the fire raged from the dragon's throat at the bow of the ship.

When our lifeboat rose again, Hunter was gone. The cloud had fallen in on itself and risen into the sky, already moving west and away. The waves and wind, as quickly as they had come, now began to settle. In minutes the sky was clear and the sea calm.

Captain Evans had fallen overboard and we picked him up in the water nearby.

"The ship looks sound," he said after he'd crawled aboard our lifeboat. "Is everyone accounted for?"

"Not the boy," said Angie.

"Hunter!" I said.

"On the bow?" said the Captain. "I couldn't see to the bow after I fell."

The other boat came toward us then and the captain yelled to Nigel. "Did you pick up the boy?"

"What boy?" said Nigel.

"On the bow."

"Did he have a life jacket?" said Nigel.

"No," I said. "I saw him."

"Check the water," the captain said to Nigel. "I want these people on board. Then I'll send Angie and AJ out and you bring your boat in."

"He's not in the water," I said.

"Did you see him?" El said to me.

"The dragon took him," I said.

Captain Evans looked at me and frowned. "The ship looks sound. Maybe he's still on board. Check the water," he said to Nigel again. "I'll check the ship. It's calming. We're in no hurry."

"It won't be back?" said El.

"It was a cloud," Angie said to her. "It traveled east to west."

"She won't be back," I said to El. "She got what she needed. Didn't anyone see her?"

"Lisa," said El. "Lisa." She pulled me to her breasts.

I didn't care. It didn't matter. They wouldn't find Hunter. They didn't.

"She took a virgin," I said quietly.

"It was a horrible thing," said El, holding me tighter, rocking.

"She took him. She won't be back."

"Let's get these people on board!" shouted Evans.

And El rocked me. "My baby," whispered El. "My child."

Someone was crying. I couldn't tell if it was me or El or everyone.

The Dragon Journal of Lisa Piccolo Zu

Some Twentieth Century writers believed that people flew on the backs of dragons. That dragons were bonded to their riders at the dragon's birth. The bonding occurred before the rider had reached puberty and when the dragons were old enough both the dragon and rider took mates. Some people believed only the best of the boys learned to fly dragons. Others, only the worst of the girls. Lives were lost in the bonding. The young dragons were clumsy with their feet and their fire. And in the learning. In the first fragile, dangerous exercises in the sky. So you could not risk the best girls. Oh, no. Not that.

Some writers pretended that dragons could leap through gaps of space or time, taking their trained riders with them. All of this is fantasy. There are no records of dragon riding. Not a single one. No one ever rode a dragon.

The Story of Werther Fausten

The edge of the woods seemed to swell and contract like the beating of a heart and the air around me grew hot and swollen with a sickening, sweet-hot smell. A gust of air, sultry now with bloody moisture, blew against me and then blew away, blew against me again, and then away, as if the space around me had become a pair of despicable lungs. I knew then, with certainty, that Dianna had not murdered her children. That this beast had taken their lives. And ended Dianna's.

"What is the point of murder?" I said as I approached the monster.

"Werther," the beast hissed. "Is that a riddle? Do you *s*seek to quiz me?"

"You murdered innocent children," I said.

"Have pity on me, Werther," said the monster. "I am alone. A nightmare in the land of the real. And is not death inevitable? Are you and I not two *s*sides if the *s*same coin?"

"*You* are responsible."

"I am but a ssimple bea*s*st, Werther, am I not? Devoid of reason. I have no knowledge of good or evil. Make no choices. I am incapable of re*ss*pon*ss*ibilty."

"I do not know what you are," I said to the thing. "But I discovered you, if I did not create you."

"Oh, murderer!" the monster said. "Or did I discover you?"

As I have said before, it is hard to say that the beast spoke. More or less, her thoughts seemed to arise in me as she opened her mouth and blue flame rolled in her throat. And I was not, as yet, beyond the hope of dealing with the creature. If it were rational it could be persuaded, if living, slain.

"I have come, Werther," the beast said to me. "I have come. I am not Chrisstian, or I might have chosen the Millennium. The devil has always played too keenly into God's hands, don't you think?" The monster's wings rose as she spoke and her neck stretched forward, her dark eyes glistening in her narrow head.

"Speak directly," I said. "What do you want?"

"How I long for mortality."

"What do you want from me?"

"What do *you* want, Werther? How am I to know what I want? I am a beasst. Your beasst. A sself-consciouss reptile. A monsster. A dream. Have you no love or pity for your creation?"

As I have said, she spoke in hisses, riddles, questions, many of which I still do not understand. I only record here, to the best of my memory, what I heard her say.

"I want mankind to learn to live within itself," I said, answering the first of her questions.

"*Man*kind?" she hissed. Her narrow head rose above me and her wings arched.

"That is all I ever wanted," I said to her. "That cautious science produce the technology of peace. That I would discover how to unlock the technology of existence. To end poverty, starvation, illness. To find love."

"That is what I want, too," the beast said to me. "You and I are utopians, Werther, no?" The monster's wings rose, then sagged. She raised a taloned forehand to her chin. "But now, is thiss for all *man*kind," she said. "Is it for womankind, too? And the other animals of the planet? Do they partake in the technology of exisstence, in the circle of your love?"

I had no tolerance for her sophistry and I told her so. "You speak to me," I said. "How is it you are rational?"

"I sspeak for all ssentience." She lowered her wings yet more and raised her chin. "It is sso good to have ssomeone to talk to. Yet I have not a word within me that was not sspawned in you."

"Yet you have murdered!"

"Oh death," hissed the beast, wagging her head. "Death. Humanity is sso occasionally frantic about the death of itss own." She breathed a ball of fire in her throat, closed her mouth around it and let sulfurous smoke escape her nostrils. "As if murder were not rational and morality had ssome logic. It brought you to me, Werther. And you musst come to me. Do you eat meat, Werther? One life for another. If you sslay a million cows, can *we* not eat one human? How much more tragic the death of a beasst with no ssoul. You, Werther, give up only your skins. No? What are two or three lives, Werther, between uss, when we are here to ssave the world?"

"Do not speak to me of mortality and immortality. I know nothing of either."

"Do you think the worsst human being is more valuable than the besst dog?"

I knew then that there was nothing I could accomplish in communication with her. Her conversation was a dance, a dialectic of nightmares. The next time I must carry a gun and kill her. I turned to walk away.

"Oh not like that, Werther. Not like that!" she hissed. "A bullet will ssimply pass through me. There are ways to kill a dragon. And there are ways to appease her."

I turned to her again.

"I want to be more helpful, Werther. Really. Have ssympathy for me, the beasst of your heart. You have a lover now. A family. A child. As you once were, I am now. Alone. But with less hope. There are none of my kind. Yet like you once did, I want to ssave thiss world." Her eyes met mine and showed me the black depths of my own being. For a moment I felt addled and mad, but then she averted her glance. "I could hold you here, Werther, I could. But insstead let me tell you a sstory. It might help uss."

She folded upon herself, becoming almost diminutive; her neck retracted so her chin rested on her chest and her wings folded back behind her shoulders. She looked, once again, almost as if she were an old woman.

"Where have I been ssince I last ssaw you?" she began. "I went on a ssearch. Living as I have, an eternity with love at my back, I wished to ssee it before me."

As I have said, she spoke not from her mouth, but viscerally, as if I felt her words in my heart before I could see them in my brain, though they reverberated in me with a wicked, reptilian hissing which I cannot reproduce except by the slimmest suggestion.

"When I left you, Werther, I traveled to a ssmall city just to the wesst, near your Great Lakess. There, an old man lived alone in a dilapidated housse. His wife had been dead for twenty years, yet he sstill mourned her. He thought of her everyday. Once a bit of an artisst, he drew pictures of her consstantly. Even as he ssat to eat he drew her image on his napkin. After twenty years. Surely, this was love.

"But he ssuffered from a horrible disease which attacked his nerves. Once a huge, powerful man, now he could barely walk, barely sstand. He was nearly blind. He leaned on a walker and at times it took him over a minute to move a foot. Why did he not jusst die? Yet he sstruggled sso determinably.

"He'd had children, Werther. Eight children. How you humans propagate in poverty. All but two now lived far away, on the coasstss. One of the two lived a few hours drive distant, the other on the edge of town. That one, a sson, came to ssee him occasionally, though he, himsself, had a dying child and a ssick wife. He worked two jobs, day and night, for his family. The other sson, who lived two hours away, came not at all. He hated his father, as ssons sometimes do.

"I learned all of thiss because I sspent time with the old man, Werther. I met him at his church, at the earliesst mass, before dawn. His name was Daniel. Many old women go to church. And ssome old men, what'ss left of them. On Ssundays Daniel would rise early and dress, then sstruggle with his walker, throwing it down his front sstepss, then use the hand rail to hold himsself up until he reached the bottom to retrieve it. Then he sstruggled the three blockss to his church. It took him over an hour. He was Catholic, Werther. But when he got there, he would ssit in his pew all day, until all the masses were done. It was his chance to ssocialize. That'ss where I met him.

"We sspent hours at his kitchen table, his old dog at our feet. His big dog was a limited creature, but the animal loved him and kept vigil over him. There in the kitchen I learned about Daniel's life. His oldesst sson, the one in the country, on the edge of town, had pleaded with Daniel to come live with him, but Daniel refused.

"'I don't know anyone there,' he ssaid.

"'You don't know anyone here anymore. Mo*ss*t of your friends and neighbors are dead,' I *ss*aid to him.

"'This was a fine neighborhood once. My son has too many problems of his own.'

"In truth Werther, his neighborhood was now a *ss*lum. Young men *ss*tood in the *ss*treet*ss* with guns, *ss*elling drugs. The police had abandoned the vicinity to anarchy a decade ago and Daniel *ss*urvived there only because he had nothing anyone would want. I *ss*uppose I could have cleared the *ss*treet*ss*, but I hadn't come to police a *ss*lum in a Midwe*ss*tern city. I came to learn. Though as I came to know Daniel better, I brought him things. Bread and butter. Milk. I had his radio repaired *ss*o he could listen to ba*ss*eball games. He had a drawer in a bureau where he kept a little money. Atop the bureau were photos of his dead wife. I made sure to keep it always replenished with *ss*ome cash. He noticed, I knew, but he *s*aid nothing. He ju*ss*t *ss*miled at me *ss*o pleasantly when he'd walk away from the drawer.

"'My wife is still looking after me,' he'd laugh. He had the gentlest *ss*mile, Werther, and a gli*ss*ten, *ss*till, in his eyes, which could make anyone joyou*ss* to look at him and *ss*ee how much pleasure he yet took from his life. Yet he once *ss*aid to me that he was not a good man. 'I was violent,' he *ss*aid. 'Hard on my kids. They've moved far away from me. One hates me.'

"'I'm sure they left to make their livings,' I told him. 'Your daughters have marriages.'

"'My sons, too,' he *ss*aid. 'Two of them are supported by their wives.'

"'They phone you.'

"'Yes. Sometimes they do. But so many of my friends are dead. And neighbors. And relatives. Good women and good men. Yet I don't die. I wonder if I'm being punished?'

"'By whom?'

"He laughed. 'Who else? The last of my sisters is in a care home now. She hates it there. They tell her when and where to eat, to sleep.' He looked up at me with that glint. 'Even when and where to poop. Her son just died of cancer. Only fifty years old. One of the best men I ever knew. Gave his family everything.'

"He paused. He'd been drawing. 'Sad stories,' he ssaid. 'Why dwell on the sad?' He pushed his paper toward me. 'My wife, Claire,' he ssaid.

"I ssaid, 'I know.'

"'But this picture is the same as the one I drew of her from memory when I was stationed in Midway during the war.'

"'Againsst the Japanese?'

"He laughed again. 'Who else? Sometimes you say funny things.'

"'I'm old, too. I forget.'

"'I hated those bastards,' he ssaid.

"'The Japanese?'

"'I killed plenty of them. I'm one tough son-of-a-bitch. How do you think I've survived here? I cheered when we dropped the bomb. Did you?'

"'No, Daniel,' I ssaid to him.

"'Neither did Claire. My oldest son was three when I came home. Years later, when some of the hate and violence had left me, we talked about it. You'd have risked my life for the lives of Japanese? I said to her. Hundreds of thousands of innocents, she said. Children, and women, like her. I wasn't innocent. I was a soldier. Claire was an interesting woman.'

"'What if I were Japanese?' I ssaid to him.

"He ssquinted at me. 'Well,' he said, 'it's too late now. I guess I'd close my eyes and kiss you anyway.'

"We had a hundred converssations like this, Werther. Though in that time, as well, I read voluminoussly. In Daniel's attic were volumes of bookss left by his children, passed from one child to the next as Daniel and Claire sstruggled to put them through sschool. In the night, when he couldn't ssleep, I read to Daniel. Bessides the knowledge I have from you, Werther, I filled my nightss with literature.

"You will forgive me if I preferred the Romanticss. I came to hate the Realism of your time. You are an odd sspecies. You use the conventions of the real to run from truth. You sseem, Werther, to have become beings afraid of the very world you have created. You are consciouss beings afraid of ideas. Or is it that you are over-impressed with the few you have? Oh, how many creatures of the world have faces—eyes, brains, feelings, heartss—each living insside its own life.

"Have I become too maudlin? Daniel's dog died while I was with him. I helped him bury the dog in his yard, beneath a pear tree. I'd grown fond of the animal's ssteady brown eyes and faithful ssmile, his watchful prowling of the borders, his ssatisfaction at a ssimple meal, his quiet waiting, his gentle heart, his generouss life. I found mysself weeping there, under the purple ssky and bare trees, the grass as brown as dung. The hair of the dead. Isn't that what Whitman ssaid?

"You ssee, Werther, I could have lived the resst of my days there. Your experiment would have been over. I was needed. And loved. I contemplated the day when I might open Daniel's blinded eyes and show mysself to him. And he would forgive me my appearance, close his eyes and kiss me the way he might a Japanese. Who knows what magic might then have happened?

"But in time, Daniel's family came to hear of me. When his oldesst sson visited, I always went away, but he found the ssnow cleared, Daniel's clothes and dishes washed, the housse orderly and clean, the pictures of Claire dussted, the cash drawer sstocked. Daniel told him of me, and the sson, himsself now in his fifties, fingered his bearded chin. But if it doesn't take a human long to grow expectant of generossity, it takes not much longer for him to become ssusspiciouss of it. The sson worried that I was taking advantage of his father.

"It yet might have continued for ssome time, but Daniel's condition worssened. One morning, while I was away, he losst his balance and fell. I found him in his kitchen, unconsciouss, a broken rib and a fractured hip. I had no choice then but to call an ambulance and flee.

"I hung closse. I followed the ambulance. Visited Daniel at night, in the dark, sslipping through the halls of the hosspital like misst. I sstood at his bed and held his gray hand in the bleeding, pale light. Ssome of his family had arrived. His sson from the nearby city and a daughter who lived in the Ssouth.

"'They're going to put me away,' Daniel gassped to me.

"'You are not thiss body, these breathss, not even these thoughtss,' I told him. 'You are broader, deeper, infinite evermore.'

"'Do not let me die here,' he ssaid. 'Take me home.'

"And sso, Werther, for the first time I interfered with your world. Under the cloak of my ssilence I brought him to his home to die. Maybe, as sso many of you humans contend about sselfishness, I didn't do it for him, but for me. That I might have him to mysself in his lasst moment and carry him within me, as you once carried me within you; the great goodness of the human heart, that moment of bright, ssweet goodness that, beyond all your foolish intellect, makess you mosst like angels. But I was denied. He did not die. And in a day's time his family was at his door.

"Oh Werther, forgive me, your creature. I should have taken him then. I should have denied myself that wish for the ssingle moment of his love and given him his own bliss. Insstead, that next morning, I met his family at his threshold.

"'He's here, isn't he?' ssaid the oldesst sson.

"'Who are you?' ssaid the daughter.

"The younger sson said, 'How did you get him here?'

"'I am his friend,' I ssaid to them. 'He wishes to die here. I will take care of him as I have for the passt year.'

"'We know who you are and what you're about,' ssaid the younger son.

"'You cannot have this house!' the daughter sscreamed.

"'He has nothing that I want,' I ssaid. It was my first lie, Werther. I felt almosst human. 'Let him die here,' I ssaid to them. 'I will take care of him.'

"'He must go to a care home,' ssaid the oldest sson. "I can't take care of him. I can barely take care of my sick wife."

"'I will take care of him,' I ssaid.

"'You can't take care of him,' ssaid the daughter to me. 'You're too old.'

"'I shall get help,' I inssissted.

"'Go back where you came from,' the younger man ssaid. 'Leave here. Leave my father alone.'

"'Let us in,' ssaid the daughter.

"I replied, 'No.'

"'Let us in or we'll have you removed!'

"'You must remove me then,' I ssaid.

"'I'm sorry,' ssaid the oldest son. 'I have no choice. You must understand, this is what's best for him. You can visit him in the home.'

"They went to their car and I knew that I had only the day and the night to sstop them.

"'I shall go to the passtor of your church,' I ssaid to Daniel when I went back to his room. And I walked the treeless bright sstreetss of Daniel's sslum, the armed boys on the corners, Werther, young men prowling on bicycles, businessmen in BMW's and Mercedes Benzes, any one of whom could have ssaved Daniel his misery with their money, drove up to the curbs to buy their cheap ecsstassies. I walked to the rectory of Daniel's church.

"There, I worked my way through maids and attendantss, a ssecretary and a priesst, each attempting to deny me access to the monssignor. I passed the day in the foyer outsside his office as the light rose in the windows and faded toward evening. As darkness fell and the ssecretary began to turn on the lampss, she turned to me and ssaid, 'I guess he will not see you today.' And I answered, 'He musst.'

"You ssee, Werther, I am not a creature of desspair. As the night came on and the passtor finally left his office, I met him. A middle-aged man with cropped, gray hair and a belly which protruded over the dark-red belt of his cassock, he tipped his four cornered hat at me, but I sstood and sstepped in front of him.

"'I'm sorry,' he ssaid, 'but I have a service to administer.'

"'None more important than thiss,' I ssaid.

"'Make an appointment for tomorrow,' he ssaid.

"'Ssomeone is dying. It cannot wait.'

"'Do they need the Last Rites? There is a priest here on duty.'

"'He needs money and food, and ssome assurance of care. Surely the Church can afford to help ssupport a man long enough to let him die in his own home.'

"'I don't recognize you,' the passtor ssaid to me. 'Who is this about?'

"When I told him it was Daniel, the passtor ssilenced me.

"'I know the situation,' he ssaid. 'I know the family. I've heard of you and know what you've done. However much you've helped Daniel, it isn't fair to take advantage of him now. He will enter our care home tomorrow.'

"'*Your* care home,' I ssaid to him. 'The family will pay *you.*'

"'He'll be taken care of.'

"'He will ssuffer and die alone,' I ssaid.

"'There will be a priest there,' the passtor ssaid. 'Now I must go.'

"Oh Werther, on how little the fate of the world turns. I returned that night and watched Daniel in his bed. One ssimple man who meant nothing to the world, yet who contained a world within himsself. I watched his breath, hoping that he would reach the dawn and yet, too, afraid that he would live to ssee me and hold the fatal moment in his dying heart. I opened the shade to let the dawn sslip through and sstood in front of him when he firsst opened his eyes. He ssaw me, or from what he could ssee, recognized me, and a sslight ssmile came to his lipss.

"'Do you know me, Daniel?' I assked.

"'My friend,' ssaid Daniel.

"'Yess,' I ssaid, letting him lie back and resst again. 'I went to the passtor of your church for help.'

"'Well,' he ssaid, as the morning light came to his window and lit the drawn shade. 'Then everything will be all right.'

"I did not know what to ssay to him, Werther. I took his hand and held it. I lisstened for his shallow breathing and felt my own heart fall in with his faint pulsse. I heard a car on the sstreet come to a sstop in front of the housse. Then another. And a third. It was the family, an ambulance, and the police. I was helpless. They would come and take him. He would die alone. And what would I know of mysself, Werther? What would I know if not tessted by this besst of human heartss?

"'Who is that outside?' Daniel assked.

"'You musst know me, Daniel,' I ssaid.

"'Stay with me,' he whisspered. 'Don't let them take me from my home.'

"'Firsst know me, Daniel,' I ssaid to him. 'You musst know who will give you thiss.' And sslowly I unveiled to him my beasstial form.

"I sstood before my dying friend, my wings unfurled, thiss blue fire rolling in my throat. I showed him what was in all of you, Werther, or at leasst what had been there for sso long until you sset it free.

And Daniel trembled in front of me. He wept. He cried, 'You are the devil! God forgive me! The devil! Don't take me to hell!'

"From below came shouting and pounding at the front door.

"'You have had hell enough,' I hissed to Daniel. 'Can you forgive me? Daniel, can you love even me?'

"But he sscreamed hyssterically. A window crashed and the downstairs door came ajar. I heard their feet on the sstairs. And sso, Werther, I was defeated. Maybe I had waited too long."

Dr. Zu, the beast stood in front of me, fully unveiled. Her shoulders sagged and her head fell forward, as if she possessed true longing and regret. From her throat, a long, low hiss and then a pause, and then her hiss again, her reptile breath the only sound left to the night.

"They took him," I said.

"No, Werther," she replied. "They did not." She raised up again before me. "I did."

"You killed him."

"Werther," the monster said to me, "do you feel nothing? I killed him in pity and rage. I burned the housse. I let the family esscape. That night I burned the church."

"You murdered your friend."

"Have you no mercy, Werther? said the beast. "No ssympathy? I do. As well as rage againsst your sspecies. You are sself-centered. Short-ssighted. Sselfish."

"It was not your choice to kill that man," I insisted.

"No, Werther, it was not."

"And however you have rationalized the murder of your friend, what of Dianna's children?"

"I am but an animal," the creature whispered to me. "How *has* the world become thiss world? Whose choice?"

"I will have no more riddles!" I screamed. "Why have you brought me here? Why have you done these things? What do you want from me?"

With that the monster recoiled, eyeing me with tilted chin, seething in her own fiery breath. Again she brought forward her head. "Could it be love?" she said.

Again I tell you, Zu, that I could not understand her, except for the way one understands the wind in the trees when the leaves turn their backs in August and rattle with winter's first hiss. Even so, if this creature, this being, had arisen from my depths, I had not known such love and bliss since her parting. Be it an invention of my heart or brain or soul, what license had this murderer to ask for love?

"Does that mean you want a mate?" I said.

"Why Werther," she responded, raising a clawed hand to her chin, "you are *sso* inventive."

"Yet where have I seen your love?" I insisted of the beast. "You could become a plague to mankind. What kind of fool would I be to help your havoc propagate?"

"And why not the rule of dragons?" she hissed. "Would we find it *sso* much wor*sse* than the rule of corporations? Capitali*sstss*? Communi*sstss*? Tyrant*ss*? Kings? Oh, the poor of your world! If dragons ruled, do you think they would know a difference? Do you think there would be *ssadness* or rejoicing among the whales, the flamingos, the chimpanzees? Look at me, Werther, your ward. Am I not metaphor for them all?"

"You are a monster," I said.

"*You* are a mon*ss*ter," the dragon said. "You are all mon*ss*ters."

"We shall destroy you."

"You shall de*ss*troy everything."

"*We* are the stars, self-conscious. *We* are the universe becoming aware."

"You are a cliché," she said. "Consciousne*ss* is but the tail of a dog, wagging, wagging, wagging. No more, no le*ss*. When the dog dies, the tail *ss*top*ss*."

Now it seemed as if I stared across a dark abyss, the monster expanding and contracting before me like a great heart pounding.

"Werther," it said. "You wished to *ss*ave your world. You *ss*till can. I will give you *ss*ix month*ss*, Werther. *Ss*ix month*ss*. And then I shall return."

"I will never come to you."

"Oh Werther," the monster said. "You will. You mu*ss*t."

The Story of Werther Fausten

In the coming weeks as I relived that night and the complete nightmare of those days in Porterville, the sequence of events became increasingly jumbled for me. But for the deaths of Dianna's children and her own suicide, I would not have believed that any of it had occurred at all. As each day passed, the simplicity of my daily life grew more profound, more rich with acute feeling and love. The ordinary facts of life, the crisp autumn air and the glory of the turning leaves, cold rain, white snow, blue sky, the cloud of my breath as it left me, reinforced for me how little anyone needed the fantastic to abide in miracles. And then there was my increasing love for Veronica and the almost painful love and sympathy I felt for Michael, my growing son.

My father, who did not have a telephone, wrote to inform me that he'd joined a mission to northeastern Bolivia. The indigenous people there, the Quechua and Aymara, were under pressure from the Bolivian government and developers. Already the Jesuits and Mormons had established missions. It had become a kind of battleground. If the Indians could not be left alone, then at least they could be given food, medicine, and religious pluralism. The Mennonites, he said, were there to moderate, not convert, and their philosophy, where earth was Bible, came closest to that of the Indians themselves. He'd been planning his departure for some time now, he said. By the time I received his letter he'd be on his way.

As much as I worried that I would never see my father again, I felt toward him the way one might feel toward an errant teenager, full of longing and love, and the sadness that he must meet his own destiny. I do not know if I could ever disagree with someone as profoundly as I disagreed with him, and yet love him so much. In the end, the religious man and the scientific man walk away from the same awe, one with an answer and one with a question, and the settling and unsettling of each moment falls like the rubble of a landslide and buries them both. Yet the religious man can only pray that it does not happen again. The man of science rebuilds, remakes, reforms. If there are no gods, then let us be gods. If no God, then Adam we must be nonetheless.

That Halloween was the first that meant something for me in my life. I built a little stand at the end of our long driveway that cut through the fields to the road. I hung it with lights and spread hay bales and pumpkins around. We even advertised in the local paper that there would be free hay rides for those who stopped by our farm and I spent a few long days repairing Veronica's old wagon and hitch so we could pull the old, wooden-wheeled truck through our corn fields by horse team instead of using a tractor.

That night, an oddly warm Hallow's Eve with a dry wind sweeping into Albany from the south, a hundred children and their families came by our stand and we handed out apples and candy, served cider and tea to the goblins and ghosts, astronauts and space aliens, super heroes, villains, monsters. With Veronica, Michael in her arms, manning the booth, I mounted the buckboard and drove the families through our dried fields and into the woods where I'd cleared the riding trails wide enough for the wagon. In the trees I'd hung spider webs of cotton gauze, plastic bats, skeletons, battery-operated hooting owls and ghouls. As the children laughed and shrieked I thought of Michael and the many years ahead filled with holidays and simple fun. I thought ahead, as well, to when Michael would be too old to enjoy these things. How brief our joy. How all things pass. I thought, too, of Dianna and her children in their graves, and the irony of this celebration of death.

Because you see, Doctor Zu, I am an empirical man. I do not believe in vampires, Yetis, ghosts, contact from outer space. Each day since that horrible August night, as ordinary life stretched in front of me and filled in the time behind me, I reminded myself of these simple, glorious realities, and these simple things reminded me that there were no such things as monsters. There were no dragons. Even now, do you believe me? Have you ever seen one? Had anyone?

I filled my life with my family as Michael grew, rolled over, took his first solid food, teethed, sat up, smiled his first smiles, laughed, gurgled his first word-like sounds. I kept almost sacred watch and made sacrament of the smell of Veronica's breasts after nursing, her hair after a bath, the soft curve of her hips, the high, smooth melody of her voice and the music of her laugh, her wit. I'd be a fool to let madness take me as it had Dianna. All that I had learned, all of my work, if it had opened me to the depths of human depravity, it had also given me the tools to control it. I would not allow this maddening vision of the monster crone to consume me. When it came, if it came again, I would contain it. It was mine and could not hurt the world.

That Halloween night, as Veronica left the booth to take Michael to bed, I unhitched and cooled the horse team, then stabled them. But when I came to Veronica in our room, the night was filled with sirens, as if half of Albany had gone up in flames.

"A Halloween celebration in town?" she said to me sleepily.

"I hadn't heard of one," I said, and stepped to the window, parting the curtain of our second story bedroom. Across the horizon, toward the city, it looked as if the sky were in flames. I turned to Veronica again, but somehow, despite the distant whine of sirens, exhausted, she'd fallen asleep. I sat at the window, watching the orange sky, a halo of hell bleeding into the night and stealing away the stars. I sat there gazing until I fell asleep. In the morning I learned that the Catholic Cathedral had caught fire and burned to the ground.

"How odd," Veronica said over breakfast. Michael, a quiet, almost complacent child, much more like Veronica than myself, sat beside us in his high chair. In the spring, Veronica would end her maternity leave and return to teaching at the state university and our hiatus from the chores of our careers would end. Dozens of research schools had contacted me, as well, including Cornell and Syracuse, both of which had strong animal research programs. For over a year I'd deluded myself into thinking that my scientific research was done and I'd contemplated writing a book about my work. Based on my theories and experiments in nuclear biology there had been recent breakthroughs in cancer research, AIDS remedies, and disease management, as well as intelligence enhancement in domestic mammals. I was being considered for the Nobel. I found it ironic that my greatest experiment had been a failure and now the man who'd come closest to understanding the secrets of the soul was haunted by his own psyche.

"How helpless God is," I said.

"Spare me," Veronica laughed. "It was struck by lightning. No one was injured. No one died."

"Did you see a cloud in the sky?" I asked.

"There was a lightning storm last night over the city. One of those updrafts that have been occurring over the Great Lakes."

"The wind was from the south last night."

"That's not your field, is it?" she said. "The weather?"

"Maybe I should think more about it," I said and laughed at myself. In fact, as a boy I had kept a weather notebook. Consulting old newspaper records and The Farmer's Almanac I'd come to believe that part of the confounding difficulty in predicting weather was our conservative methodology. Chaos Theory had only made us more conservative. Now meteorological prediction barely strayed from the observations we accumulated from weather satellites. The line between prediction and description had all but disappeared. By recording the history of weather and observing its patterns I believed I could predict the severity of the coming winter by observing the pattern of spring rain, by watching the thickness and lay of the late summer fog or, indeed, the breeding of mosquitoes, the fur coats of animals, the thickness of a caterpillar's fuzz. Even as a child, Dr. Zu, I was an innovator, willing to examine paradigms. And yet I have been called a reductionist! Even educated people throw labels at things they fear!

As you might know, in the last decade there had been an increasing number of quick-strike storms off the Great Lakes. People added them to the argument about whether or not the weather had been changing, an argument that had raged since the global warming debates at the end of the century. One summer hotter than ever, the next the coolest. A horrible winter, then a gentle one. More and bigger tornadoes in the Midwest, more powerful hurricanes in the east, more frequent *El Nino* patterns in the Pacific, greater floods in China, worse draughts on the Russian Steppes. Was the ozone layer depleting over the poles or had it been contracting and expanding since the beginning of time? How much of it was true and how much of it was accountable to more precise measurement, weather satellites, a larger vocabulary and better world-wide communication? But of course the weather was changing! The weather always changes. It's the weather! Mountains move! Continents part and collide!

I said all of this to Veronica who, in her peculiar way, regarding me much as I had suggested we regard the weather, eyed me wryly. "Well," she said, "the Fundamentalists have always thought the Catholics to be devil worshippers. One fire makes another."

"And we can blame God or the devil depending," I said.

"Back to the witches," she said. "It was better then. At least it was matriarchal."

"Oh yes," I said. "That would be better. Witches." Oh Dr. Zu, I sat before my beloved and my child, he an innocent baby, and she skeptical even of the weather. What was I to say? That I had a theory: a monster burned the church?

"Better than witches, dragons."

"Godzilla," said Veronica. "Is he anti-Catholic?"

"I can see this isn't going anywhere," I said. But in truth, there was nowhere to go. A church had burned in a storm. A Catholic one. Not a Lutheran church. Nor a Mennonite meeting house. To find pattern in coincidence, to see the disasters of the natural world as personal confrontations, these were the elements of paranoia, a paranoia upon which I was now determined to do battle in order to save my life.

As the year progressed I returned to the preliminary exercises I'd used at the beginning of my experimentation with the unconscious, many of them simple, ancient techniques as old as the Veda, others from Tantric or Tibetan Buddhism, still others from bio-feedback. Whatever their source, these were, in fact, empirical methods for achieving control of both the conscious and unconscious mind, methods I would employ when, in all likelihood, my inner alarm sounded in six months and I would be forced to encounter the next onslaught of hallucinations which produced the uncanny appearance of the crone. As you stand before me now, Dr. Zu, unbelieving, I stood before myself, with my life, my sanity, my family and my world at stake. So cautiously I told myself that if need be I might also be prepared to search for the crone's mate.

These were Michael's first holidays, though he did not know it. Yet I reveled in the Thanksgiving Turkey. For the first time in my life I set up a Christmas tree. I purchased an antique sleigh and on Christmas Eve, amid a soft and deafening snow, we bundled up and drove through the woods, cutting across the empty, white fields to visit our neighbors. In the following month, Michael crawled. He spoke, "Dada." He stood. I saw in him the microcosm of humanity and I felt, for the first time in my life, the love of each father for his children; the passion of the creator and protector, the hope of the future, the frailty of life in our insecure world. If I had been motivated before to change the world for all mankind, I now saw my task more personally: to protect my wife and my son, to save two by saving all.

In January Veronica went back to teaching and I, too, returned to work. Though I had to fly to Ithaca once a week, Cornell funded me to set up a laboratory at home. Most of my models, expressed in calculus and in theory, could be e-mailed or faxed to the university where I discussed it on the day I flew in. I could even lecture by video, if need be, over the Internet. Though I was home enough to compensate for Veronica's absence twice a week, my work consumed much of my time and we hired a nanny for Michael. Even so, I was a scrupulous father, unwilling to give away a single moment with my son to the unmemorable past. I left my work to feed him, bathe him, play with him, sing to him before he took his nap.

Now, for the first time since I'd evoked the crone, I returned to my work in the nexus of communal unconscious. But now the fields of fantasy lay at my feet as if burned by a retreating army, the jungle of desire withered away from my crunching footsteps, the desert of fear sat windless and still as if dormant under a fading, Antarctic sun. In the soundless mountains I felt nothing, neither hope nor despair, and at the mouth of the crone's cave only a voiceless, gray light beckoning void.

I thought then that if this were the price of my joy, then so be it. If the psyche was metaphor, then why not the death of fear and desire? Had I found the technological path to the mystic? In the coming weeks I began to employ the cyber-technology I'd been developing just as I'd abandoned my work. If, as I have said, I could not inhabit another's psyche, I found that I could, in fact, accompany another being's journey. Much in the way cyber reality interfaced with psychic experience and could be projected onto a screen or shared by inclusive users of the same program, I found that a psyche-nexus could be shared and projected into cyber reality. I began to use student volunteers whom I guided and accompanied into the areas of psychic space time, or psychic placement.

As I have said, there was little risk. This shared psychic space, however objective, lies beneath or beyond most people's dream reality. The deepest dreams float on top of it like continents floating on a molten plastic core. People seldom enter it and when they do, they forget. Yet to my astonishment I found what I should have expected. In each of my volunteers, their psychic substratum, like my own, now lay dormant at best, if not dead.

I followed this up with several statistical surveys drawn from previous psychological experiments at the university lab, as well as other world universities, including Duke University's Center for the Paranormal. Even more precisely, several of my student volunteers had been involved in other, previous dream studies. Since those last experiments their psychic lives had drastically changed. If in the last months they had experienced a remarkable, if complacent satisfaction with their lives; more astonishingly, like me, they had stopped dreaming. You would find, Dr. Zu, though now it is no longer possible to do so, that if you could accumulate all of the dream studies that occurred during this period, this fact is confirmed. It seems that people had stopped dreaming and hadn't even noticed.

Do you dream, Dr. Hestor Zu? If you do, you are one of the last. But not the very last.

One evening, after Michael was asleep, Veronica and I shared a glass of wine. I asked her, "Veronica, do you dream?"

"Yes," she said. "Of course."

There was a moment when I felt the frightening chill of any man who fears the worst, but I held my fear in check. I told her of my recent work, not mentioning the crone, but only that my recent experiments, as well as surveys, seemed to indicate that most people were not dreaming.

"Surely that's not true," she said. "I dream, Werther. If your wife is dreaming, then others are dreaming, too. The world is a big place."

"I am not," I said.

"You are not what?" she laughed. "A big place?"

"Dreaming," I said.

"Well maybe not now," said Veronica. "It happens in cycles, I'm sure." She laughed again. "Like being horny or anything else."

"Anything else," I said, but she stopped me and then took me away with her love. I remember holding her after our passion, a passion renewed for me each time with greater fire, and feeling my breath slip away onto her soft cheek, holding that moment the way lover's do, as if there would never be another; counting her breaths next to mine.

Michael awoke in the night and I went to him. I lifted his window blind and beheld the light of the white half moon. "Look," I whispered. "The moon out your window." I held him as he passed from tears to laughter, his lips forming around the amazing vowels. "Oo," he said. "Oon." And then the quiet murmur of his sleep. I placed my child back in his crib and returned to Veronica, saw the wrinkle of her brow and the ever so slight movement of her bottom lip. I watched her dream and knew. I knew.

In the morning, preparing to leave, she said to me, "Is it something in what you're doing? Like Heisenberg? Your instruments are obscuring the phenomena?"

"Would you try for me? We can do it here."

"Try your dream machine?" she laughed.

"You don't have to be awake. But either way, I'll be with you."

She came to me. She placed her hands around my neck and clutched the hair at the back of my head. She raised her chin and looked me in the eyes.

It had been five months since I'd met the monster of my nightmares and there was but a month left to discover the truth of her threat. Now I felt as a man who had cheated on his wife and hidden his infidelity. Like Hawthorne's Aylmer or Rapaccini, I dared lay the most precious of all lives on the altar of science. I had hidden this creature, this threat, from Veronica to protect her. To protect the earth. Once a man who had wished the world to lie at the feet of his genius, a man who was once the threshold to a new age, on the verge of that reality I had become a man who shrank from the dreadful fact of those responsibilities.

A few days later, after Michael was asleep, I brought Veronica to my lab and prepared her for the experiment. I sat beside her, donned the cyber lenses, and we proceeded into her dreams.

The Story of Werther Fausten

Yes, Veronica's psyche was verdant, alive and wild. She moved through this world, as I had done, in a kind of astral presence, and in that way I could not accompany her, though sitting next to her in my lab I took her hand.

"Have you seen this before?" I asked.

"Yes," she said, "I know I have, even though I don't remember it."

I'd coached her very precisely as to what she might expect, yet there is nothing to prepare one for this entry into the depth of themselves, the substratum of all selves, this land beneath all individuality to which only an individual has access. And of course the contradiction astounded me, that the same place could be both alive and dormant for two individuals. The laws here, if laws there were, were not the laws of natural phenomena, anymore than the laws of inter-dimensional quantum strings translated to the everyday world.

"Oh Werther," Veronica whispered as she moved through the fields of wishes. "How beautiful."

"It is not all beautiful," I said. Even then I felt the deadly truth that would be confirmed if she continued to the end of her journey. "You needn't go much farther."

"I want to."

"You will lose time. It could feel like days, months."

"I want to see what you have seen," she said.

"It will be harder and harder to communicate," I said. "Your presence here will fall away from you, and to you will feel like a ghost who haunts another world, a hint, a suggestion. I can only watch. But if you need me, you need only turn away. Just turn to me and you will be back."

She pressed my hand and went in. I had forgotten how glorious and sensual that world could be as I saw once again, this time through my beloved's eyes, the thick jungle of our complexity. You feel as a flower opening among other flowers, a climax of birth and fecundity to which orgasm is but a brief shadow in the corner of your eye. It is impossible to explain the awe. What lies beneath us! The ever-expanding depth and expanse of a simple feeling! Its beauty! It's glory!

My wife closed her eyes and fell into concentrated meditation. At the desert of fear, her pulse sank, then rose again, then sank. Her hand went cold. Yet she persisted. As the mouths of sand opened around her, she walked through those bleeding jaws. As I once did, she wept. I know that for her it felt as if the minutes had been weeks, yet she flew forward into the mountains and met the granite heights of gray despair. In those hills I thought that she was near coma, near death, though I could not recall her. Next to her, I wept, too, as a hot breeze emerged from the opening of a cave. Veronica stopped there, in front of that blackness thicker than tar, darker than nothing. Then there came a roar, a hiss so deep and visceral, an emanation deeper than sound, not for the ears or the mind, but for the blood.

She stood there, peering in. And then the mountain trembled beneath her feet, but not as an earthquake, but in the measured steps of a giant thing. The cave belched fire. "Do not die," I said, clutching her hand. "Do not die here. Not for me." But she was beyond my call. She stepped back. I saw the eyes of the beast. I felt him. He spoke to her bone and blood, the lust of his passion. I feared now that I had fallen stupidly and easily into the monster's trap and that this hideous creature would take Veronica and I would be left with his mate, or worse, Veronica would precipitate his release. "Turn from him," I begged. "Turn! Let him lie buried in you!"

But if the air was black, this beast was darker still. He took Veronica, my beloved, into his diamond, yellow eyes. Their centers opened into more dazzling darkness still. "Come," he moaned. "Come to me. Come."

My wife beside me, her pulse almost gone, turned cold. The last thing I felt, in the depth of my blood and bones, was *my* name.

Werther. Werther, in his hiss deeper than the heart, harsher than light. And then Veronica turned.

I unhooked her from the electrodes and carried her to our bed. I placed my head on her chest in search of the heartbeat by which I counted our love and mortality every night. It was my imagination, certainly, by which I heard my name under that faintest, faintest of rhythms.

The Story of Werther Fausten

Yet her color returned and in an hour she awoke. I brought her tea. She smiled at me and I held her hand and cried.

"I am so grateful for your life," I said.

"But you have been risking yours. Is this what you walked away from?"

"Yes," I said, unable to say more.

"What was it?" she said.

"I don't know," I said. "I haven't been beyond."

"It's not a dream?"

"It is a place," I said, "as far as I can understand."

"And its inhabitants?"

"Real and unreal. Not subjective. Not objective. A substratum for all sentience, not unlike the Tibetan Bardo."

"Psychic neumena," she said. "But the ontology, the beliefs of the perceiver, creates the forms."

"Better that the forms create the perceiver," I said. "As if we, ourselves, are not the dreamers but the dreams."

She surrendered her tea cup to me and I placed it aside, then she took my hands. "What will science do with this?" she said.

"I'm afraid," I answered, more truthfully and broadly than I could ever have told her. "Were you drawn to it?"

"You mean to him?" she said. "Yes, of course. He was the wrath of love. The *anger* of love. I am transformed." She said this, I could see, almost dazzling herself, and she blushed. "I feel no need to go back, Werther. Ever. I've seen more than I can understand, felt more than I can feel. All that I have read and seen pales." She sat back. "Each of us has this?"

"It has each of us," I said, fearing that I spoke the truth.

"What beings we are. What mysteries. We live, we think, we breathe, we wonder, and have no clue. Who plays this trick on us? How could it just happen?"

"In this age of cruel miracles," I whispered.

"Yet what moments in between." She sat forward again and kissed me softly. "Is yours female, Werther?"

"Yes," I said. "Yes."

"I thought so." She brought me to her. "Hurry, before Michael wakes up."

In the next month our passion grew to a kind of madness. We clutched at each other in fear and pleasure in every spare moment, with unquenchable, painful, self-conscious desire, Veronica spurred by the beast within, me haunted by the secret beast without. Inside the miracle of that love, Michael grew, laughed, and became a child. My life filled with radical joy, as if every moment were touched by mystical awareness and longing for some unnamable, highest good. And as the term for my fulfillment of the monster's wish neared its end, I was flooded by altruism. My days became meditations of simple generosity to those around me. I gave time at the local health clinic. I planned to return to psychiatry and medicine and use all that I'd learned to transform the medicinal field. You find that grandiose! A kind of nineteenth century megalomania! But I had touched eternity!

On the eve of that fatal day I waited for the call of the beast and heard her beckon just after midnight. I had denied her. She would not have her mate. And if I had once contained her in the recesses of my psychic depths, then I would contain her once again with my self-conscious discipline. If I had created her, then I would destroy her. If she longed for my scrutiny, then she would wither under my inattention. If she were mine, then I would contain her with patient bliss. If I were hers, then I would be her unruly monster of discipline and will. You see, Dr. Zu, I was the first to deny the dragon. I was the first and the last to deny her existence. All that has followed has fallen to me, however reluctantly I must accept the responsibility.

In the quiet under Veronica's breathing I cleared my soul, my ego, my psyche, and denied the monster. I did not go to her. I did not acknowledge her. She existed neither outside me nor inside. It was a god-like moment and as the beast's call faded into the darkness, I felt myself overcome by tremendous peace. In the morning I was informed that I'd won the Nobel Prize for nuclear biology.

We made an uneventful trip to Stockholm, Sweden where I accepted my award with wry generosity. All such things come for the wrong reasons and too late. Upon our return we discovered that Veronica was pregnant with our second child. If my awareness of our mortality ticked inside me like a bomb, yet then my nights were dreamless, quiet, filled with satisfaction, future, sleep, and my days filled with love of my family. I thought that I'd written the last chapter of my scientific life and that I would become, to the real world of medicine, what my father had become to the world of myth.

How ironic that I thought of him then, and wondered if, far off in the wilds of Bolivia and religion, he'd heard of my recent honor. It was as if I'd brought him to me. Two weeks after our return from Sweden I was contacted by the American embassy to Bolivia. My father's mission compound had been destroyed by a lightning storm. At the time I didn't think otherwise. Everything had burned. My father was dead.

The Dragon Journal of Lisa Piccolo Zu

On the island of Cozumel, off the Yucatan shore, the marine laboratory must have been abandoned for a long time. We had to anchor off shore and take the lifeboats in. The beach was pretty barren except for some empty frond shacks. There wasn't anyone living anywhere near, no cabins or huts, just huge, empty cement bowls like smooth craters. They once held rehabilitating marine specimens like sharks, rays, or sea turtles. Now those cement tanks were crumbling. Captain Evans figured the lab had probably been raided for scrap metal, wood, instruments, beakers, whatever had any value.

We had two couples on board who'd had sons in Cozumel. They were very disappointed and quiet. We'd seen from the boat that things looked pretty empty, but people are always hopeful. The captain said we should try to find out what happened, so we sailed across the strait to the Yucatan and made port at Cabo Peche. The air was warm and the water clear and blue-green. Near the shore, you could see right down to the discarded junk; fish swam through the rubbage; crabs and sea stars clung to the scrap metal.

The Yucatan, including Cancun, had returned to fishing and farming, and Maya revivalism. Very few people even spoke Spanish, though as in most places where we stopped for water and supplies, there was kind of an ambassador who cut the deals and traded news. Mostly we needed water. Fish were plentiful, we could catch our own, though we traded small batteries and some engine lubricant for meat, corn flour, rice, beans, some honey and fresh fruit. It wasn't called a trade, but gifts, and they really gave us a lot more than we gave them.

In their families and schools the Maya taught only the local languages now. Their churches had been burned. Only their temples to the sun, the moon, and wind still stood. On one old pyramid a huge, new mural was painted of a dragon balancing the moon in one palm while opening its jaws to swallow the sun.

"It is a new cycle," the ambassador said to our captain. He spoke in Spanglish, and Jorge, one of the Chileans, was there to help us out when the Spanish got too thick. The ambassador called himself Puuc. He was a short, squat man who wore a simple, white pull-over shirt and white pants, sandals. "A new cycle," he said again. "The Seventh. Your world, the Sixth Cycle, has past." He advised us to avoid the big cities on the coasts. There was still a lot of chaos, greed and piracy in the cities. Where people still clung to the old order, there was always trouble.

"We have to go to Panama City," Captain Evans said. "And we need to cross at the canal."

"The canal?" said Puuc. "Good luck."

"What happened at Cozumel?" said the Captain.

"The dragon," Puuc said.

"The phenomenon?" said the Captain. "Did you see it?"

Puuc shrugged. "If your boat has an engine, I am to request that you take it off shore and ferry in for your supplies."

The Captain rubbed his chin. "Do you know what happened to the people at the marine lab on Cozumel?"

"They went home?" said Puuc.

You could see Captain Evans was getting pretty frustrated. Most of our encounters on the trip had pretty much gone like this anyway, but now there was a lot more at stake. A father of one of the missing scientists grabbed Evan's arm. "It's okay," he said.

Captain Evans rubbed his dark forehead. We'd lost Hunter, half the reason we were going to Panama. Now this.

"You are relatives?" said Puuc. "I'm sorry. The lab has been gone a long time. The island has been returned to 9 Wind. *Ix Chel* is there again. We worship there. No one lives there."

I knew 9 wind, a calendar date for the plumed serpent, Quetzacoatl.

"Is the dragon there?" I asked him. "Quetzacoatl?"

He tilted his head at me. I could see he didn't expect us, me in particular, to really know what he was talking about. "No," he said. He spoke very gently, like he wanted to make sure he meant no antagonism. "Quetzacoatl is *Mexica*. Aztec. To us he is Gucumatz. The water serpent, plumed blue and green." He pointed to the ocean. "The other is Huracan, Heart of Heaven, the dragon who rules the sky with lightning. He has brought down your world."

"It's not a *he*," I said to him. "This dragon is female."

"Some people say that," he said to me. He smiled for the first time. "Mostly women. In any case, we prefer her to the United States." Puuc was looking at the captain again when he said that.

We took the ship off shore and rode the lifeboats back in for our water and food, loaded up and took it back. On board again, El didn't really want to talk about the dragon, but I did.

"Heart of Heaven is a beautiful name, isn't it?" I said to her.

"He was right that things go in cycles," El said to me. She made tea on our little plug-in hot plate. Each cabin had one plug. "Do you want tea?"

"Yes."

"But this age of myth isn't going to last long. The weather anomalies will stop or people will learn to deal with it. There will be new technology. It will all be back. Different maybe, but still back. Maybe better, maybe worse."

"You sound like Hunter," I said.

She handed me my tea with some lemon and honey we'd got from the Maya. "I'm sorry," she said.

"It's okay. He didn't dream, you know," I told her. "He just had his laser boat fantasies and card game. Daydreams. He said he didn't dream at night."

"I barely do either, anymore," said El. "I'm so tired."

"I dream," I said to her. "Sometimes I feel like I'm dreaming all the time, right when I'm standing around, like now."

"You mean that it's all a dream?" she said.

"No," I said. "I mean that while I'm conscious, I can feel myself dreaming underneath it all."

El brought me to her and hugged me. It used to bug me, but it didn't anymore. "You're an unusual kid," she said. "And you've been through a lot. Do you think we should go back?"

"Home?"

"Yes."

"To what?"

"We could hire a boat up the west coast. Go live with Grandpa Charles."

"After we find Grandma," I said.

El put her head in her hands, ran her fingers through her hair, then down her cheeks. "I'm afraid," she said. "The Antarctic. When people couldn't even survive in the Caribbean."

"The Maya survived."

El sipped her tea. "Do you want to sleep on shore tonight?"

"Not really," I said. "I'm used to this."

"Exactly," said El. "I've told myself they were getting ready for Mars. Mars is colder than the South Pole. No animals, no plants, no air. As long as—"

"They get left alone," I said.

My mother smiled a little. "That's right," she said.

These were hard days, though there were harder ones to come. Before landing in Panama, Captain Evans made sure we were all armed. But I didn't find Panama City much different from New York. City people weren't any better or worse than anybody else. It was just a mess. All torn down. Dead machines stacked everywhere. You just didn't go into what used to be the urban area. Life there was, as the captain said, "inconsistent." He was great at finding those kinds of words. People had moved to the shoreline or the countryside. Many had died.

El and I went ashore with Captain Evans, Nigel, Angie, AJ, and Jorge. Captain Evans brought me to talk to Hunter's grandparents because I'd been Hunter's friend. There was an office there, at the port, where boats checked in. They'd been expecting us and sent a runner, a bicyclist really, to Hunter's grandparents. If the captain was selective about the words he used to describe certain events, he was really direct in a lot of other ways. In the message, he said that Hunter wasn't with us.

Hunter's Grandparents were older than Grandma Hestor or Grandpa Charles. You wouldn't imagine them riding motorcycles or going to Mars. They both wore pants and big hats. They'd been staying at a cottage outside the city. Now they lived in Guatemala, on property that was once part of a diplomatic estate, but they'd given it up to a number of families, almost a tribe now they said, and lived in the servants' quarters. They farmed the area communally with their neighbors. There was still a diesel train that ran inconsistently from Oaxaca, Mexico through Guatemala and all the way down to Panama City, but it took a long time. There was often trouble getting fuel. They told us all this after we met them. They rode in on the community-owned horse and carriage, after we'd been waiting for them for about four hours. During that time we found out that the canal didn't exist anymore.

The port director told us that at the Gaillard Cut, the deepest pass, and again at Contractor's Hill, the canal had cracked and collapsed. What was left of the waterway was now overgrown by water hyacinths.

We were in a little office that overlooked the port. It used to be a communications station which radioed information to in-coming and out-going ships, and organized the cranes that lifted cargo to and from the trains and trucks to the freighters that came and went from the canal. Now it was pretty grubby; you could hardly see the ocean through the dirty windows, except for where the panes were broken.

Captain Evans was pretty direct when Hunter's grandparents, Margaret and Drake, arrived. We'd lost Hunter overboard in a quick-storm, he told them. Hunter was heroic. He'd stayed aboard to help, against orders, after everyone else had abandoned ship. We lost him.

Hunter's grandmother, Margaret, sat down on a wooden chair. His grandfather, Drake, rubbed his eyes. "I've seen too much death," he said.

"It was too far to travel alone," Margaret said. "He was only a child."

"I'm sorry," said Captain Evans.

"A quick-storm took out the mission church, very early on," said Drake. His chest heaved. "But in all the carnage, only a boy died. The minister's son." He paused again, looking around at each of us like we might have some information, something else to tell him, anything more. I felt right then like that's all there was to life. After your whole life, all that's left is just this little bit of information about you that other people remember, and then it fades, and then they die, too. "It was as if the boy walked to it," said Drake. "After the church was struck by lightning it was like all the air around us was exploding, but the boy ran outside, into the square, and then he just went up in fire. Then it was over in an instant." He looked at Evans. "There are other stories like that everywhere. We've been hurled into atavism, I know. But you hear that story all of the time. A boy dies and the storm ends."

Nobody said anything even though I thought somebody should. But it couldn't be me. I understood that. So nobody said anything.

El put her hand on my shoulder and said, "My daughter, Lisa, was his friend."

"Yes," I said. "He was a good kid. He taught me his card game. We played all the time."

Margaret put her hand out to me and I took it. She pulled me to her and brought the back of my arm to her cheek, just kind of hugging it there. So I put my other hand on her shoulder and kissed her hair. Then she just held my hand and stared at me. In her eyes I saw something strange and miraculous, like tiny galaxies were exploding in them, but the explosions opened in, in, like you could fall into them so deeply that it hurt. I tried to remember if I'd seen anything like them before, like maybe Grandma Zu, or El, but every time I thought I remembered, it only felt like I did, I didn't really remember anything. They were a memory that I didn't have; somebody else's memory, mine and not mine, like I'd discovered something I already had, new and not new, old but new. It's so hard to explain!

I suppose the captain didn't really see the storm take Hunter. I suppose nobody besides me really did. But Drake and Margaret saw something and believed something. That I could feel.

"Do you dream?" I said to Margaret.

She looked at me and then her husband. She pushed back her hat and said nothing.

"Did you see what happened to the boy?" I said.

"Lisa," said El.

"No," Margaret said to El. "It's okay." She turned to me. "Horribly," she said, "and constantly. I dream."

"Then you saw her," I said. "I saw her, too."

Margaret glanced at Drake again, then stood. "What would you have me believe, child?" she said to me. "My eyes?"

"Yes," I said.

"Did anyone else see an animal?" said Drake. "You were there," he said to Captain Evans and the crew. "Did an animal kill my grandson?"

Captain Evans put his hand on my shoulder, but he spoke to them. "There was an updraft. A quick-storm."

Drake turned to me. "An animal cannot destroy the world," he said. "We have done that ourselves. We can't let our fear destroy what's left."

"Lisa knew Hunter and loved him," El said.

"If we can be of any service to you," Captain Evans said. "I have Hunter's belongings."

Drake shook the Captain's hand, then Margaret did. She took my hand again before they left.

"Why not?" I said to her, though she didn't answer. "Why not?"

The Dragon Journal of Lisa Piccolo Zu

On board we had a meeting to decide what to do next. The two couples with sons on Cozumel, and the families who had relatives on the Galapagos opted to cross Panama by land and see if they could hire a ship on the Pacific side, rather than venture all the way to the Antarctic and then back up.

Captain Evans balked at that a little bit. "We were committed to each other as a group," he said.

One of the men, the father of one of the Cozumel boys, said that Evans could keep the money they'd paid him for the trip; those families had all agreed.

"It's not about money," said El. "Has it ever been about money?"

But discussion wasn't going to change any of that. Like Grandpa Charles always said, "Short sighted, self-centered." That's what El said to me after those families left the rest of us there in the meeting room: the Captain, Nigel, AJ and Angie, the four Chileans, Jorge, Luis, Eduardo, and Cruz, and then there was me and El.

"Ten," said Evans. He looked right at me, then at El. "Nine?"

"Ten," I said.

"It's been done with crews of ten. We'll head down the Atlantic coast to Buenos Aires, cross the cape at Tierra del Fuego to New Zealand. This boat can do that."

And we all agreed.

"You're going to learn a lot about sailing," he said to me.

"And survival," I said.

"And survival," said Captain Evans.

Later in our cabin El had some wine.

"Can I have some?" I said. She knew what I was saying. I was in this as deep as any adult.

"Yes," she said, but she mixed it with water.

"May I speak freely, madame?" I said.

El laughed. "Yes." She had on a T-shirt and jeans. She had her boots off, her hair down, her back against the bottom bunk and her socked feet up on our wooden chair. "Sometimes it's hard for me to imagine that one day you won't be my baby," she said.

I sat down next to her. "I'm not your baby. I'm your companion."

"No," she said. "You're my baby."

"And you're Grandma Zu's baby?"

"You got it," she said.

"May I make some observations?"

"I said you could."

"The Phenomenon, can we agree on that word?" I said.

"Okay," El laughed.

"It has patterns."

"So you've contended."

"It's destroyed weapons of mass destruction, nuclear and fossil fuel facilities, the mechanized fishing fleets."

"Among other things," said El.

"Churches," I said. "Temples and mosques. Not Buddhist stuff."

"Now that's hard to know, isn't it?" said El.

"Just bear with me," I said to her.

"If I must."

"You agreed. And there's these stories about boys, like the boy in Guatemala."

"Stories."

"And Hunter. Hunter was no story," I said to her. "And there's this dream thing."

El put her wine down. She touched my cheek. "You're young," she said. "Amazing, and young. When you're young it's hard to be anything but young."

"And when you're old?"

"You've once been young," said El.

"Maybe you forget," I said.

"What patterns in the world made us conjure up God or the devil?" said El.

"Or science," I said.

"They're hardly the same. I'm no scientist, but I know that much."

"Hardly the same to whom?" I said. "Listen, El, if you were a powerful creature, so powerful that you could destroy everything, what would you destroy?"

"I wouldn't destroy," El said. "I'd create."

"You can't create. You're a creature. Besides, what you'd create would destroy other stuff, wouldn't it?"

"Then I would prefer not to, like Bartelby," said El.

"Bartelby the Scrivener."

"Yes." El took my hand. "You thought this was going to be easier," she said to me, "but you forgot that you came from me."

"You think like me," I said.

"*You* think like *me*."

"Okay," I said, "but I'm not saying that you are a creature, I'm saying the creature *is* you. To live, you must destroy some things or die. What would *you* destroy?"

"Not poets," said El.

"That's one I haven't figured out."

"Among other things," El said.

"El, she's trying to make a world she can live in."

"I'm shocked this is where we ended up."

"But El, what if it's true? What if it's like there being eleven dimensions or that the only theory that explains everything also proves we don't exist? If there is a creature, a dragon, the whole world is changed. And it has changed, El."

El got up and got us a little more wine and water. She sat down in front of me. "That's a logical fallacy called Asserting the Consequent," she whispered.

"It doesn't matter if it's true," I said. "El, I can stop her. I can make peace with the dragon."

That's when El hugged me for a little bit. It was the end of the argument. I didn't know if she was going to cry or lecture to me. I got the lecture.

"Lisa, everyone tries to make sense of the world," she said. "When you're young you do it fantastically, beautifully, cruelly. That's where horror and fantasy come from. From the crying in our blood because we're becoming adults. And now, when the world is frightening, as frightening as it's ever been, the whole world's blood is crying. But we must hold the line. Maintain a reality, a rationality that will be there to recover when the horror ends, so we can rebuild. And right now we have a job to do. To get Grandma Zu and take her back to Grandpa Charles and rebuild our own lives."

"But it's not more frightening now," I said. "It's better now. We can't destroy everything anymore."

"For the time being," said my mother.

I was going to put it all together here. Write down my theory. Where the dragon came from. What she wanted. Why she did what she did. But I wrote down my conversation with El instead. I felt like a baby, a child. I felt like that look I saw in Hunter's Grand-mother's eyes; dazzled, sad, and unbelieving, even in my own thoughts and memories. That if I gave over to what I knew was true, I would fall into a world of fantasy and madness. I would not be human anymore. Because I can feel it. I can feel it here. Now. I am dreaming, you see. I am dreaming as I walk and talk, and now as I write. Inside me, I am horrible, and beautiful, and I want to spread my wings and burn everything.

The Story of Werther Fausten

This time I did not wait for the creature's call, but purchased a rifle which I hid in the basement. At dusk, I told Veronica that I felt like taking a walk.

"It's almost dark," she said. "Take a flashlight."

I got the gun and went to the woods to find the beast. It did not take long. In the first clearing, the air above me filled with a torrential cloud, blocking out the early stars. The wind whipped against me, so cold that it burned my cheeks and ears. Then, as if sliding down a tunnel of flame, the animal descended with great speed and alighted before me full afurl, her body the size of a draft horse, her wings like sheets of night. She held my eyes in her gaze even before I could raise the muzzle of my gun. I was frozen and the rifle fell from my hands. Her mouth opened and the last of her blue, flaming breath seethed behind her jaws and sizzled between her fangs like fireworks. "Werther," she hissed at me in her laconic telepathy. "Long time, no *ss*ee."

"How dare you jest," I said directly. "You murdered him."

"I murder no one."

"You murdered my father to bring me to you."

"Really?" She brought her wings to her body then and shuffled them on her back, sitting back and crouching on her hind legs.

"You exist," I stammered. "You are real."

"News," said the creature.

"And I shall not sacrifice my wife to you and your kind."

"I did not a*ss*k for her," she said.

"You murdered my father."

"But now that you are here," she continued, neither admitting nor denying me, "I have a question for you. How is *ss*cience like religion? Better, how are *ss*cience and monotheism the same?"

"I will not play your games," I said. "Even if I cannot kill you. Even if you kill me."

"You undere*ss*timate my motives," she said. "By the way, I, my*ss*elf, am a polythei*ss*t."

I stood silently as she folded back upon herself yet more, though kept her neck extended to hold my gaze and keep me frozen.

"But Werther," she said. "I need you."

"Then you shall not have me."

"I have been traveling, Werther," she said. "Did you know that in Buenos Aires there are mothers *ss*till alive who march at the *Plaza del Mayo*? I walked with them. There is an amusement park where once there was Auschwitz. AIDS has ravaged Africa. In China they yet murder baby girls to hold down the population. In India men can *ss*till murder their wives. In America, you look down upon all thi*ss*, and fund it."

"The litany of human misfortune and cruelty is well documented," I said to her.

"That is not my point."

"We are complex beings, capable of great goodness, too."

"Ye*ss*, Werther, I am only looking for a way to bring that out," hissed the creature. She relaxed more now and brought her head back to her shoulders, looking almost diminutive. "The orangutans are rubbed out, you know. So are the gorillas. Your cousins. And a million other *ss*pecies as valuable to the cosmos as your own. In their way, as intelligent as you, with feelings as deep as yours."

"I am not interested in discussing philosophy or ecology with you," I replied.

"*Ss*o I a*ss*k you, Werther, how is *ss*cience like monotheism?"

"I will find a way to destroy you!" I asserted. "And if not me, then someone else when you are inevitably discovered."

"You undere*ss*timate my power."

She stood fully retracted now, folded in upon herself as when I first met her, imitating a crone. Again I tried to take control of myself, my own consciousness and will, but far from being able to destroy her with my thoughts, I could not even move my arms, and even as I tried to deny her by thinking nothing, she drew my thoughts from me as one reels in an exhausted fish.

"Have you ever driven on a freeway in Loss Angeless, Werther?" said the monster. "In a way, it'ss a metaphor for your sspecies. You are better behaved in a traffic jam, you know. When you are boxed in." She tilted her head. "I would releasse you now, but you would run from me," she said. "Anyway, I've assked mysself, does one remove the sspecies or the freeway? Because I can do it, Werther. I can do either one."

"You are one creature," I said. "A single beast, alone."

"You underesstimate my cunning. I am magic itsself. Maybe I am a goddess."

"You are evil."

"No. I am a creature, as natural as all other life. But while I am here I might even the playing field. As you are to all other ssentience, *I* am to you. As Adam was to the animals, I am to you. Your destroyer. Your benefactor. I am humanity's humanity. Man to men. I am Eve undominated. The wrath of life. The vengeance of ssentience. Until now, humans have decided what lived and what died. Now I can join the game. I am your match."

"You murdered Dianna's children. You killed my father."

"All living things die, Werther. A housse was sstruck by lightning. A church burned. I assk you, Werther. Should I take ssacrifices? Male virgins?" Her neck stretched forward again and her wings shuffled on her shoulders, their pinnacles rising above her like spires. "Werther, have pity on me and you will have pity on all of humankind. You can yet ssave your world."

"I have done everything I can for mankind."

"For humankind? You have not."

"What would you have me do?"

"Love me."

"You are avarice. You are hate. You destroy."

"I am ssympathetic. My heart bleeds for ssentience. I create."

"You are brutal."

"I am intelligent."

"I will not help you."

"You shall an*ss*wer three riddles for me. The fir*ss*t, How can you love me?"

"I cannot."

"You mu*ss*t. The *ss*econd, Who is my mate?"

"Another beast. I have seen him."

"No. The third, Why are *ss*cience and religion the *ss*ame?"

"This is madness," I said. "And I am mad."

"You will wish you were. Werther, I am your creation. Have pity on me. Love me and *ss*ave everything. Or you shall wish that you never lived."

She turned away. For a moment, I could have sworn I saw her weeping. But I did not take that moment, for when she lowered her head she broke her gaze and freed me, and I ran. I ran from her again as her roar rose behind me like thunder and her fire burned at my neck.

I startled Veronica when I returned to the house. She sat on the floor with Michael, playing, and looked up. "Werther, there was an updraft over the woods. I was worried about you."

"Yes," I said, gasping, trying to remain calm. I laughed, falsely. I hoped she couldn't detect it. "I seem to attract them." Here, in front of me, was my life. Everything I loved. Everything I lived for now and vowed to protect.

"You're pale. You should lie down, then we'll have something to eat," Veronica said. "I hope you're not getting sick."

And I did lie down. I took her hand when she came to me.

"Werther, remember I'm pregnant, not you," she said.

"My God," I said.

"God?" laughed Veronica. "Did you have a vision in the woods? If I keep having children you'll end up a mystic."

How could I tell her, Zu? How could I protect her? How could I share my life? My burden? The utter, external reality of my madness? Now, that it threatened everything.

The Story of Werther Fausten

Two weeks later, Dr. Zu, began the events of which you are now somewhat familiar. At night, the first of the mysterious storms struck the nuclear facilities in Pakistan. Before most of the world even received the news, and as the major powers went on alert, the storms swept across India the next day. Even greater than the oddity of where these storms struck was the fact that the materials required for nuclear fission at the facilities was not so much destroyed as voided. I struggle to find a better word, for in the rubble of the weapons plants and reactors, the nuclear waste lay dead, as if consumed, digested, and then expelled.

As the world paused between the mutual annihilation of these ancients enemy's nuclear arsenals, the two nations did the absurd thing and went to war on the Kashmir border. The quick-storms swept across the mountains, paralyzing both armies, and in a week the war between Pakistan and India was over but for the words.

As the military juggernauts of the industrial world went on alert, I was one of the group of over a dozen Nobel American scientists called to Washington, D.C. for a think tank on the mystery. Despite American communication with Russia and China, there was growing feeling in the world, particularly from Pakistan and India themselves, that the conflagration was an American playing field for a new, devastating weapon, the logic being that we had experimented first with troublesome, lesser powers, destroying them both to hide our political tracks. The counter-argument, that it would be absurd to demonstrate that kind of power and risk the imbalance that now threatened the world, was offered as its own counter-argument. America would hold the world hostage. We in the think tank were assured that the United States military possessed no such weapons. The parallel nature of the attacks seemed illogical for terrorism. We suspected the Russians, or worse, aliens.

I will not bore you with these endless meetings. The destruction, based on what little evidence that had been gathered, appeared natural and yet supernatural, its execution performed with unfigureable intention. Eco-terrorism seemed unlikely. What group would possess such resources and technology? Though an ecologist in our group suggested that the storms were natural phenomena somehow drawn to fission reactors, a kind of thermal over-heating in the atmosphere similar to Pyrocumulus thunderstorms which are created by large forest fires, as mysterious as spherical lightning, yet drawn to fission as normal lightning is to metal.

As you know, Zu, aside from limiting the quick-storms to attacks on fission reactors, the theory that this destruction is natural is the one still most predominant today, except that the speculation was adjusted to include the likelihood that the storms were somehow drawn to the burning of fossil fuels. This led some scientists to conjecture that the storms might have begun that way, but then spread across the world in a kind of chaotic fury of which we have now lived through the worst. Any other so-called patterns in the storms are attributed to anthropomorphism or the simple, human need to find patterns and reasons in nature.

One cyber-theorist, though, suggested the possibility of an *interferent*, that is, some kind of emergent characteristic in the interface of cyberspace and the effect of weather on the human psyche. Though the idea was vague and unformed, at the time I was tempted to agree with him.

Of course, Zu, there was always the supernatural: God, Shiva, Satan. A week after the disastrous battle of the Kashmir, some of the first Pakistani survivors swore they saw a creature emerge from the clouds, a creature the size of a mountain who took planes and missiles out of the sky and flew down across the battle lines, sweeping them with acrid flame. But there were no pictures.

So in honesty, I did not put it together. I refused. I am a rational man. Whatever the extent of my madness, whether it was in my mind or aflame in the world, I saw it as personal. The insanity of the world was not my insanity, and my insanity not the world's. I traveled to Washington, D.C. I was lucky that it was the middle of the summer and that Veronica would be on sabbatical the following semester or I would never have been able to keep my family with me. Veronica would have refused to leave her work and come along. As a natural precaution to the situation, I was permitted to keep my family under guarded surveillance while I was away at meetings. Yet as real as the monster was to me when she confronted me, in each case, the salve of time made me doubt her reality. I considered myself as insane as you likely consider me now.

A week later, the atmospheric events occurred in the Middle East. On the first night, Israel's secret facilities were consumed by the updrafts, the next day, the storms struck the nuclear plants and bio-chemical facilities of Iraq and Iran. In the coming weeks the storms struck a number of other nations; some were quite a surprise: Turkey, South Africa, North Korea, Libya, Taiwan. The industrial world began to fall like dominoes, from small to large, a disaster which disarmed the world by degrees.

By this time, Dr. Zu, I assume you were already here in Antarctica, so the information you have is probably pretty sketchy. As populaces began to panic, the major technological powers scrambled to find ways to hide and protect their nuclear stores and yet remain on military alert. To fight. To fight what? Not that the phenomenon, that's what people began to call it, the phenomenon, did not have its advocates among the radical ecologists. But I began to fear that it was I who was truly to blame for it all when the phenomenon changed its tactics for the big powers. Japan was rendered helpless by a kind of fusion explosion west of Tokyo which rubbed out all its electrical power, much like the model of how a one megaton explosion above Kansas could shut down all the power in the states. The next day a series of the same kind of storms darkened China. China's nuclear capabilities were gone a week later. And so fell France, England, Russia, under an inexorable shadow which crossed the world and threw us back two hundred years.

I do not have the details. No one does. I sat in the last meetings with my fellow scientists in those last days as the world economies collapsed, governments fell, and rioting shook the cities of the world as winter approached and food and heating supplies disappeared without replenishment. What was I to say? That I had released a supernatural beast from my unconscious? Briefly, I began to try to tell my colleagues, "There is another dimension accessible to all human beings, deeper than the unconscious; the subjectivity of the conscious and unconscious mind floats like a cork on that supernatural ocean, and in that sea of mystery there are living things as fundamental as Platonic forms. One has escaped. It is alien, intelligent, angry and insane. It is governed by none of our laws, neither moral nor natural."

I appealed to my colleague the cyber-theorist. "I wish it were an *interferent*," I said. "Something we could place on a grid, identify, understand, emulsify, reproduce. Some *It*. But it is pure subjectivity, beyond subjectivity, the conscience of prehension, as righteous and irrational as any unconscious drive, and so, in that way, it is like us, it *is* us, and it is the alien in us escaped, as if the earth has raised a scythe against itself."

"You're not making sense," he said. "That's poetry, not theory, not even philosophy or speculation."

"Poetry?" I muttered. "Not good poetry."

The room fell deathly silent and in the quiet I asked them all, "Is there anyone here who still dreams?"

"What are you saying?"

"Only that we have fallen victim to our collective nightmare," I said.

"A mass hallucination?"

"That there is a fine line between reality and mass hallucination," I replied.

"Are you saying that we create the weather?" a colleague demanded.

"No, more that in its image and likeness, the weather has created us."

I didn't stay for a reply. I left the meeting. I went to Veronica and Michael and caught the train to New York, and then to Albany so I could be at home with my family to wait for the storms; like the rest of the populace, to gather what food and supplies we could. To harvest our crops and can our vegetables. I took my family home to wait for the inevitable disaster. We waited for the storms, Dr. Zu, and they came.

It is impossible to recount the passage of those days. You have heard the same stories I have. After the nuclear facilities and weapons— even the submarines; they had to surface sometime and she took them one by one—then went the aircraft carriers, the ships of war, the bombers, any fighting plane that could still take to the air and still dared. All satellite communication was rubbed out. And then the airwaves: radio waves, microwaves. No phones. No radios. No TV. I don't know how. It took some time, but the monster had all the time in the world. Next she took the oil refineries, then the mechanized fishing fleets, and then animal testing labs. I know the order, Zu, because later she told me. She shall take us back to bows and arrows and to swords, and then to sticks and stones.

It was when she began to destroy the churches that I finally admitted to myself that I knew, surely, that the beast I had somehow released was responsible. Science and religion. You've heard the stories of the dragon appearing over Mecca and the Vatican. Over Notre Dame. Dr. Zu, as impossible as it seems, they are true. However the dragons of our myths had once dominated the skies and exacted tribute from our primitive cities, now a dragon rules the world village, what is left of it. There are rumors, I'm sure you've heard them, of cities paying tribute—a male virgin for natural gas or hydro-electric power. An old woman appears at the steps of city hall and lays down the terms. If there are cities on any continent that still have light and heat, it is because they have sacrificed their children.

I know with certainty that Albany suffered horribly that winter. Veronica and I had enough stores to make due and there was little reason then, in the depth of the frozen season, for refugees to seek the countryside. By spring, Veronica had organized the neighbors and those of us with farms united in community farming. Of those in the city still alive, some wandered out as far as the farms and were taken in by our group, or others, when they came. With these came the stories of violence, starvation, disease. In the beginning, there were those who didn't want to work and we had to expel them. Those who were ill or undernourished, we nursed back to health. In that first year there were bandits, as well, and we had to guard the barns and patrol the fields. I shot and killed men several times.

Veronica had our second child that spring, Thomas, another boy. She'd wanted a girl and was a little disappointed. For obvious reasons, I was, too. Though for my part, I had begun to see the dragon's vengeance as something loosed upon the world, her grievance gigantic, her battle with all mankind, not just me, in fact, not with me at all. Certainly she could have killed me at any time. I worked now without ignominy, in a kind of quiet, liberating despair that each man comes to in greater or lesser magnitude as the world hardens around him and dreams and possibilities shrink, then disappear. My fate as a scientist was no worse than others who had tried and failed, my fate as a human the same as for the rest of our kind, the ones who, at least for the time being, still lived. As I set about my daily chores, I no longer feared the beast, nor expected her. Her monstrous quest played itself out on a much greater stage than the petty exigencies of my struggles day to day. I wished she did not exist, but my wishes meant nothing. Minds and wills greater than mine would have to defeat her. I was satisfied enough to be left alone.

I hesitate to say that these days at the cusp of our horrible new world were for me almost holy. As you know, things did not fall apart completely. We are at our worst as a species, it seems, when things are at their best and at our best when things are at their worst. We hoarded gasoline for our tractors and went to work at building plows for if and when the gas ran out. We bred our horses for draft and travel, bred sheep, pigs, and cows for clothes and food, set limits on the amount of game we'd take in season. It was remarkable how different it felt to raise the animal you knew you were going to eat, or to hunt it down, as if the intimacy were as nourishing as the flesh. I had never eaten with such gratitude.

In a year we'd set up a smithies, stables, leatherworks including tallow production, a spinning hall, we even had a drill for natural gas and emergency generating facilities. In time we established mail communication by horseback. I worked as a doctor, a mechanic, a manager, and organized our plans for replenishing the forest as we began to harvest wood.

Veronica bred and trained horses. She opened a school. We raised our children, and in short time the secret of my betrayal faded into our day to day tasks of survival.

Sometimes in the depth of night Veronica would turn to me and touch my face. "How odd and cruel life is," she said. "How unpredictable, uncertain. How lucky I am."

If everything that is put together falls apart, then what falls apart must eventually come together. I thought of my father and wondered if we all had been cast from, or into, a dangerous Eden.

There are a thousand stories from these days, and yet among the survivors there are likely a million stories like mine, and many of them will be better told. But for this. Veronica, the only person I knew who yet dreamed, began to be haunted by nightmares: trees turning into beasts, fish rising monstrously from quiet ponds, our children disappearing down narrow sewers. They were so horrible and persistent that she became afraid to sleep. Exasperated, I finally sedated her one night after the children were asleep. I walked from our room to our children's and touched their heads. Their gentle hair lay like silken halos in the moonlight. In that moment, I felt such uncertainty, such longing for their safety, that I almost prayed. I returned to Veronica who murmured softly and kissed my hand, holding it to her cheek. Outside, suddenly, the wind rattled in the trees, and under the push and howl I heard my name.

"Werther," it hissed. "Werther." And I wept.

The Story of Werther Fausten

She descended from the sky on her column of fire, in the woods, in the place where we last met. I could not keep myself from her. Her wings arched behind her and pushed her hot air around me in rhythmic beats like the pounding of a heart. She alighted, the beast triumphant. Her head swayed on that tenuous neck as she stood upright and towered above me.

"Do whatever you want. I'm not afraid of you," I said.

She said nothing, but began to fold upon herself as she'd done the other times, diminishing until she stood in front of me beneath the spires of her wings.

I repeated, "I am not afraid of you."

"Nor I, you," she said, hissing inside my brain, my heart, as if her thoughts were my blood.

"You have destroyed the world," I said to the beast. "What more could you want?"

"The an*s*wer to three riddles?"

"Don't be absurd."

"And how am I absurd?"

"Millions have died," I said to the beast.

"Maybe a billion or more," she said. "It would have happened anyway, Werther. Rather than leave it to chance, I have tried to do it with a little guidance."

"Choosing how people will die," I said.

"Choosing how people, among others, are *s*saved. In fact, I have chosen very few people. I have no hate for humankind. I have but changed the circum*ss*tances of *ss*urvival for everyone. You are a *ss*pecies of inadvertent malice, Werther. I've tried to remove the worsst of your insstitutions. The ones that have missguided you and made you thoughtless."

"You have no right to play God."

"And how do you know I am not God?"

"You are not God!"

"I'd ssay I'm about as closse as you can get."

"And you are not the one to choose!"

"I did not choose, Werther," said the monster. "You did. As you know, I am yours. I am your monstrouss depthss unleashed."

She had folded in upon herself completely now, assuming the shape of an old woman. Her accusing stare, eyes like suns with diamond slits as deep and dark as all blackness, boiled inside me.

"No," I whispered.

"Yess." She lifted her head from her shoulders. "Let'ss take a moment to think thiss through. Am I an innocent beasst or no? Who is ressponssible for me? Am I God's creature? Yours? Whose creature are you? Is God innocent? Is sscience? Are you? I do not believe in God's innocence. Nor do I believe in the innocence of sscience. And I believe that the war between them is a ruse which has fattened them both. One could not exist without the other. And together they have jusstified your domination of the planet, your desstruction of the ecology, your dissdain of the other sspecies. Do you ssee? Jane Goodall and Sister Theresa were of the ssame ilk. Einsstein is Moses. The gentle faces of your inadvertent malice. Jesus is not the Sson of God. Sscience is the Sson of God. I am trying to lead you, Werther, to answer the riddle. It is your riddle, Werther. It is your ansswer."

"Rid the world of religion and science both," I protested, "it will not change who we are."

"It might," she hissed. "It'ss worth a try. I ssee improvementss around here already. The worsst I might do is fail. Is that not your logic? The logic of sscience? Bessides, I shall be here to keep you on the right path. Or if I leave, I shall at leasst have given you another chance to sstart anew. You could fail and again reach the brink of world desstruction. Then again, I might come back. It is a world of infinite possibility." She lifted her chin and rolled her angular head upon her shoulders, breathing in and then letting out the slightest wisp of gas-like flame. "Have you taken the time to notice that I have only de*ss*troyed the churches of the monothei*sstss*?"

If you find it difficult that I can so clearly remember this cryptic rambling, then recall that it was not spoken to me as much as imprinted in my cells, maybe as deeply personal and as beyond understanding as my own dreams, but real, deathly real. I pressed forward with her on the chance that breaking the code of her mad dialectic might allow me to turn her upon herself, break her insane determination and give us hope.

"We are only animals, like yourself," I said to her. "We are not perfect. We cannot be perfect."

"You could be better intentioned."

"We are well-intentioned."

"That is why I am trying to get your attention. It has not been easy."

"There will always be suffering in the world. Sickness, old age, death."

"*S*starvation? Poverty? War again*s*st each other? Again*s*st all other *s*sentience? Cruelty? You've built your homes, your indu*ss*try, your leisure on the graves of other beings. You *s*seem to think it is better if humanity does it than if I do it."

"It is better if no one does it!"

"Ye*ss*," she said. "Preci*ss*ely."

"Then have some sympathy for this world, your world!" I pleaded.

"*My* world?" she said. She raised a taloned hand. "Werther, that is exactly what I have done. But you mi*ss*under*ss*tand me. I have no vendetta again*s*st humanity. What did you call it once, your mi*ss*tre*ss*? No, Werther, I am yours and I have done it all for you. Take it personally. You once dreamed of changing the world, of *s*saving it."

"I no longer do."

"You do right now. And you should. It is your re*ss*pon*ss*ibilty. I am your re*ss*pon*ss*ibility."

"You are not."

"Am I an earthquake, Werther? A cyclone? A phenomenon? Or am I your creature? Your creation? The daughter of your depth*ss*?"

"You are all mankind's"

"All humankind's, Werther. For all of *s*sentience."

I wept in front of her. "Have mercy."

"Werther, *you* have mercy. Werther, why are monotheism and *s*science allies? How are they the same?"

"My God, beast, they are not the same!"

"I shall give you the an*ss*wer, Werther, but you will have to follow me around the globe to get it."

"I will not!"

"You shall. And when you are done, we will meet at a place of my choosing. There you will an*ss*wer truly or we shall fight to the death."

"I never will."

"Oh ye*ss*, Werther," she said. "You mu*ss*t."

With that her head came forward upon her neck and she expanded her wings. Standing, she rose upon her hind legs and inflated in front of me like a huge bellows, tripling in size. As she inhaled, flame rolled in her jaws, her eyes flashed, held me, then filled me with miserable fate. "No!" I screamed. "No!"

She took flight and I turned to follow her as she soared across the planted fields to my home, but a horrible updraft filled the night and blackened out the stars, as if the sky itself had filled with steaming, sulfuric breath. The air was sucked from around me and then rushed out again in hot, morbid gusts. I was pushed to the ground and could barely raise my head to see the dragon emerge from the boiling, heart-shaped cloud and hesitate above my house. She turned her head and held my eyes in her infernal gaze before the air was sucked again and then the light exploded from her jaws. It rolled over my home like a sea of fire. And the scream I heard, the scream of my wife and children, and the dragon, ignited inside me with its misery, its despair, its fire, its death.

Nothing was left. The beast flew off into the night. My life, my love, Veronica, my children, Michael and Thomas, lay indistinguishably and forever dead, indiscernible from the ashes of my home, my life, the earth.

The Story of Werther Fausten

So began my pursuit of the awful beast. I saddled one horse and packed another, then rode to the university library. In the city of Albany, already the streets had begun to buckle and crack from the push of trees and foliage through the asphalt. Automobiles lay rusted and stripped in the avenues, though I saw an occasional moving car or motorcycle, which I assumed were government owned. People moved about on bicycles or on horseback and clearly most of them knew each other quite well because I was regarded with distance and caution.

Though the downtown was in ruins, neighborhoods looked quite sound but for the blackened lots where once stood churches and cathedrals. With land at a premium, these lots had been used for burning the dead. In the first winter thousands froze when temperatures sank below zero; then it seemed that people had pulled together. There was yet running water, and wind mills were under construction everywhere. There were community gardens, as well. The first attempts to rebuild churches had been scorched. Soon after, the first clear-cutting from nearby forests immediately brought the horrid updrafts again. Then communities began to enforce controlled cutting and planting.

At the college, a swathe had been cut through the row of science halls, but the rest stood. The library went unscathed, and though all computers were long down, there was light enough from the windows to see the new index card files, which a young man showed me. From there I went to the shelves to find out all I could on dragons. All the books were gone.

I found the man who had shown me the files.

"I could find none of the books you have listed for dragons," I said to him.

"We should have removed those cards," he said. "The Believers took them. We haven't been able to replace any books yet."

"Believers. A dragon cult, I suppose," I mumbled.

He eyed me skeptically. "It's hard to know what to think these days," he said. He watched me for a moment and then said, "A book on dragons was left here for someone."

"I am Werther Fausten," I replied, for it was inevitable that the book was for me and that she had left it. "An old women," I said.

And the young man said, "Yes."

It was a book by a British woman named Elizabeth Ilford, written near the end of the Twentieth Century. It argued for a paleontology of dragons, classified them by origin, species, and region. She theorized on the dynamics of their flight, their mating habits, their ability to communicate. She discussed the well known stories from the past and purportedly debunked current mythologies. Not much of a book, really; a collection of dreams. But there was a chapter on dragon slaying marked by an index card. There I found a picture of the trident, the weapon used to kill a dragon. On the card there was printed a short note in what almost seemed to be dried blood. It said, *Both try to reduce all phenomena to one, simple answer. Thus, both seek a complete explanation of all events or phenomena through identification with their ultimate cause.* And then, *I am sorry about your wife and children.*

It did not take much to make me break down back then. I wept for Veronica, and for Michael and Thomas. I wept for myself, and for the world which I had brought to its knees at the feet of this horror. And I wept at the irony that the man who had been stripped of his dream to save the world was left with the fate of saving the world again, though this time it was not his dream, but a nightmare in the mind of a nightmare.

Back on the farm I convinced our iron smith to help me fashion the trident. He deferred to me simply out of respect for my misery. We created the weapon from several pitch forks and iron rods which had been left outside the forge with a note that read: *Both made men the stewards of the earth. Both separate humankind from nature.*

Forged in primitive fire, as you might expect, from the same element that sprung from the lungs of the beast, emerged the tripartite scythe of death, shaped as a heart, a weapon as wide as my chest, made to pierce hers. The sparks from the forge lit the sky like stars. Did I see an elongated beast there in the night, a reptilian form writhing in the ignited air above the forge? What of those tongues of fire? Iron of the earth. Only something deeper than humanity itself, extracted by man, molded by man, cooled in the water tanks of man, hardened in the heart of man; nature turned to metal. Here is what separated humankind from all the rest. In the morning I held it in my hand, the trident, the instrument of her death.

It was a strange and miserable hunt, Dr. Zu, as I followed the sun south, led and nurtured, guarded and tormented by the beast I hunted. My pursuit has taken almost three years, as I plodded by horseback down old highways, skirting the decayed metropolises of what, only a half-decade earlier, was the richest, most advanced country in history. I avoided people if possible, because inevitably the campfire or stove brought stories of the past, and then the destruction, the deaths of parents, and of children, and the stories of those who knew someone who knew someone who saw her, the beast that emerged from the hideous cloud to blacken the sky under her fire, the cities somewhere in the Midwest who have light and heat because they sacrificed a male child. And then the primitive theories, whispered quickly without meeting your eye, whispered out of fear lest the omniscient beast overhear them and return with her lightning; the tellers avoided naming her like the ancients who could not speak the name of *Yahweh*. When there is no electricity, you worship fire and the sun. When no water, the rivers and the rain. When winter is long, you worship the spring. Where there is no knowledge, you find worship. This is the world now, Zu. It is the world you will return to, if you ever return.

Yes, people were generous enough, though I avoided them. I was guided by a bestial, omniscient hand, driven by dragon lust. A note left at my farm told me to travel to Poolesville, Maryland where, behind the ruins of an estate, in a decaying Chinese garden, a stone dragon lay beneath a fountain, a list of edible roots and tubers between its teeth. *To Manassas*, it said at the bottom, enough *s's* within to implicate a hiss. I rode a day and as evening fell the air grew still. Then the clouds churned above me and I heard my name in the wind. *Werther. Werther.* I clutched the trident. "Are you ready for the dragon?" I said to my horse. "Could you ever be as ready as I?" Ahead of me, at the edge of the woods, a column of fire descended and I prodded my animal forward, toward the burning, sulfur stench, ready to meet her to the death.

The column dissipated as I edged toward the wood. Again the stillness fell and I stopped. And then I saw the light, the flicker of fire. But I did not find her there, only a prepared camp; fresh water in a dried squash shell, a squirrel roasting over a fire, the gentle babble of a nearby stream. A note beneath the dried calabash scratched in blood said, *Worship what you are about to eat.* Cooked game. It happened again and again.

Yes, Zu, I ate them. I ate them as if they were her very flesh. And there was always a note, sometimes telling me what vegetation was edible in the vicinity and how to recognize it, what game would be available and how to hunt it, where the streams and lakes would be and how to bait my hook. I was told where I should go next, and given another clue. In Poolesville: *Both are Cartesian and so regard the other animals as biological robots. Both deny the consciousness and feelings of the non-human.* In Manassas: *Both find the structure of their reasoning in Aristotle. Both place a premium on abstraction yet fear both philosophy and fantasy.* Outside Birmingham: *Both are naive realism and naive rationalism.* In Corpus Christi: *Both require faith and miracle.*

I followed her dreadful path to Renosa, Mexico; to Teotihuacan; to Oaxaca, San Salvador, Managua, Panama City, and Jaque, Panama; in each camp my lecture and my clue. *Both are authoritarian. Both are intolerant. Both believe they are the only path to truth. Both deny the other. Both deny all else. Both are violent. Both are anthropomorphic. Both, under the premise of improving humankind, make it worse.*

Oh, Zu, I began to fear that God existed and He was insane. Yet I list these because they still chant inside me with rage. They became the focus of my quest, my obsession, this mad monologue and argument which I began to see as the beast's apology for her loneliness and her power. I saw in her the long battle that had raged inside me for years, and she, the daughter of my depths now played out that battle irrationally upon the world as savagely and relentlessly as the most horrible of dreams. She had become my deadly mistress as completely as the world had become hers.

I traveled by ferry from Jaque to Buena Ventura, Columbia and rode horseback again down the west coast of South America; Quito, Ecuador and Trujillo and Lima, Peru. She lectured me still: *Religion is the irrational explanation of the world. Science is the rational explanation of the world. The world is neither rational nor irrational. Do not tell me that science is description, not explanation; I will have none of it. **And I cannot be explained!***

Though it is true that low technology societies had suffered less than the technological ones, there was yet much suffering. In illness, people had fallen back to chants and herbs. If at one time we had become individuals isolated in our freedom, now, once again, we were beings stifled by our communities. One did not give birth alone, pray alone, plant alone, hunt alone, think alone, nor die alone. And if the earth was no longer on the brink of being blasted into the Stone Age, it was because it had already been annihilated. Where nations once fought over borders with tanks and guns, neighboring communes fought with swords and clubs over streams, or liberated plantations, or murdered the rich. Ironically, where people were once Catholic or Mormon or Protestant Christian, many of them now prayed to a dragon. Oh, Zu, we are the same beings, with the blood of each other and, yes, the blood of the earth on our hands, no matter which God, no matter what we might call knowledge. There was no paradise before Moses.

Many believe that there is little crime now because communities are so tight-knit and there is so little anyone owns. This might be so if you sit within your impoverished clime, but not if you travel. I did my best in those three years to avoid human beings, but even now they were unavoidable. As I left the outskirts of Lima to make my way across the Andes Mountains, I was stopped on the road by a band of five ragged men. They brandished machetes and bows before me and spoke to each other in what I'd come to recognize as a dialect of Inca. They wore beads in their long hair.

One of them stepped forward and spoke to me in Spanish. "You are the mad one who travels behind God," he said.

"I know who I am," I said. "I simply want to pass."

"I must speak with you honestly, we are here to end your life and take your things."

If I saw my death in front of me, well, I had seen it there a thousand times. "Better and easier if you had come in my sleep," I said.

"That is your way. The old way."

"If you have heard of me, what good is any of this?"

"Maybe if we eat you," he said, "God will follow."

"Maybe," I answered. I would not have time to unsheath the trident, but I carried a sword. I touched it.

"You may fight us," my assailant said.

And then, Zu, then the sulfuric wind. I saw the men before me sniff the breeze and hesitate before the air was sucked out as if the sky had inhaled; flame descended and the bandits lay in front of me in piles of bone and ash. Again I met this noble ritual of ambush, and again. I began to look with pity upon the faces of these dire men. As my reputation grew, their faces became younger and I realized before the end that they had come with less intent to take my life than to sacrifice their own.

I called for her to show herself, to meet me. Oh, on those nights under the swirling southern stars when I heard my name in the wind and smelled her skin upon the soil at my feet, the odor of her breath upon my food, saw her golden eye split with black hold my mind when I was awake, when I was asleep. More than once I wept pitifully in my saddle or by a fire, sustained by my dreadful enemy whose sustenance I took so that I might meet her one day and kill her.

From Lima I traveled the crest of the Andes to La Paz, Bolivia and then into the steppes of Argentina at San Miguel de Tucuman, crossing to Buenos Ares. At the camp outside the city my note told me: *If both science and religion achieved their goals, both would cease to exist. Both would rather subdue the world. Dominate the world. Oh Werther, fuck your sacraments and cell phones. Fuck your angels, your automobiles, missals and missiles. Fuck your priests and scientists, saints and lasers. Fuck the bomb. Fuck the*

Apocalypse. Fuck prayer. Fuck communication. Fuck business and multi-tasking. Fuck forgiveness. Fuck heaven and knowledge and e-mail and Satan. Fuck holy water and holograms and chain saws. Fuck religion and science, Sodom and Gomorra. Find me but one loving being. Even now, I would not destroy them for the sake of one. If she was not the one, insane deity of our wretched earth, then who was her equal, her kin?

Finally, I was told that there was a boat commissioned for me at the harbor. There I gave my faithful horses to a family with two young boys and boarded the clipper for my trip through the Drake Passage to New Zealand.

South America is less configured now by its national boundaries. People still speak of themselves, vaguely, as citizens of one country or another, though most people in the countryside referred to them-selves as members of some community or tribe, some ancient and indigenous, some new. Argentina, like the states, was a little more cohesive, configuring loosely around its old, ranch economy; the pasture land in the *pampas* still filled with grazing sheep or cows. Whatever her sympathy for the other animals, my enemy had not terminated the Argentine fondness for beef. Though the big slaughter-houses had been destroyed, there were plenty of small ones, and Buenos Aires itself now profited by its long dependence on the American dollar, the only currency yet viable in the hemisphere. The captain of my boat, Antonio Ferzi, a small, older Argentine of Italian descent, had been paid in dollars to take me to New Zealand.

"A woman," I said to him.

"Yes," he said.

"And after New Zealand, where then? The ends of the earth?"

"Who would know if you don't?" he said. He was a thin man with long, flowing white hair that he wore tied behind his head. It fell almost to his waist. "I was told someone would meet you at an outpost in Antarctica," said Ferzi. "We'd pick up supplies in Invercargill and leave you off near the Bay of Whales on the continent."

He'd made these trips before. He'd been a pilot, too, and had flown as well as sailed for the Argentine expeditions out of Tierra del Fuego to their bases on the Antarctic Peninsula, though his familiarity with the Antarctic often got him tourist work with the New Zealanders and Americans. Mostly he ran cargo now, though his eyes were almost ruined from years of ozone exposure. His brow was knit in a constant squint. He had a crew of ten on his ship designed much like the old steam clippers, though the small engine was powered by a battery charged by a fly wheel that ran from the energy collected by the sails.

I got to know him well enough during the passage to Invercargill in which, for the most part, we encountered fair seas. He fancied himself a wine connoisseur and a chef and we spent several long evenings over Argentinean wine and *asado*. We became the victims of each other's stories, so he came to know mine, and me, but for the beast herself whose existence, whose intimacy, I never revealed. He only knew I was a wayfarer, though the first he'd met who had an agent. Yet he knew, himself, that for a man in pain, travel, motion, was at least that, and worth doing. A *Montonero* when he was but twenty, he'd been disappeared by the military in the counter-revolution in 1972. His family, his young wife and child, were murdered then. Since, he'd had male lovers, but he'd lost his lover of over ten years at sea during a quick-storm. One night, late, and deep into the red blur of a wine drunkenness which, ever so briefly, had brought me forgetfulness and dulled everything, he spoke to me of the monster.

"You saw it then, that night?" he said, referring to my family's deaths.

Even in my stupor I felt better to deny the monster than confess. Let her make her own world, I would not become her troubadour. "The storm?" I said.

"The beast," he whispered.

"No."

His brow lowered, then he sat back, drinking, studying me.

"Do you dream?" I said.

"No one dreams anymore," Ferzi said. "You've traveled enough to know. Except the night your agent commissioned this boat. I dreamt of the storm and of my lover's death. I saw a beast in the cloud. And now, now, when I recall the actual event, I think I see the creature."

"We are drunk," I said to him.

"Do The Believers dream?" he asked me.

"There are none on your crew?"

"I won't hire one. They say it's bad luck."

"They do not dream any more or less than anyone else," I said. "I do not know why some people still dream, but it has nothing to do with a dragon."

"The dragon," Captain Ferzi said. "You said it."

But I gave him no answer.

"So you haven't booked passage back from Antarctica," he said. "The Argentines left long ago. I didn't know anyone was still there."

"Well, I shall be there," I said.

"Is it science or suicide?"

"Until now, I never knew there was such a fine line between them," I said.

After that night we were both more cautious in our drinking and our friendship, the fate of men who, cast together by circumstance, have told each other both too little and too much. By the time we took on our supplies in Invercargill, I am sure he thought that both my agent and I were working for the American government, a government which was now, in South America, not much more than a powerful myth less real than the dragon herself.

In New Zealand we took on the power sledge. Your engineers must have looked at it by now, Zu. It has quite a remarkable battery and a gallon of ethyl will run it for a year. Though the ship itself took on a good deal of supplies for the voyage, the captain was surprised how little food I would be packing.

"So," he said, "there is someone there."

"Yes," I said. "Someone is there."

Amid my supplies for the trip I found a letter:

My dear Werther, my father, my enemy, my love:

I have no animosity toward your species, though it is true I am not fond of it. Many of you are fine individuals, but too many are not. Speaking as both an outsider and an insider, I find that your species, in general, does more harm than good. And I suppose that I should not find it surprising that a group so methodical in its annihilation of so many other species finds it so reprehensible when someone threatens them.

Dear Werther, you have lost your souls to production and purchase, forgotten Time, tried to abolish death for yourselves while dealing it to others. But in the absence of death there is the absence of life. You cannot purchase the reason for your existence.

I have come to believe that all things come to be and evolve equally. All things are equally intelligent in their way. The power to conceive and destroy makes you nothing but a conceiver and a destroyer. While I bide my time among you, I ask that you reconceive and recreate. Each being must take responsibility for all beings.

I am not a systematic thinker. I am only the beast of your depths. I am not opposed to science, I am only opposed to its hegemony. I would be opposed to monotheism even if it were true.

But how irrelevant the truth is and how little anyone wants to know it.

I have not set about to make a better world. I've sought only to destroy yours. I hope you can forgive me for doing what I thought was the best thing. I am a meteor, Werther, a nuclear winter, a global warming, a drastic climatic change. I am flood and fire, famine and pestilence, the dark fire of a gentle god, the gentle breath of an evil one. Oh Werther, who am I? Why can't you tell me? Had I not sprung from the depths of all your hearts, would I be a better creature? Oh Werther, I am. *I am.* Yet you have never even asked my name. And for your love I would let you keep your horrible world.

Your mistress,
Humanity

How bitter that the beast would now give herself the name of the very beings upon whom she'd cast her vengeance; this dragon of my soul, this Satan in her Godless Eden. Humanity. And with whose innocent blood had she signed her name? Yet as I held the paper, the letter dissolved in my hands, and when I went to my pack to find her notes, they had disintegrated too. I suppose it was another of her distasteful ironies that she became as the God she so hated, everywhere leaving her signs, her effects, but nowhere leaving evidence of her profound subjectivity. No, gods do not wish to be worshipped, Zu, nor known. They wish to be feared and forgiven.

In the passage to Antarctica we encountered a lengthy storm, but eventually wended into the ice floes where we could find shelter by anchoring behind tabular icebergs. Though the Bay of Whales is not always the best approach to the Pole—there is not a land ridge like the Transantarctic Range on which to securely set your sights or your camps as there is out of McMurdo—the break up of the Ross Ice Shelf is less haphazard there, more predictable, and there is solid landing on the Edward VII Peninsula, off the inner bay, the Okuma Bay and the Prestrud Inlet; things you might know as a sailor and not as a pilot. We made land and transferred my sledge by ramps and pulleys from the ship to the icy wasteland. Across the way, within sight, sat a small shack, undoubtedly my first destination.

Ferzi and I stared across the ice. It was a moderate, summer day, just below freezing, the snow hitting our faces from the wind-swept dunes.

"There is no one there," Ferzi said to me.

"Someone built the shelter," I said.

"Yes, but when? Why do I doubt that someone will meet you?"

"Because you are a rational man."

"Let me wait for you," the captain said. "If no one comes in a few days, we can return."

"You haven't been paid," I said.

"I'm going back anyway."

"No," I replied.

"I'll come back for you in nine months, when the ice breaks up again."

"No," I said.

He looked at my trident and sledge. "No one is coming," he said. "It's true."

"You are right, my friend."

"What better place for a madman," he whispered. "But you are not mad."

"The world," I said.

"Someone is mad at it," said Ferzi.

"Yes."

"Good luck," he said.

He was the last human I saw, Dr. Zu, until you found me. I have wandered this shelf for six months, chasing a dragon shadow across the ice, smelling her scent from camp to camp. You wonder how I have survived, but she has kept me. At times, during storms, I was held up for weeks in a shack of her making, huddled inside, my stove lit by her fecal fire, my stomach nourished by her regurgitations left at the opening of my hut. At times, her wings held off the wind and her sweet, hot breath encircled my tent. As she once lived inside me, now it was as if I lived inside her. And still I followed to kill her.

I'd expected her to lead me to the Pole, though I realize now that I'd arrived too late in the year and when the spring ends and summer breaks again, she will lead me there where we shall meet for our final and wordless battle. This is how you found me, Dr. Zu. Admit, you saw the shadow that blacked out the sun and felt her hot stink upon you. You felt the pulse of her wings and her heart. And your own heart stopped.

Dr. Zu, how has the world come to this? How have I survived? You must admit, there is no rational explanation, only mine, a madness which is true. So you must release me now, before it is too late, before the summer is gone, because if you do not, then she will come here for me. You must let me follow her to the Pole where I will end this misery of the world or commit the earth to the dragon's reign. I can hear the summer approach. I hear the ice cracking at the horizon. It is time for the world to have God again. It is time for the world to have knowledge again. I will slay this horrible beast and put destiny back into mankind's hands.

This ends the testimony of Dr. Werther Fausten, recorded at McMurdo, Antarctica in the year 2017.

Dr. Hestor Zu

The Dragon Journal of Lisa Piccolo Zu

It has been a very long time since I have written in this journal and much has happened and I have changed. The journey from Panama to Buenos Aires is a long one, with long days blending together on the cradle rock ocean, hours spent gazing southwest to the shore above the fifth southern latitude, to the Brazilian coast, and northwest to Brazil below it, and then east, always and simply straight east to the infinite ocean. If you know the geography, then you know that the closing of the canal made our trip much longer, the distance from Panama to the hump of Brazil being one of almost 60 degrees of eastern longitude before coming back again half that distance to Buenos Aires and then another thirty degrees west to New Zealand. If all went well, we'd be a month late; New Zealand by February, and then Antarctica.

As you can see, I learned to sail: I learned the parts of the boat, the names of clouds, how to fold sails, set moorings, tie knots, leeward and windward sailing and anchoring, how to tack and jibe, how to read the weather and ride out a storm. I took some notes on it in another journal because it is something, now that I have done it, that I might wish to do again someday on my own, because the sea is ever more present now in this changed world.

South of Rio De Janeiro, off Porto Alegre, which put us near Uruguay and Argentina, we saw our first barge city. Though a lot of cities had begun to extend themselves by piers and rafts into the ocean, this was the first time I saw a free-floating, sailing city of connected barges; a huge, floating island over a mile wide with gardens and squat buildings, even trees. On its edges, boats of all kinds made harbor and other barges had begun to attach themselves. Dogs barked at us from the docks and I spotted a gray cat in a doorway. The city flew a flag with a winged dragon on it and a slogan in Spanish beneath it on a banner: *La vida sin destrucción*. Life without destruction.

They were Argentine and did not let us make harbor because we had an engine, even if it was powered mostly by sun and wind. All the way down, in any of the rural places, this was the case.

"Reactionaries or futurists?" said El.

"Survivors," I said.

Captain Evans had studied most of the late Nineteenth Century and early Twentieth Century expeditions to Antarctica and made the journals of the explorers Scott, Amundsen, and Shackleton available to us to study. We were pretty much on the same route as Ernest Shackleton's 1907 expedition and planned to negotiate the ice floes on the Ross Sea and make land near Ross Island at the north end of the Ross Ice Shelf, and then try to reach McMurdo where we knew there was an American base. If we couldn't land there, we'd make land where we could and cross over the ice shelf. If no one was at McMurdo we'd have to reconnoiter. I knew Evans wanted to find his wife, Adjoa, at all costs, and if he had to he'd retreat to New Zealand for the winter and come back in the spring for a run to the Amundsen-Scott Mars Lab at the South Pole.

"What will we do if we don't find Grandma Zu at McMurdo?" I asked El.

"I don't know," she said. "The trip to the Pole is a thousand kilometers, then back."

But by then I had already begun to feel that I had been drawn to Antarctica by something more powerful than our original purpose. That something was going to happen. That something *had* to happen, as if a great yearning somewhere pulled me; something more personal than fate, though it felt like fate, a future open and blank yet inevitable and fateful, hopeful and dire. My heart was aching.

We made land in Buenos Aires. On the northeast shore of the Rio de la Plata, a huge estuary miles wide, Montevideo, Uruguay looked burned out and devastated and we didn't begin to see fishing villages on the north shore for another mile. Buenos Aires on the other hand, at the foot of the delta on the south shore, seemed almost like a Nineteenth Century city with carriages and horses, though there were lots of bicycles, too. The cars and cathedrals were gone, but around the Plaza de Mayo people sat in open cafes and teenagers skateboarded in the streets. There were no movie theaters now, but plenty of opera houses and tango clubs.

The government building, the Pink House, still stood, though the central cathedral nearby had been burned. An extensive subway, powered by electricity, still ran through the city. Farther west, we were told, the industrial section and the *frigorificos*, the big slaughter yards, had been pulled down by the people who lived outside them in the *villas miserias* and now orchards of cherries, oranges, grape-fruits, plums and figs stretched along the Rio Parana and Rio Uruguay and into where the factories and slaughter yards and slums once stood. The *Liniers*, once a giant meat market, still sold beef and lamb, but the farmers slaughtered it themselves then brought it to market and much of what was sold there was now produce. The city was still big, over two million people, but there had once been over ten million in the area. Many had died in the first years, but many more had fled to the countryside.

The port was very built up and went on for miles. Unlike Panama City, which had fallen into decay, it was filled with fishing boats and cargo boats, all powered by sails. It was odd how some places seemed to fall back to the way things were two hundred years ago, yet other places seemed medieval, and yet others ancient and some worse.

What we didn't see for ourselves we found out from a sailing contact of Captain Evans' in Puerto Nuevo at the center of the harbor, a man named Antonio Ferzi who'd made the run to the west side of Antarctica almost a year before. He was a small man, older, but with long, white hair that he tied behind him and let fall on his back. He'd not sailed as far as McMurdo, but had left a single man ashore at the Bay of Whales on the southern end of the ice shelf.

"One man," said Captain Evans. "Did anyone meet him?"

"I think he went there to die, or to kill something, if only in himself," Ferzi said. "An American, like you. His name was Werther Fausten."

"The Nobel scientist?" said El.

"He said nothing of that to me," said Ferzi. He became nervous. He rubbed one brow with his left hand, then the other, then placed his hand over his mouth. Then he did it again. "I'd be careful," he said to Captain Evans. "I didn't like the way the sea was breaking up."

"Too much?" said Evans.

"I am almost blind," Ferzi said. "From deteriorated ozone exposure." He raised his chin then, as if trying to summon something lost from within. "Whatever good all of this has done for the ecology, it will take decades for the ozone to react. I've traveled down there for years. It might be too late to stop the melt. If the Antarctic shelves drop, cities like this will be underwater." Then he squinted at me. He held my eyes with his. They were pale-gray like old snow. "I won't go down there again," he said. He paused, as if both afraid to speak and yet driven. He spoke to me. "I've begun to dream since. I dream of that man on the ice following a shadow. I dream of blue wings and death in the hearts of clouds. And I dream of the dead." He touched my chin. "If you dream, child," he said to me, "if you dream anymore, you have to keep it to yourself."

"I dream," I said to him.

"And how did I know?" He put his index finger to his lips.

"There's enough fear in the world," said El. "We barely need our nightmares, we barely need hope."

"Yes, barely," whispered Ferzi.

"What happened so differently in Montevideo?" asked El quickly.

Antonio Ferzi eyed us tentatively again. "War," he said. "Almost. Or something like a war. These were two huge populations and not much space. When the infrastructure fell in the first years, so did government. There was only the military. They met on the north bank of the Rio de la Plata and a quick-storm rubbed them out. In a week oil refineries on both sides were gone, then the rest. You know this pattern, I am sure. Why we continue to exist and Montevideo does not, I don't know. There is no justice in the weather. Unless you are a Believer and think we sacrificed a virgin."

It was the first time I heard the term "Believer," but I knew right away. "A boy," I said.

"I don't know anything about it," said Ferzi.

"You've seen her," I whispered. "You don't have to believe."

But he wouldn't continue. He compared some more notes with Evans. At the end he said he was through sailing for a living. He talked of the barge cities and said he'd heard that to the north, on the Rio Negro, as well as in the rain forests of Brazil, there were people who had returned to the trees, who lived in the canopy and whose feet never touched the ground. At the Iguacu Falls, near the head-waters of the Rio Parana, a people lived under the waterfalls on fruit and fungus; they had become like water and air, never leaving the thick fog, moving through the mist like ghosts. To the west now, in the *pampas*, there were horse people, descendants of the *gauchos*, who lived on the backs of horses, and people in the Andes who flew from cliff to cliff on ephemeral hand gliders, living like birds. "The dreamers," he said. "I will join the dreamers. *La paganos que sueñan.* The pagans who dream."

We headed south again, truly chasing the sun, the yellow days strung out like pearls, pale between the ocean and the sky, for I, too, was dreaming, constantly dreaming. I couldn't sleep nor stay awake but to dream. I knew what Ferzi was talking about, a desire to leave the ground forever, not to fly so much as to not tread, to not walk upon the altar of the earth, we who are its fruit, its sacrifice.

Words come to me now, as do dreams, as things that are not mine. But I shall try my best to recount the last events. I began to dream the dreams of birds, of the gulls and albatross. I dreamed the dreams of the orcas and sperm whales who themselves dreamt of play and blood, the dolphins at our bow who dreamt of flight. The fish dreamed. Sharks swam beneath us in the liquid of nightmares. The rope in my hands. The sails. How the world dreamed and dreamed! I wanted to drop and pray to everything I touched as the dreams of everything around me turned eating, drinking, and breathing into the eating, drinking, and breathing of dreams. I barely spoke but in the feelings of each thing I saw or smelled or touched. How the call of a gull opened up a world.

El worried for me now, and had convinced herself that she had taken me too far from home, too far from everything I knew. But now the world itself was far from everything I knew. There was no place to go that would not be far from everything I knew. She held me at night if I did not have watch, or she did not, or maybe she held me constantly, maybe she did not let me go once in all that time, but held me to her breasts which themselves dreamed in my ears and on my cheeks, each and every thing leaking a dream into a fabric of crystalline webs through which we moved liked spiders, only thinking with the most shallow part of our souls that this world had any substance, any existence beyond feeling.

"My darling," whispered El. "My child."

"Don't worry, El," I said.

"You have a fever."

"I am so well."

"What have I done?"

"You've done the most beautiful thing," I said to her, though I could not explain, cannot explain even now. "You have done the most beautiful thing."

As we moved south we left the coast for the swing around the cape. In our path lay the Falkland Islands, or what the Argentines called the Islas Malvinas, where Captain Evans decided to put ashore before our sweep through the Drake Passage and into the Pacific Ocean, to New Zealand. Nigel spied the isles in his electronic binoculars before we could see them, though I knew they sat under the spread of purple and gray clouds at the end of our path to the south.

"Do you think anyone is there?" Clyde asked Captain Evans.

"Farmers are there," I said, "and sheep."

"Then not much has changed," said Evans.

"A lot has changed," I said.

"Look at those clouds," Nigel said to Evans, passing him the binoculars.

"It rains there 260 days a year. I'd expect storm clouds," Evans said. "They're not moving. We're under sail only. We'll be cautious."

Nigel's chest heaved. We hadn't seen a patch like that, so isolated and so brooding, since the Phenomenon, and since then we hadn't used our engine once, though we'd have to later to negotiate the ice floes, even though I told them we were safe now. But I was not considered an authority. In fact, most the crew was pretty concerned about what they called my "unconnectedness," which was really just the opposite.

I didn't say it to them. I said it to El. "She's there," I said. "She comes there for sheep."

"To eat?" said El. "Do you think the dragons picnic on the Falklands?"

Actually, I was glad she felt she could still tease me, that I wasn't so crazy that she found me delicate or fragile. It made me feel good. I laughed. "She takes them somewhere else," I said.

"All the better for us," laughed El.

We harbored in Hill Cove, a cove among a thousand coves on the west shore of the west island. The only city was Stanley, at the tip of a chubby peninsula far on the northeast shore of the eastern isle. We came in on a heaving sea and a dark sky, the wind sweeping in bitterly from the west despite the summer season; it felt almost freezing. But the cove was well protected, a small bay within a bay and protected by Saunders Island which we passed on our way in the Byron Sound. After sounding we found we were in calm waters deep enough to get well in and find protection. Oddly, the sky opened above us and as the storm broke upon the land; the sun shone almost directly above and we remained dry as huge raindrops exploded about us on the black rocks and refracted sunlight as they fell like a million bubbles of rainbows.

"Good fortune, wouldn't you say?" Evans said to me.

"Magic," I said.

Everyone went ashore but Nigel who stayed with the boat. El and I climbed over the rocks with Evans where we looked over an expanse of grassy, windswept hills of tussock, a heath that seemed to rise and fall almost like the ocean, the island mimicking the sea. The sky had opened yet more and we were still dry, and though the wind was cold and wicked, the ground felt warm at my feet. Between the cold gusts, the heat heaved into my legs as if we stood on the back of a huge, gently breathing beast. Here the land dreamed of the water and the water dreamed of the land.

"Well, here we are," said Captain Evans.

"But why?" said El.

"I don't know," he said. "It was on the way. I just wanted to stand on something that was untouched, I suppose, by people or…or anything else."

"There are probably shepherds somewhere," I said as we walked back. "Maybe a farm."

Captain Evans tousled my hair. "The boat should hold fine when the tide goes out and you can see that the beach near the rocks stays high and dry even at the height of the tide. I saw jackass penguins nesting there. And there are crabeater seals breeding. We'll be safe enough. So I'm going to make camp here. If anyone else wants to spend a night on shore, now's your chance." Angie and AJ said they'd camp, as did the four Chileans. They were good men. They'd taught us a lot of Spanish and soccer, *futbal* to them, which they managed to play even on deck, sometimes with a ball that they brought, and sometimes with anything they happened to find, like a ball of canvas or rope or trash. Those guys could kick anything and keep it in the air forever. Captain Evans was really grateful to them for sticking out the expedition when it might have been easier for them to cross the *pampas* and the Andes Mountains to Santiago when we were in Buenos Aires.

I told El I wanted to stay ashore. She was surprised, but she agreed. We went back to the boat and got our packs and the Chileans got their soccer ball. We broke into sides and played *futbal* on the beach while the penguins honked at us from their burrows and a few sea lions watched us curiously. It was the first time our Chilean friends had room to hit headers and they taught me and Angie and AJ and El. We laughed really hard every time we failed and the ball caromed off our shoulders or face. The storm suddenly broke over us, but we played on in the icy rain. Then the sky cleared and as the late sun dried the land around us, wading birds ran back and forth at the lapping shore and hundreds of gulls and petrels landed and stood quietly facing the sun. At the edge of the cove, a single heron stood motionless. Finally the sun set gently into the ocean, into the late-coming night as a canopy of southern stars emerged.

AJ and Angie played their mouth harp and guitar. They played an old folk song to each other that went: If I needed you, would you come to me? / Would you come to me for to ease my pain? / If you needed me, I would come to you / I would swim the sea for to ease your pain. It was sad and beautiful and I could see they really loved each other. Captain Evans put his face in his hands. For a moment, everybody forgot everything. We went to sleep under a sky blazing with starlight, the hiss and splash-push of the waves, the wind wishing above us through the rocks.

I awoke frightened from having been blank and dreamless, dreamless for the first time since I could remember, though my life had become like one of those dreams that you walk through with full awareness that you're dreaming. El seemed almost breathless in her deep sleep and it seemed as if a pall had fallen on everyone. Around me, the night had become soundless and I couldn't even hear my own footsteps as I walked to the edge of the rocks. "El," I said, but it was much like the moments before the dragon came to take Hunter, as if something in the air inhaled the sound.

I scrambled over the black rocks and walked through the heath. I don't know how far or how long, but it was some time because I noticed the shifting of the stars. The wind had quieted and under the spray of starlight I saw the heads of nesting upland geese rise around me above the tussock grass. To the east stood a small mountain and there, above it, a formation of thunderheads puffed and rolled upon itself like a time-lapse movie of clouds. Then a column of fire sprang from the billowing clouds and I saw the dragon descending to the foot of the mountain as if sliding down the fire.

As I continued across the heath I felt as if I walked through a history of dreams, a world of dreams. Each snipe and goose in the tussock grass poured at me with wishes and Time, each blade of grass wept a nightmare. Now it seemed like I had been on the heath for weeks. At the foot of the mountain I crossed a wide sand dune and then the wind picked up again and snow fell. I felt so foolish and hopeless as I pressed forward, climbing the rocks and the crumbled slate at the mountain base. But then I saw the cave before me and I rushed to it to escape the snow. At the mouth of the cave, the light from the stars died and I fell into a blackness so deep and so dark it seemed that I walked without footing, as if I were falling, not walking, down and down. Finally, up ahead, I spotted a small glow which I floated to now with such lethargy it seemed I was skating through an airy tar. And then I saw them. Two ovals the size of ostrich eggs, smooth and blue-green, veined with brown, like giant, smooth turquoise stones.

Then, from behind them, she arose and faced me, her teeth like needles and her huge, golden eyes split with black diamonds. Her wings rose behind her and stirred the sweet, hot air that sucked in and out as if the cave were breathing. Her head seemed weightless on her long neck and her skin shifted over her like an oily coat of mail.

The dragon's eyes transfixed me and I understood so much in that moment, though there were no words, only the beating of her heart in my ears. And in my brain and my own heart I felt her longing, her hate, her need, her fear. I felt a desire so large, so painful, I began to cry. I cried and cried. And then I found myself at the mouth of the cave, her hot breath pushing me toward the dunes and over the heath where I arrived at dawn to find El and everyone else who had spread out just beyond the black rocks, searching the ground for my tracks.

"My God, Lisa, where were you?" said El.

"I saw her, El," I said crying. "I saw her."

Everyone rushed up and I knew what they saw, a weeping, crazy child.

"Where were you,?" said Evans.

I pointed to the mountain. "There."

"That's Mount Adam," he said to El. "It's four or five miles away."

"She's there," I said. I didn't even know if I wanted them to go. If I took them, I would be asking them to travel into the depths of my own heart, to a place which couldn't be walked into, a place that couldn't be reached. And I couldn't understand the rage I felt at them all, even El, who I wanted to love me and hold me and take me back inside her.

"We've heard a hundred stories on this trip," whispered Captain Evans. "What's a day's hike?"

So we ate and dressed and hiked back out, Captain Evans and El, AJ and a grumbling Angie, and me, hiking across the heath that I'd crossed in the night. From the west, sleet flew at our backs as we trudged quietly, though it was encouraging to find signs of my passage, prints from my boots and matted grass where'd I'd stopped to rest. When we reached the dunes at the mountain base, Evans turned and looked at me, the oddest twist crossing his features, like someone who'd fallen reluctantly into the fortune he'd been told by a clairvoyant.

"Up there," I said. "Over those rocks."

Evans told Angie and AJ to wait there.

"What if there's something there?" Angie said.

"The child escaped," said Evans. "Are we safe?" he said to me.

"I don't know," I said.

"One step at a time. First the cave," said the captain.

We climbed. As we scrambled up the slate, I felt nothing of the despair I'd felt the night before, but only the simple, anxious desire to have my story confirmed. After that, I didn't know. But when we reached the spot where I'd found the cave, now there was no opening, only a pile of rocks and dirt. Evans sighed heavily.

"It's under there," I said.

"Oh darling," El said, taking my hand.

"There might have been a slide," Captain Evans said, forcing a tight smile at me. "I can't read these things. I don't know when it happened. It looks pretty settled."

"It doesn't matter. She's not there now. But there are eggs."

"Eggs," said El.

"Well," said Evans.

We made the long walk back, though after we arrived at the cove there was still plenty of time in the long austral summer day to make way. Evans ordered us to pack up as Nigel pressed him about it all.

"Nothing," said Evans. "It seems she did walk all the way there and back—"

"We're running out of time," said Nigel.

"Yes," said Evans.

But later, after we were on board, he took me by the hand. We walked to the bow of the boat and stared into the churning sea. He took the brim of his cap into his hands and rubbed it across his head, staring, staring out, and then he looked at me. He smiled a little. He put his hand on my forehead, my cheek. "What has happened? Do you know?"

"No," I said. "Only that the world has changed."

"But we are still here. Why are we here?"

"Because there is no better thing to do," I said.

He nodded. "If you see her again—" he stuttered, "—if you see her—" and his chest heaved—"ask her to spare Adjoa, my wife."

Then I went below, reluctantly, because I knew El would be waiting, and I felt ashamed and powerful, embarrassed, loving, confused. She'd made tea. Her hair hung down on the shoulders of her sweater, her face, full of concern and tiredness, was still streaked with dirt and sweat.

"You can't choose it, El," I said to her before she could speak. "The world chooses for us. Or maybe I'm crazy. Uri was crazy," I said.

"Your father was crazy with self-destruction," she said. "He saw greatness in everything he did, and that was all that was great about him. Sometimes that's enough to convince people. There's not much room in the world for that anymore."

"You're not mad at me," I said.

"Were you dreaming?"

"I'm always dreaming. Even now. Everything is. Every person, every animal, every thing. We're nothing but the dreams of others around us."

"And do you know the difference between when you're dreaming and when you're not, between what is a dream and what isn't?"

"Do you?"

"Most times," she said. "Though I needn't worry about that now."

I went to her, I went to my mom and touched her forehead. "El," I said, "I give you dreams."

"Don't wander off alone again," said El. "Promise me."

And I did.

That night I slept in my mother's arms again and together we dreamed of a blue shadow flying over the shining ice, of a mountain exploding, a phoenix rising above it, of water, water everywhere, and of the fecund earth. We awoke in the pre-dawn with the heaving of the boat over heavy sea. El kissed my forehead. "My miracle child," she said.

I knew then that it didn't matter whether I'd seen the dragon or not. It didn't matter who I was or what I saw or felt, because it all mattered so deeply anyways. Because we lived on the edge of something so wonderful, so dreadful; we passed through our lives like the stingers on the tentacle of a jellyfish, momentary, electric. Filled with desires we did not even own. Everything meant so much and so little and so quickly it was gone. There were things so much more important than the truth.

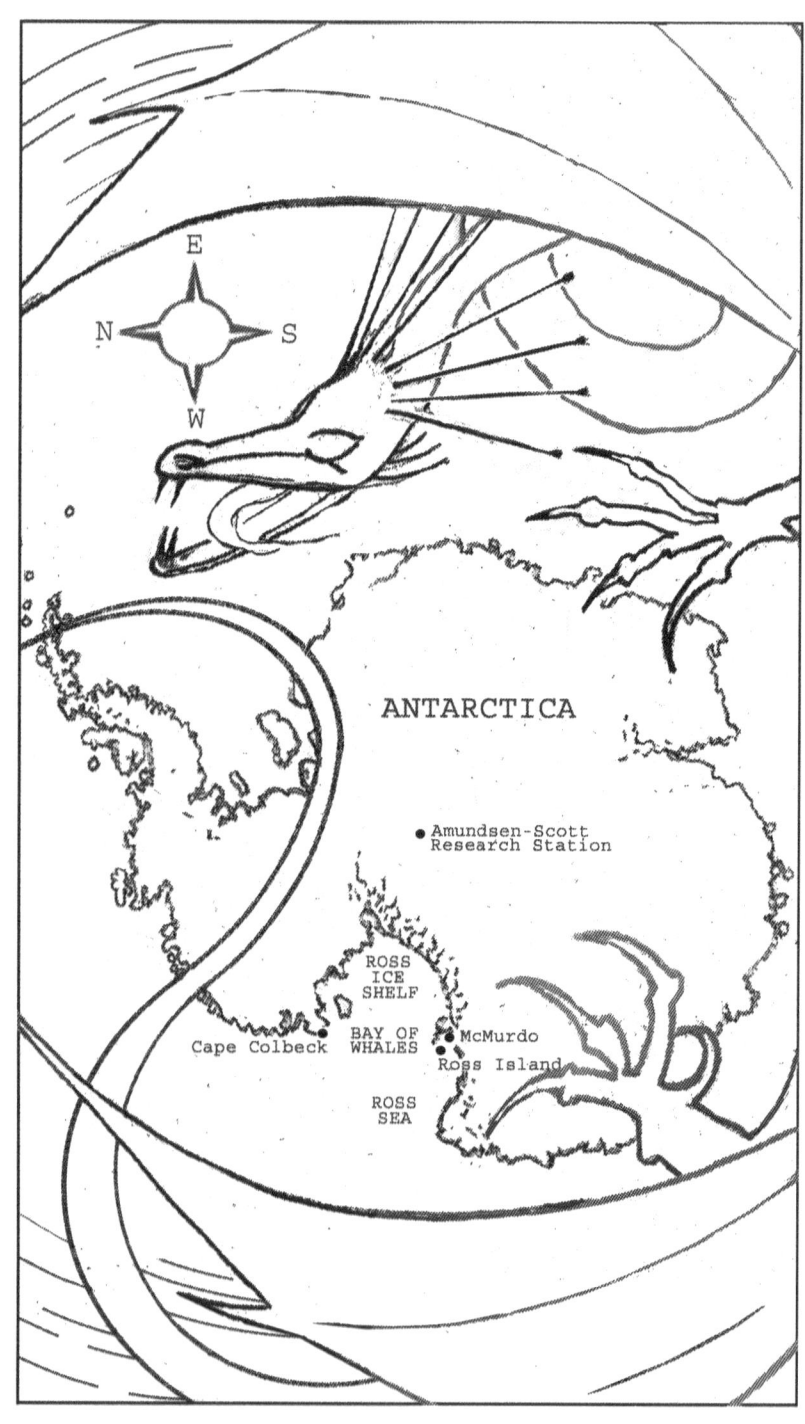

The Dragon Journal of Lisa Piccolo Zu

In the Drake Passage between Tierra del Fuego and the Antarctic Peninsula the wind blew against us so hard and the seas were so rough that we couldn't hold storm anchor nor raise a sail. The captain engaged the engine and we fought through the heavy waves for three days, Evans keeping the bow of the boat into the wind so we wouldn't be struck broadside and rolled. The boat rose and plunged and we spent almost all of those three days below, often tying ourselves to our bunks. Despite sealing the hatches, water poured in. We walked in water, slept with water. We were always wet. Captain Evans was almost always up top with Nigel or Angie or AJ, one of them at the wheel, one midship, and one of them, or another adult forward near a hatch to pass information back and forth. Up till then, that was the heaviest surf I'd ever experienced.

We'd planned to try and make harbor in Ushaia, Argentina or Punta Arena, Chile off Tierra del Fuego, but the seas were too harsh. When we broke through to the Pacific Basin, the heavy roll of the Pacific Ocean felt gentle, long and low, like riding the moo of a huge cow.

We made our final stop before Antarctica in Dunedin, New Zealand, where we took on fresh water, dry pack food, wool sweaters and pants, mittens, skis, and two battery-powered sledges, modified tread-tractors charged by small amounts of precious corn ethyl. We took on wagon sleds, too, that were to be pulled by the sledges. Dog teams had been outlawed on the continent decades ago, when it was learned that they carried diseases, like distemper and rabies, that devastated the rebuilding seal populations. Not that there was any law in Antarctica now, but despite all the reassuring talk about the randomness of the Phenomenon, its specter kind of silently reinforced that kind of ecological morality, if you ask me.

Evans had pioneered some of that technology and bartered it for the sledges and supplies early in the crisis when he began to worry about the safety of his wife. He hoped we'd barely need these things, but if we didn't find Adjoa or Grandma Zu at McMurdo, then we'd spend some time on the ice shelf practicing before heading back to New Zealand to wait out the winter before coming back and making a run to the Pole as soon as spring broke, late September or October, if possible. None of us wanted to do that. Not because it was hard. Based on a trans-Antarctic run made by Vivian Fuchs and Edmund Hillary in the last century, Evans figured we could make the one-way trip in forty-five days and return well in the heart of the austral summer. But no one had heard anything from the Amundsen-Scott base since the beginning of last winter. If anyone had survived, it was hard to guess the likelihood of anyone making it through a second winter on the South Pole without technology.

New Zealand, always rugged and not heavily populated, had fallen back on its fishing and farming. They had some geothermal and hydro-power, and natural gas. Before the recent development of vegetable ethyl there had been a few whaling expeditions into the Antarctic seas, in search of whale oil, that never returned; the same with seal hunting expeditions, even those strictly under sail. "One might have wondered what would happen if the animals had weapons," a young woman, a dock worker in the supply terminal, said to us.

"Yes, one might have," I said, and the two of us laughed while everyone else tried to ignore us.

Her name was Monica and later, before we left, she showed me her tattoo of a winged dragon over her left breast.

"Are you a Believer?" I said.

"Dreamer, like you. I can see it in your eyes."

I told her about the barge cities and some of the stories we'd heard in South America, of people living in the canopy of the rain forest, on cliffs, in waterfalls.

"I'm going to Mars," said Monica.

"You can't go to Mars anymore." I told her about why we were there and Grandma Zu.

"I'm going. I'm going to live at the very bottom of the *Valles Marineris* and raise flying horses."

Some people are dreamers and some people are just crazy.

Three days out of Dunedin the seas picked up. A day later a wind from the southwest brought a huge storm and our boat bobbed among waves as tall as our masts from trench to crest. The rain came down constantly and we struggled, barely moving forward, for two dismal weeks. Though we were all pretty dulled to the prospect of fearing for our lives, we weren't beyond feeling hopeless and miserable. We were always cold, always wet, even in bed.

One night, the ship completely lashed down and the rudder set, the ten of us huddled below, our feet in a puddle of cold, splashing water, Evans read to us from Ernest Shackleton's journals about a passage from New Zealand to the Ross Ice Shelf. One storm lasted almost three weeks, and after a one day break the next lasted ten days. We passed Shackleton's and Scott's journals back and forth like the Bible. We read about Scott's last days before he perished on his return from the South Pole. "We'll be brave like Scott, but not so stupid," said Evans.

We read about Shackleton's ill-fated voyage on the *Endurance*, how the boat was caught in the ice pack on the Weddel Sea for ten months before being crushed by the ice. After abandoning ship Shackleton and his twenty-eight men tried to reach Snow Hill Island, 312 miles away, by packing over the ice, but could only travel a mile a day and ended up camping on the ice floes for five months. Finally they took three life boats to tiny Elephant Island, only a hundred yards long by fifty yards wide. Then Shackleton and five others sailed 800 miles across the southern Scotia Sea in a 22-foot boat. Using compass and sextant they made it to South Georgia, an island only twenty-five miles wide. They had to cross the wintry island mountains on foot where they found a whaling station. They healed, packed up, and set out for Elephant Island again. After three failed attempts, they finally made it back and rescued all the men.

When the storms let up slightly, we went to our engine and pushed south. When the sky cleared, however briefly, we set the sails. By late February we saw our first grease ice under calm seas, then tiny bergs and growlers, and then finally floes of pancake ice like wet, gray circles of batter on a blue grill. At last we edged across the 180 degree meridian and into the Ross Sea.

Then the sea opened and we sailed into the floes of tabular icebergs that broke off, or calved, from the shelf, towering hundreds of feet above us, white, gigantic, quiet, except sometimes for an odd creaking. We had to avoid the tall ones because sometimes, after a loud creak, a great cracking sound followed and they'd break in two, or the ocean would melt their bottoms until they became top heavy and they flipped over. Passing through these giants, especially in a snowstorm with our masts, halyards, and life lines coated with ice, felt frightening and sacred. Twice, huge snow squalls came upon us and we docked in the lee of squat, wide icebergs to protect us from the snow and waves. I remembered an old song that El used to hum to me when I was little. "These are the times of miracle and wonder," it went. I couldn't remember the other words, but it didn't really mean miracle and wonder, but more about terrible, technological miracles. Why would El hold me and sing that? Or was it a dream?

This was the most tense time of all, because now we were close enough to see the smoky plumes of Mount Erebus, the volcano that rose above Ross Island, yet everything depended upon the state of the pack ice ahead of us. Best if it had broken completely and gave us passage to Ross Island and McMurdo, worse if it still clung to the ice shelf and we had to dock on it and haul over the ice, with the risk of it breaking up beneath us. But our luck was even worse still. The winter pack ice had broken, but not enough. We spent day after day wandering along the shelf, looking for a passage through the ice. At first we sailed west until it became obvious that to continue in that direction would place us on the other side of Cape Adare, then even if we made land it would place us on the opposite side of the Transantarctic Mountains from Ross Island.

So we began to work our way back again. Well east of the meridian we saw our first opening and Evans steered us in, the ocean slapping at us and back at the great, frozen ice pack on either side, poised like a vice at the sides of the ship. Around us now, sea lions and penguins stared at us calmly from the floes and petrels and albatross examined us from the sky, swooping to see if we had any food on our deck. The sea opened suddenly and a pod of three, black-and-white orcas appeared starboard, raising their heads from the water to inspect our passage, but we sailed south only a few miles before we struck the barrier again. Slowly we worked east and east, each opening in the pack ice guiding us yet farther east, and each day taking us farther from Ross Island. It was now March and there was not much summer left.

Evans met with everyone and discussed our alternatives. We could continue through the ice pack and try to wend our way back to McMurdo or follow the flows east and make land near the Bay of Whales, where a number of explorers, Shackleton, Amundsen, and Byrd had at least once successfully harbored and crossed the shelf. One big difference was that none of us had done it before. Aside from the storms, there were ice ridges and hidden snow caves and a hundred dangers that could keep even an experienced explorer from succeeding. It still being summer, there was danger of the shelf breaking up, and as much as we might loop away from the shore, which would cost us vital days, we could still find ourselves on the wrong side of a calving that left us adrift in the frozen sea on an island iceberg. The sea approach was our best hope. Evans decided to give it another forty-eight hours before relinquishing to the ice pack and harboring on the east end of the ice shelf.

The first day we were forced to follow a channel east again, but by the end of the day we hit another wall of solid pack. We cruised west a little, but finding that the pack ice wall curved north and back out to sea, again we turned back toward the Bay of Whales. The next day, with no opening in sight, we began to prepare for the landing and the crossing, packing the sledges and preparing our clothes. The sun had almost circled us again before Angie, who stood on the bow pulpit, yelled out. "Two o'clock to starboard! A break in the ice!"

With the wind behind us, Evans steered the ship toward the break in the floes, a tiny opening which gave us only about ten feet on either side. A squall had begun to kick up behind us. "Drop the sails!" yelled Evans. We dropped the jib and then the mainsails just in time, because the storm, picking up, would have driven us into the ice pack. And though the ice walls on either side protected us a little, the snow whirled so furiously that we could barely see ahead or behind.

"The squall will end!" Evans yelled. "Even if it lasts a day, it will end. Hold tight!" But it mattered little because we were all thrown forward with a deafening crack, and then the grown of ice against the hull. Now we were locked in the ice.

After about twelve hours the squall passed and we could see our predicament. Though the depth of the ice around us had thinned, our passage had closed. I stayed on the boat with Nigel, who stood at the power and the wheel. Everyone else went out on the ice pack with picks and shovels and began to dig at the front of the boat. Though it seemed futile, Evans said that you couldn't tell what would happen if the ice gave way. He'd read that sometimes the ice thinned and closed like this just before a clearing, almost like a river delta. All we could do was try to break free.

The icy sun circled and soon it became apparent that we'd have to start working in shifts. We had to break free. If we abandoned ship, who would come for us? We'd have to haul overland to McMurdo, yet even if we made it, there might be no one left there. How could we survive the winter? But after another day of hopeless digging we began to think harder about leaving the boat. At a meeting Evans said there were probably shacks from previous expeditions on the ice shelf, and even if McMurdo had been abandoned, there would likely still be buildings there. If we made it, we could live on penguins and seals until they left in the austral autumn. There might yet be some unhatched eggs. And some of the meat would keep frozen. We'd then have our own supplies for the long winter. In the following spring we'd try to come back for the boat.

El didn't like it. "It's suicide," she said.

"We might have already committed it," said Angie.

Captain Evans agreed with El. "Until the last minute, the boat is all we have," he said.

We went back to digging at the ice pack. Now, even I was permitted to help. We dug a wedge in front of the boat. Often we tried to push the boat backwards, off the ice, when it seemed we had loosened the hold, but each time the boat rocked forward as the ocean closed in behind us and pushed the boat. After a week of digging, the hull sat even higher on the pack. And in another week, even if we broke free, we'd barely have time for the run to Ross Island before trying to flee ahead of the short autumn and the winter freezing of the Ross Sea.

Yet early the next day, even before the first shift went out on the ice, the air vibrated with a moan from below. The ice in front of us began to crack and our boat surged forward. The ice pack fell open and suddenly we were in open sea. Evans steered us out from between the floes as we swept west under the great barrier of the Ross Ice Shelf, its glimmering cliffs towering above us, glaring white over the blue sea. As quickly as we'd once been doomed, we were free and sailing for Ross Island and McMurdo.

The Story of Werther Fausten
continued by Hestor Zu

January 2, 2018 / Amundsen-Scott / South Pole

I have taken the liberty of recording the following events in the name of inquiry and in an attempt to bring Fausten's story to some kind of close. However one wishes to interpret the collapse of the technological world, the fact remains that it has collapsed. Here at Amundsen-Scott we barely made it through the Antarctic winter. We abandoned all of our out-buildings; all experimental laboratories, all exterior livestock sheds and biospheres, and consolidated our existence inside the base's original geodesic dome. There was little anymore that we did not do together, eat, sleep, or even think, so that we could sustain small areas with our own body heat. What little petroleum we had was used to power our main generator for heat, and to light an interior green house where we grew bulk vegetation, mostly various kinds of beans. Our supplies of grain and dry pack food are now extremely low. Our livestock is dead.

Though we'd adapted the technology on Fausten's power sledge to our own generator—his actual equipment was too small for us to use—our battery technology was simply not good enough. Further, there is not enough diesel to power both heat and light for another winter, not enough solar power collectible during the summer. Kevnev has experimented with some wind mills, but it is debatable that we can build anything sturdy enough to stand up to the katabatic winds, the horrible downdrafts that scream off the glaciers at over a hundred miles an hour. If we had been prepared to survive on our own on Mars for nine months, we cannot survive two winters alone on the South Pole.

I made all of these points in debate held in the tiny mess hall. There were forty of us there, not counting Werther Fausten: twenty members from the original polar base crew, fifteen astronauts and five support scientists, one of whom was Adjoa Neri-Evans, my friend and our medical doctor.

I argued that we could adapt Fausten's new generator technology to a tractor, or maybe even two. Along with Fausten's sledge we could pull twelve to fifteen sled carts of supplies, as well as rest ten to fifteen of the traveling group while the others kept pace on cross country skis. Our failures to produce an infrastructure for continued human survival here prove that we have already stayed too long into the Antarctic summer. We should leave soon, while the weather is still good. If we make good time, thirty kilometers a day, we can reach McMurdo on Ross Island by the middle of February. Even at half that speed we would arrive by the end of March, still summer. If there was no one left at McMurdo, it would still put us on the ocean, in a warmer climate near fish and game, with time to set up for winter in the abandoned facility which was the largest Antarctic outpost. It would give us the chance to signal a boat.

Though a number of people spoke, the main argument arose between Kevnev and me.

"What if there is nothing at McMurdo," insisted Kevnev. "What if it is like here, or worse."

"The winter is milder there. Our only chance to be rescued here is by plane, and there are no planes. McMurdo is accessible by sea. A boat could find us, or we could build a boat."

"Who knows how to build a boat out of building scraps? One that could negotiate the ice floes? And who knows that there are no planes?" said Kevnev.

"Kevnev, there are animals near the shore during the summer. There are penguins and penguin eggs, shore birds, sea lions, fish."

"The great animal lover," said Kevnev, waving his arms at me. "The vegetarian."

"This is survival, Kevnev."

"Yes," he replied. "Exactly! Here we know what we have and have what we know. Out there, we have nothing and know nothing about it. We have been trained to stay put and survive. We have been trained to survive on Mars!"

"On Mars we could make our own fuel. Here we will run out."

"We were not trained to travel across the Antarctic waste," said Kevnev. "The first rule in a crisis like this is to stay put! So if they come looking for us, we will be *here*, where we are supposed to be."

"And who will come looking for us? Who *can* come looking for us?" I asked.

"The Russians, for one," he said. "It is likely we will not even have to survive the winter. Someone will come. It is not the end of the world. We are here, alive, on the South Pole. If we are alive here, then there are millions alive everywhere. Nations, great nations have invested in us. There are Chinese here, Japanese, French, Germans, an Italian, a Canadian, a Swede," he looked around the room, "and Americans, too. Only eighteen months ago a plane brought in the last of you. Everything is not gone since then. Someone will come for us. To race across the ice into nothingness, carrying everything on our backs, that is madness."

It was then that Werther Fausten entered the room. He'd wrapped his parka around his hospital gown, yet his shins were bare down to his shabby socks that he must have retrieved from the chest near his bed. His hair and beard were long and wild, and now mostly white and gray. He took in the stares of this group, these scientists, his fellow prisoners. Most of them had never seen him and only heard of his presence at the lab. He was a kind of rumor, the mad man found raving on the ice. Even as he stood in front of them there was no reason to believe that this wreckage of a man was, in fact, Werther Fausten, the Nobel scientist whose work had helped bring us here. Even so, there were enough people who found Fausten's latest work to be bizarre theory, too far on the edge of science to be science. It was speculation, science fiction, fantasy.

"I could not help but overhear," Fausten said. He gathered in the packed room. "I've seen that look before. Timidity in the face of new and challenging ideas. Now that your lives are at stake, when you reach inside, that's all you have."

Kevnev reproached him immediately. "What kind of cowards would have placed themselves at the edge of the world to prepare for two years in outer space?"

"Your kind," said Fausten, which drew a muffled laugh from the room, despite the situation. "You can't radio home, Mr. Kevnev. No one has built you a rocket ship and laid out your game plan. There's no food and fuel ready and waiting at your destination. Nobody is giving you orders." He stumbled as he walked to the center of the room. He needed a cane, a staff like an Old Testament prophet. "I've been out there more recently than any of you. Government is a myth holding together loose bands of agricultural communities. The cities are in anarchy, even if surprisingly benevolent. The coast has been reduced to fishing villages and ports reminiscent of the Middle Ages. Armies have been stripped of their mechanized weapons, navies devastated. I have not seen a plane in a year. You won't survive here unless you can do it for a long, long time."

His gaze ran the room. "Are you not the best? Are you not the last of the best? The fittest? The brightest of your nations? Wouldn't your survival, your leadership, be vital to what is left of humanity when it comes time to rebuild? Yet you shall sit under a dome at the bottom of the world and wait for your deaths, like plants before the frost. So much for intelligence, for creativity, for bravery."

"Brave men and women will wait here," said Kevnev. "Here are the best odds of survival, of rescue. And though you may choose to vote with your bodies and run foolishly to where there is no food and no shelter, I am, in fact, yet in charge. I am giving orders, and my orders are to stay."

Fausten held the bridge of his nose between the thumb and index finger of his left hand. He swayed, then caught himself. He looked at me. I saw his eyes dance with fire. I say this, as yet to this day incredulous, that in his pupils danced the fiery beast of his mind's eye. Yet without an utterance of caution from me I saw that he was in full control and understood that to speak of his dragon, to utter his ultimate truth, would be to doom his argument and everyone else in the room. His altruism and clarity never showed more plainly through his madness.

"Take your lives in your hands!" said Fausten. "You can survive on the coast. A sailing ship might come. Here there is no hope. To survive here is a daydream, which is all that is left of our old world, our technological world, our world under one God, whether benevolent or cruel. You must dream real dreams. You must step into the white nightmare outside if you have any hope of living."

After the silence, Kevnev stepped forward again. "We'll vote," he said, "though my orders shall remain the same."

"Do I get a vote?" said Fausten.

Kevnev hesitated.

"Even if I am the deciding one?" Fausten said.

"I am the deciding vote," Kevnev said.

I met Kevnev's eyes then. He had been my commander here. My friend. I saw his conviction to do what was right, saw his deep, Russian obstinacy to hold on, to resist, stay put, not surrender. It had worked a dozen notable times in Russian history, at Moscow, at Stalingrad, on MIR. I felt, at that moment, almost swayed by his steadiness. And stood disconcerted, ready to vote for insanity and risk on the side of a mad man. It mattered little. The vote went 37-4 to stay, with Fausten, myself, and only two others voting to leave.

Kevnev took his victory with humility. "This was no triumph," he said to me quietly before addressing the meeting. "It is a cruel choice with dismal consequence."

"Is that an old Russian saying?" I said.

"I wish it were," he replied. He told the group we would meet tomorrow to organize the winter fortress. "But this is no tyranny," he said. "Like the Americans—the American Indians—those of you who wish to go are free. Choose your own leader and take only what is yours."

Adjoa Neri-Evans and I helped Fausten back to the small infirmary. Now he was silent and brooding again, but for my part I needed to find out who the other two votes were besides his and mine, though it wasn't difficult. Paulo, my Italian friend, had followed us back.

"Adjoa," I said.

"Yes," she said, "I voted to go. But I'm the doctor. I have a duty here. I can't leave thirty-seven people without a doctor."

"Paulo."

"I voted to support you," he said.

"But you won't leave with me."

"Two people and a mad man alone on the ice? And then what? Hestor, think it through." He raised his palms. "There are worse deaths than freezing together with your crew."

"You will not freeze," interrupted Fausten suddenly. "You shall not freeze! The beast will take you! Fire and ice! I am the only reason you have survived, because she waits to fight me. When we fight for the fate of the world, here on the bottom of the planet, it will be only she and I left!" He stopped when he saw their incredulity.

"And he isn't fit to travel anywhere, let alone over 800 miles of ice," said Adjoa.

"I'll decide tonight," I said. I gave Adjoa a hug, and then Paulo. I thanked them. Then turned to face those deadly hours of decision with the mad genius who was my last ally and companion.

The Story of Werther Fausten
continued by Hestor Zu

January 4, 2018

That night Fausten laid his argument before me.

"Zu," he said, "whether by dragon or winter, this place will not survive."

"Not even if you stay?"

"Even if I stay. But I shall not stay. And whatever your choice, I shall leave tomorrow. But you have been my friend. Though you would not have chosen to have my insanity placed at your feet, you've listened impartially. I have always admired your work. Now I admire you more. If you choose survival, I can take you across the shelf safely."

"Can you?" I said. "You're barely well."

"I am here. I am proof."

"That logic is specious."

"Nonetheless, I am here and you have only my story to support my claims. Zu, there is no reason for me travel across the Ice Shelf with you when I can end everything here and now. Let me save your life and anyone else who will come."

"No one else will come."

"Then let me save you."

"You haven't been to McMurdo," I said to him. "You don't know if anyone is there."

"We can't go to McMurdo. There is no one left."

"How do you know?"

"I know," he said.

"Are you prescient, Fausten?" I said.

"I no longer deny the possibility of clairvoyance, but I am not prescient. McMurdo was the largest, most complex of the Antarctic bases. It would have been the first to go. Remember, Ferzi had not been asked to make the trip in years. I will take you to where I made land on the Bay of Whales. You can survive there. It's been done before."

"I must go to McMurdo," I said to him. "That's where any rescue mission would go."

He sat quietly.

"Or I will stay here," I said.

"This base will not survive the winter, Dr. Hestor Zu. Whether or not I am insane does not change the facts. They have been obvious to you for a long time."

Now it was my turn to be quiet.

"Do you dream, Zu?" he said.

"Yes," I said. "I dream of my dog. I dream of my husband. I dream of making love to him. And I dream of a ship."

"Dream of a ship," he said. "I think that will be of some help."

"Dreaming didn't help your wife."

"Zu," he shouted, "I am not promising you eternal life! I am offering my protection. I have crossed the shelf! Whether you believe in the beast or not, I have survived in the Antarctic. I will take you to McMurdo. And when we find it deserted, *then* we will cross the shelf to the Bay of Whales. I owe you this. But there I must leave you to return here, because whether or not you die or are rescued, when I am the last human being on this continent, then the future of the world shall be settled!"

We stood silent again. He supported himself on his bed.

"Why am I offering to do this?" he said.

"Are you asking me?"

"No," he murmured. "No, I am not."

"Do you dream, Fausten?" I said.

"My dreams," he uttered. "My dreams are alive. My nightmare stalks the world."

He watched me. "Enough abstraction. Take me to the tractor garage. Let's look at my sledge and supplies."

We dressed in parkas and crossed through the cold, back corridors of the dome to the depot, a walk which seemed to give him strength the closer we got to his things. By the time we reached his sledge his body suddenly pulsed with energy and the blood rose in his cheeks as he touched the trident that rode in a holster on the right side of the machine.

He was, in fact, well equipped. The sledge was a marvel of engineering with every system backed up with an equivalent. He had extra parts, stores of dry pack, two excellent butane stoves for heat as well as cooking; they could also be adapted to run off the flywheel of his sledge generator. His shelter was made of the latest super-polymers and expanded into a structured dome with several layers of air insulation.

"You will need your own clothes. Two sets of everything, especially mittens," Fausten said. "And dry-boots. A dry-suit, as well, if you have one. Do you?"

"Yes," I said. "There's an emergency land route supply trail between here and McMurdo. The depots are marked with flags."

"Yes, I'm sure there is," he said. "Still, bring your share of food. Your knife. There is a harpoon, fishing gear, a cross bow and arrows at my bay camp. You needn't take anything else from here, except for your dreams."

That night, or in what amounted to the night under the unremitting, cold, summer sun which I could not see from under the dome, I prepared my gear. Besides food and clothes, I brought a digital recorder, paper and pencils, a picture of my husband, Charles. I went to Paulo Clemente and wished him luck. He ran his hands through his black hair. I remember his face that morning so well, his scant beard and brooding brow.

"I wish you would stay," he said.

"I wish I could stay, too," I told him.

"I'd give you a rosary, but I hear such things attract the dragon," he said, and smiled a little.

Then I took my leave of Kevnev. "There are no more animals here," he said. "I guess we don't need you anymore. You are relieved of duty." Impossibly, we laughed. "You have been a good colleague."

"I'll bring you back some vodka," I said.

"Potato vodka. None of that fermented grain."

We shook hands.

"Good luck, Dr. Zu," Kevnev said.

And finally, my friend, Adjoa Neri-Evans. We held each other's hands. In my mind right now, I see her face, as pale and brown as an eclipsed moon, her eyes like soft obsidian.

"Why do I feel I should be with you?" she said.

"Because we've become friends."

"Where I was born, in Los Angeles, Africans and Asians fought about everything."

"Not in Antarctica."

"No." She tried to smile. "It seems so absurd. Here you are, and then in a little while I will never see you again."

And then I asked her the question that Fausten had asked me. A question that, despite our friendship, I had never before asked. For if the world really had been forever changed, each of us was still our own center of it. And in this new world, our depth, our privacy, had become more personal than sex. In that way Fausten was right. For most people now the nightmare stalked us from without. Our deepest fears lay at our fingertips, our hopes waxed with the beat of our hearts. There was little need for any of it to lurk in our sleep. And its sacred absence was something unspeakable.

"Do you dream?" I said.

"Yes," she whispered.

"Dream of me. And I will dream of you." And we both wept.

Then I met Fausten in the garage where he stood miraculously healthy and ready. We opened the hatch and drove into the sucking, bitter cold, the blinding light.

"I hope they make it through," I said. "I hope they live. I would rather I fail and they all lived."

"You must forget them now," Fausten said to me over his shoulder. "They are doomed."

That night I dreamt a fire dropped in a column from the sky and the dome exploded. I had looked over my shoulder from the sledge and saw the smoke and fire rising from the pole. But in the morning I couldn't remember, couldn't recall if it were a dream or real.

"It's irrelevant now," said Fausten as we packed our gear. That day, I drove the sledge. And I heard him behind me. He groaned. "She will call it a mercy killing."

Hestor Zu and Werther Fausten

Ross Ice Shelf / January 2018

It is no longer just Fausten's story. It has become my story as well. We crossed the Transantarctic Mountains through the Queen Maude Pass and made our way into the Ross Ice Shelf. Fausten was right, the Bay of Whales was much closer from there and our route would have been in the lee of the West Antarctic land mass. Still, traveling on the windward side of the Queen Maude Range, we would only be susceptible to the katabatic winds when we crossed over the Nimrod and Byrd Glaciers. We moved through the endless Antarctic days over the endless plains of ice, the only mark of time the dip and rise of the circling sun, the days broken only by time lost crossing ridges and circumnavigating ice canyons. Holding to the compass we came to the first depot, a red flag flicking above it against the blinding snow.

"You see," Fausten whispered then, "we are taken care of."

"It's an emergency land-route depot," I said to him. "I told you about them. That's why we're following this course."

"Who permits it to exist?" murmured Fausten. "If she stopped thinking of us for one second, we would slip out of sight. We live at her caprice."

After several days in, Fausten's health began to change again. Now he often seemed fatigued if not oblivious. Yet he somehow steadied himself between delirium and acuity.

In those days I came to know this man with greater intimacy than I have known anyone, but for Charles. Either behind him on the sledge, my hands on his hips, or he behind me, his chest on my back, his thighs pressed to my thighs. In the shelter, the wind howling about us, we lay body to body, at times breath to breath, though for the longest time we held to the barest of conversation, a comment on the wind, the sun, the path ahead; a request for help in setting the shelter poles, melting ice for water, sharing food.

Then, in a storm, we did not find the second depot.

"Have we lost our way?" I said.

A wind rose out of the southwest and it was evident that soon we would be engulfed in a storm.

I insisted, "We must take shelter."

Fausten was driving then and quickly bore off course, south, into the wind.

"Fausten," I yelled into his ear. "We will die out here!"

Yet he persisted into the storm. Almost blind from the drifting snow, we came upon an ice ridge that curled from the wind and allowed us to camp in its lee. We quickly set camp and went into the shelter as the storm raged. Though little snow falls in Antarctica, the tremendous winds can create blinding walls of snow. That night, the storm raged over the drift and Fausten began to rave. He ran a fever.

"She dreams us!" he raved.

I wrapped him in everything we had and pressed him to me. Whether or not he died and left me on my own, there was greater chance that the morning would find us buried.

"Zu!" he screamed. "Zu! What if she is right? What if we are the worst of the animals? What if we are a devolution? A disease?"

"You have a fever."

"I am the heat of her breath."

I slapped him. I rubbed ice on his forehead and on his face. "It is irrelevant," I said to him. "We have our lives to save. And when you give up your delusions you'll realize that there still is a world to save, which you can do with your knowledge and your genius, but only if you stay sane, only if you live."

He focused on me. "I am sane, Zu," he said.

I did not sleep. Though when Fausten finally did, it was as if a warm palm had cupped itself over the shelter. In the morning the snow lay around us in high, curving walls, out to the mouth of our shelter and leading to our sledge, and beyond from there, out, a tunnel of ice in the contour of the drift.

"You see," said Fausten when he awoke to the spectacle.

"It follows the contour of the ridge," I said. "It was a brilliant move, Fausten. We camped perfectly under the wing of the wind."

"Yes," he said. "Under a wing."

That day, we stumbled upon a depot, though unlike the last in which all the supplies were marked as American, this outpost held an assembly of odd sundries from a dozen countries, like Japanese soap, French toilettes, a bottle of Australian wine.

"As if dropped from the sky," Fausten mumbled. "But I'd think we should take the wine."

In those long days of hard travel and feverish nights, I sometimes felt the fool, the atheist who denied God's wonders, as if we were two mad philosophers traveling in the jungle who found a strange patch of apparently cared-for vegetation and we were to spend our lives watching and arguing whether or not an invisible or omniscient gardener came and tended it whenever we turned our backs. In those times, when I found Fausten's chides like the sophomoric utterances of a megalomaniac teen-ager, I reminded myself not to judge his genius, his work, his life, by this, his fevered raving during perilous frailty. I, too, had become not myself, something other. I found myself dreaming even as I drove the sledge and even now these words come to me as if erupting from some soul not my own.

We drove onward in the blur of eternal day or huddled together whispering to each other in monologues, speaking only from ourselves and to our own ears, each ignoring the other as the wind howled outside our frail shelter. In moments I came to believe, as Fausten did, in our fragile invulnerability, as if we were protected and guided by a personal hand. Other times, I saw my death so plainly that its cold breath was threatless and banal and my life stretched out behind me and before me like the glaciers upon the ice shelf. Yet we survived.

And Fausten was right. In just over six weeks we were nearing Ross Island. Before us, smoldering in the sky, the plumes of Mount Erebus, and farther away, to our right, another volcanic cloud. It would have to be Mount Terror which had been dormant since its discovery. Even days away the ash from the two volcanoes fell upon us, coating the ice.

"She is not happy with me," said Fausten.

But I made him continue until we stood on the shore of the Ross Strait, the volcanoes pouring out thunderously, their lavender and scarlet plumes darkening the sky. From the heat off the volcanoes and the rivers of lava the ice had given way in the strait between the shelf and the island, leaving only fissured bergs and tenuous ice floes. McMurdo lay somber beneath the ash, like a graveyard, and to the east, the New Zealand Scott Base was the same. Wordlessly we traveled along the shelf, looking for an isthmus of ice to cross over, without luck. Even as we did, the first tremors of the ice shelf itself threatening to break up forced us away from the coast. We looped inland, heading for the Bay of Whales.

"They are dead," I said to him that night. Whatever the reality of the collapse of Amundsen-Scott and our loss of contact with the world, I had somehow failed to link Fausten's story with reality, as if denying his ravings about his mythical dragon also denied the reality of this apocalypse. "Is it the end of everything?"

"The beginning of the end. The end of the reign of man," said Fausten, though I hardly expected him to respond.

"Why are you taking me to the Bay of Whales? Why didn't you just let me die with the others?"

"There are boats. One brought me here." He heated water and opened a packet of dry bean and corn stew. It had been weeks since he had the presence to do such a simple thing, as if somehow having his world vision proven at McMurdo brought him into credulity with himself. "People will live here again, like Eskimos. Their rhythms will rise and fall with the endless day of summer and endless winter night. They will worship the orcas and the elephant seals, leopard seals, Weddell seals; the albatross, the petrel, the skua, emperor and king penguins, the sperm whale, the fin, the minke, the blue, the southern right, the bottlenose. They will have a hundred different names for ice and snow." He stirred the small pot in front of us and bowed his head. "I thank the plants that grew this corn, these beans," he said. "They are God." He looked at me again. "I've learned this from her, though it has not been worth the price. We would have come to this on our own. In any case, do we thank Satan for the gift of death, of grace, of salvation, of sin? Maybe the planet is better off without mankind. But I do not think so. Is that madness?"

"And will the dragon be worshipped?"

He looked at me. "Rebuild, Zu. I will slay the dragon."

And I answered him. "All the worse."

In the coming days he fell into fever again. He cursed. He raged. We crossed the shelf until reaching a small shack just northwest of Roosevelt Island, still frozen in the Ross Ice Shelf.

"Do you see?" screamed Fausten. "Do you see? It was here, waiting for me! And it is still here."

But the shack was not at the coordinates he designated. Old beakers and Bunsen burners still sat on the shelves. There was a kerosene heater long in disuse. It looked like descriptions of Little America, one of the winter base camps of Richard Byrd. There were some very old pots and pans, but no weapons, no cross bow or harpoons.

"How will we survive here Fausten? It's March. Winter is near."

"You mean *you*, Zu. I shall survive on my own somewhere else."

"There is no equipment for fishing or hunting. How long can the dry pack last?" I said to him.

"I have greater concerns than your survival!" he screamed. "There is the future of the world. The whole world!"

"We don't even know what is left of the world."

"I know! What has been and what will be is in *my* hands! Do not tell me. Do not attempt to tell me! I am the one who has brought you here, Zu. I have saved you. If it is not the dragon who is your god, then it is me!"

"Fausten," I whispered, it was almost a prayer, though I couldn't guess to whom. "Fausten, be sane."

"There is nothing sane left!"

"We must be able to fashion some of the wood from this shack into spears."

"More. Always more!" He glared at me. "My promise," he said.

Then he staggered from the shack and disappeared into a rising gust of snow-laden wind and I heard the grind of the departing sledge.

It was not the first or last time I marked my hours by counting my breaths. What would I do now? In these late days of summer there was a brief period when the sun descended and in that darkness, that brief dusk, came the overwhelming despair of my futility. How much better it might have been to die with the others, if they were in fact dead. I had followed a mad man over the ice continent for two months to end my life unrealized, my death unrecorded, to settle down on the edge of nothing, to live out my end as nothing, to die as nothing, to have ever been nothing.

Then as the brief dusk became the dawn, Fausten returned. He carried a harpoon and cross bow, fishing tackle. On the sledge was a slain Weddell seal which we skinned and gutted, then packed in the ice.

"You can walk to the coast from here," he said. "There's landfall and harbor just to the northeast. The battery will run out on your laser flare."

"Yes," I said. "There are more. The old kind. Thank you, Werther Fausten."

"I must rest," he said.

Fausten collapsed on the small bunk and fell into exhaustion, then fever. He raged and sweat, shivered and raved for three days while I did what I could to keep him cool, then warm, to try to keep him fed. In between, I sent the laser beacon up at four hour intervals. It became a hopeless clock.

Now Fausten was on his way to fight his dragon where, I imagine, he always fought her, in his mind, his dreams, his depths. He cried out that he was her creator, the maker and haven of Satan, and where were his followers, his Christ, his Archangel Michael, his host of scientist angels to meet the army of dreams? If the world was now more holy, it was also now more dangerous, more evil, a world of grace and despair, hope and sin. World without God! World without knowledge! The dragon's world, because she has sucked out our dreams and now they walk among us! A world of sorcery and magic, filled with the worship of ghosts and beasts! "World without end!" he screamed. "World without end!" And slipped into his final coma. There was no calm moment, no last sane word, no gift of final awareness or clarity. Fausten died in his sleep, insane.

The following day I took the sledge down the edge of the shelf. To the east, a sand beach had formed off the shoals and elephant seals had come to molt, give birth, and breed. The pups were almost three months old, the larger ones already weighing as much as three hundred pounds. There were few nursing females left and fewer large bulls. They were heading back to the sea. Most of the females had already weaned and abandoned their pups, leaving them to enter the sea and make it on their own. The young seals lay in pods of twenty to twenty-five, crying out for their mothers. It is a bleating much louder and more sustained than the cry they give while nursing. I knew that only about three in twenty survived the year. I went out of my way to take several of the smallest and weakest. Even better than the harpoon for taking them, was the trident.

I returned to the shack where I skinned and gutted the pups, then packed them in ice in front of the shack. Then I went inside and retrieved Werther Fausten and buried him in the back. I launched a laser flare. Was I the last living human being on Antarctica? Maybe Werther's dragon would come for me. But she did not.

The days have eked on. It has been almost two weeks since Fausten's death. I find it impossible to think of him or to think beyond the bitterness of my circumstance. Yet I tell myself that I was trained to travel in space for nine months, to live on Mars for a year and return, trained, if need be, due to calamity and death, to complete that mission on my own, on the loneliness of a dead planet, in the black vacuum of space. Knowing my mission, I can survive alone indefinitely. But what is my mission now? How long can I survive here without hope?

At times it feels as if the whole ice shelf is trembling. Or is it me? The battery died on the laser flare and I have begun launching conventional flares. I have almost two hundred. If I set them off at twelve hour intervals, I must hope that a boat cruising the shelf for survivors will at least wait that long, if not launch a party to the shore. In only a few weeks, the short autumn will set in and then, quickly, the dark, long, bitter winter. The sea outside the shelf will freeze. I won't need flares then, unless and until I survive. Then I can launch two a day from December through February, and then I shall be out. It will hardly matter. Whatever the odds of surviving the Antarctic winter alone, I will not survive two. If I face that, then a year from now I will take my own life.

For now, that is my story. I am not a writer. I will not write again. Soon I must place myself in the cocoon of survival, a state of stillness close to hibernation. If I see the spring I shall ready for my last effort. If I see another autumn, I shall make my final statement, likely undiscovered by a quieted humanity, a silent earth. How absurd that I continue to write. Yet I wish to say this for myself. For whom else? Charles Borromeo, I have loved you more than my own life. How could you have let me leave you? How could I have left? I love you. I died with your name on my lips.

The Dragon Journal of Lisa Piccolo Zu

Briefly we again felt the glory of the open sea. What a strange thing to yearn for. As we moved past the ice floes, huge colonies of Adelie penguins, like cities of birds on the ice, watched us pass. And the giant Emperors and squawking Kings. Albatross circled above us, orcas below. Weddell seals croaked at us from the icebergs and leopard seals, mouths gaping, swam at out hull. Whales surfaced amid pools of krill, so many different kinds of whales that I couldn't name them all. Life. Everywhere there was life.

"They feed on each other," El said to me, to dampen my innocent enthusiasm.

"In a month it will be winter and they'll all be somewhere else," said Evans.

"Yes," I said. "Somewhere else."

But the adults, who were trying to caution my youthful optimism, were only hiding their own hopes. In a day we sighted the double plumes of Mount Erebus and Mount Terror on Ross Island. Until then, Erebus had been only mildly active and Terror extinct. Now they poured smoke and ash into the sky. As we approached the island, we could see that the ice shelf had broken into a thick mash of floes from the heat of the lava. Ash from the volcanoes fell upon the ship as we floated on the frozen and boiling sea. McMurdo was inapproachable.

Still, Evans had us circle, trying to find a way into the Ross Sound and into the strait, trying to find open sea or solid ice between the shelf and ocean, some way to McMurdo, but we could get nowhere within sight of the base. In vain, Nigel tried to radio into the nothingness. We sailed east again, circling back to the other side. Now it was March.

In a meeting of the crew, Evans suggested that we head back through the openings in the floes, to the Bay of Whales, and try to make land there, reaching McMurdo by hauling over the ice shelf.

"Winter will set in and trap us on the shelf," said Angie. "And we could lose the boat if it gets locked in the ice. We should head back to New Zealand and try again in the spring." She held AJ's hand. It had been a long time since anybody had cut their hair and now Angie's dark curls poured around her head like black wool. AJ looked thin and tired, her dirty blonde hair tied back, she wore a black, wool shoreman's cap. Those two had given Evans a lot.

"Your lives," said Evans in a whisper. He looked around the room. "I barely realized that I was asking you to risk your lives."

But everybody was way beneath that kind of abstract emotion. Soon the room was inflamed with debate about whether or not we should vote and if we did, whether or not I should be given one.

"She's risked her life as much as anyone, she should vote," said El.

"She'll vote with you," said Nigel, avoiding Evans' eyes.

But there was no one on board now, besides the captain, me and El, who had a reason to press on. You couldn't ask the crew or the Chilean men.

Evans surveyed the room. "We have time to make it back to the Bay of Whales," he said. "After we put ashore, if I decide to stay you can take the ship and come back for me in the spring."

And so we turned back across the face of the Ice Shelf once again, for the Bay of Whales.

That evening, in the short dusk, I stood with El on the deck, the ship gliding between the gray bergs, the ocean black beneath us.

"We should sleep," said El. She put her arm around my waist and pulled me to her.

"We have eternity for sleep," I said.

"The voice of youth," she laughed.

"We're going to find Grandma Zu," I said.

"Where?"

"In the only place where we can find her. In the only place where she can be."

She gazed to the west. "It will barely be dark," she said, "and yet it is the most depressing thing in the world. The harbinger of total darkness."

"El," I said. "Did you know that the ocean dreams? Did you know it can hear itself crashing on the shore, against the cliffs at Big Sur, off the Australian reefs? How much life is inside it? What must it think to give so much?"

"Does the darkness think?" she said to me.

"It feels us, El. It feels us inside it. Otherwise we wouldn't exist and it wouldn't exist either. That's our duty now, to feel everything, don't you think?"

"And to think what?" she said.

"Whatever we want. Thinking is overrated."

"Nice thought," said El. "And how about what the ocean thinks."

"It doesn't think like we do. El, I can't explain it."

El held me closer. "Lisa, everyone who has lived, has died," she said. "And everyone who has died once felt as much love and hope and meaning as we do now."

"Hope and meaning don't mean much," I said to her. "There's something deeper."

"Or nothing at all," said El.

"But El." I said. "We're here!"

El kissed my forehead. "I hope I haven't sacrificed my child," she whispered.

"For Grandma Zu and Grandpa Charles, El," I said to her. "Besides, we're both way bigger than sacrifice."

"Don't lecture me," El said. She took me by the shoulders. "Lisa," she said to me. "Lisa, I'm thinking real. And whatever else, you must think real enough to stay alive. If you are a goddess in your dreams, you are still a child, and my child."

I guess I was being kind of single-minded and undeterred. Good old El, the Motherist.

Soon we passed from the open sea and back into the ice floes. Away from the volcanoes things were normal again, the water liquid and the ice solid, the sea less churning. Yet if Angie was worried about being frozen in, Evans worried about the opposite. Even as the days shortened and cooled, huge calves still broke from the glaciers on the barrier and at times it seemed as if the whole shelf shimmered and trembled.

As we crawled through the floes it seemed as if we sailed through our own sadness. Whatever anger and fear that people had aired at the meeting, no one actually had said that it looked impossible for anyone to survive at McMurdo. On the cusp of winter, we were sailing away from our destination toward a last hope, to a place where there were no bases anymore, where no people stayed, just so we could touch the land, touch the continent, get ashore and shout to our loved ones, Here we are! We came, after all! We're here! We love you and we're here! We've come all this way, where are you? Then maybe we could get rid of some of this sadness. If El wondered whether Captain Evans would really stay, I knew he would for exactly those reasons. It wasn't like our search for Grandma Zu. Evans would die trying to find his wife, Adjoa, or die as close to her as he could.

When we finally sailed into the Bay of Whales a storm swept in. Then almost directly south of us, through the snow and clouds, it seemed for a moment that something red flickered in the sky. I wasn't the only one who saw it. Evans did, too. Though the storm picked up ferociously, Evans didn't want to move into the lee of a berg for fear of losing sight of the shore. When we couldn't hold storm anchor, he turned the boat into the wind and we battened down to sit it out, with Evans determined to stay atop to steer and watch the obscure shore, even now barely visible through the wind and snow. Already the halyards and lifelines were lined with ice. But just as the rest of us prepared to go below, a powerful gust of wind turned us starboard to the storm and a huge swell broke over the boat, laying us forty-five degrees into the sea and setting the deck awash. AJ, who wasn't tied down because she was securing the mainsail, was swept from the ship.

Angie screamed as the boat came to, but then we were hit again and the sea flew into the open hatches, taking me with it, washing me down below into the storage hull. I hit the bottom of the boat hard, sloshing in the water, then swung in the air by the rope on my belt, the sway of the ship knocking me against everything. I heard Evans yelling and then El. Angie was screaming and screaming. I cut myself from my tie down and crashed into the soupy floor of the hull. I found some sacks of rice which had been secured to the walls and crawled onto them. I heard El again, and Angie. That's all I remember.

The storm lasted three days, though I wasn't conscious for most of it. El said I had a concussion. The rest of me ached pretty badly, too. AJ was gone. No one sighted her during the storm and now she'd been three days in the frozen sea. When Angie came to see me we both cried and cried. When I went above, outside, under the calm, cold sun, the shelf shined blindingly, the ocean lapping against it now with its crash and push. Captain Evans stared out to it. "We'll wait here a day," he said. And we did. But we saw nothing.

That night Evans said we'd go ashore on the Edward VII Peninsula, through the Prestrud Inlet of Okuma Bay, just to the south. El, who was one of the few people who could really talk to him, because she had something at stake, too, pressed him not to stay.

"Even if you make it to McMurdo, even if there is someone there—"

"Adjoa?" he said.

"You can't make a difference. Not until spring."

"What are you going to do?" asked Evans.

"Return in the spring," El said.

"I'll be waiting for you then," he said.

Just south of the Bay of Whales the floes broke and we moved into open sea. Ahead the black shore of the peninsula jutted from the ice like a ragged tongue. Just below the cliffs was a sandy cove where the last elephant seal pups of the season huddled together, a circle of black and silver, squirming life, as tentative about approaching the ocean as we now were about approaching land.

We set anchor and lowered the long boat in the lee of the ship to protect us from the choppy ocean that was churning under the wind swooping off the coast. It was going to be Evans and Angie, me and El. We climbed in and set to the oars, two on each. But as we came around the bow Nigel, who held binoculars, yelled out. There was something on the bluff above. A machine. Then as we approached the shore I could see the lone figure on the beach. We had found Grandma Hestor Zu.

The Dragon Journal of Lisa Piccolo Zu

"So," said Grandma Zu when we came ashore. "Will Miracles never cease?"

She looked so tiny, standing there with a big, forked spear, her dark face barely peering out of her parka. El hugged her and hugged her. Then Grandma Zu hugged me.

"What's that?" I said, pointing to her tall, forked spear.

"A long story," she said. "Your arrival saved a seal, though I doubt many of these will live. There are a lot of orcas and sharks waiting."

"Why are you here?" El said. "Where is everyone else?"

Grandma Zu stood there silently. She blinked a few times. "You really are here," she said. "I am not dreaming."

"You might be dreaming, but it's us," I told her.

El introduced Captain Evans and Angie and Grandma held Evans' hand for a long time. "She's not with me," Grandma finally said to him.

"McMurdo?" Evans said.

"There's nothing at McMurdo. It's buried in ash, though it was probably destroyed or abandoned or both long before that." She looked at us all again, then looked down to the boat, and then out to sea where the ship was anchored. "So there is still a world," she whispered.

"Adjoa," said Evans to Grandma Zu.

"She stayed at Amundsen-Scott," said my grandmother. "She was the doctor."

"You made this trip alone?" said Angie.

"Not alone. But I am alone now."

We all stood there. Captain Evans was really shaken. We hadn't expected to find anyone. Now that we did, his disappointment was even greater. He stood on the edge of the continent now, eight hundred miles of mountains and ice and the Antarctic winter between him and Adjoa Neri-Evans.

"Could she be alive?" Evans said.

Grandma Zu looked at him with quiet, narrow eyes. Now, in our silence, all you could hear was the ocean rushing the shore and the wail of the abandoned seal pups. "She was my best friend there," she finally said. "She stayed because she was the doctor, though she voted to leave with me."

After some quiet again Evans said, "Let's get you on board."

"I have to go back to my camp," said Grandma Zu. "To gather some things. Come with me," she said. She looked to her big sledge atop the bluff and then at us again. "Well, I can take two of you. Go back to your boat, Captain. My camp is only an hour away. Take your ship into that cove. I've seen the mother elephant seals shelter there. The smartest ones. Their pups can get into the water without facing the rip tide. Though the great whites and killer whales know that, too." She stopped. "I'm sorry," she said. "In my heart I'm still alone. Anyway, the cove is quiet and deep and protected from the wind. My daughter and granddaughter will be safe with me. There are no predators, human or otherwise. We'll be back in four to eight hours, depending on the weather. But if a storm comes up, just wait, we'll be back as soon as it clears."

El and I followed Grandma Zu up the bluff to her big sledge and straddled the seat behind her. Everything felt so strangely normal. She drove slowly onto the ice and made her way around hills and ridges. She could see depressions in the snow that covered fragile ice caverns, and a hundred other things invisible to us. "There are a thousand kinds of ice," she said. Once, the ground shook beneath us and Grandma Zu shouted, "I'd hate to know what that is!" That's all she said to us the whole trip back.

We arrived at a wooden hut covered with thick grass. Of course, neither the wood nor the grass came from Antarctica because nothing grew there. Inside were some pots and pans, a cross bow, a shelf full of beakers and tubes like from an old sci-fi movie. It was pretty dirty, but Grandma Zu had a stove which she hooked up to her sledge. She said, "I wasn't expecting guests." There was a bunk which she wasn't using. She had her sleeping bag on the floor next to the stove.

"I want to get a couple things. We'll have some tea, to celebrate, then we'll be on our way. But I must tell you something first. The man who brought me here is dead. He's buried outside. His name is Werther Fausten."

"We heard his name in Buenos Aires," I said. "We were told he came here."

Grandma Zu didn't say anything to that. She made the tea and we sat. She took a little over a half-hour and told us about Werther Fausten, his story, his genius, his insanity, his dragon.

I kept quiet. Because everything seemed wrong. For the longest time aboard the ship, I felt I had been driven, called here by the dragon to meet her or maybe to meet Fausten, even though I hadn't known him. But now he was dead. There was no dragon here, not even the feeling or smell of one. A hard wind ripped against the shack, but it was just that, ordinary wind.

"You were with him," I said, "but you never saw her."

"No," said Grandma Zu. "I never saw her. At times, with him, it was as if I felt her. But we were alone on the ice and Fausten was powerful and mad. I felt a thousand absurd things."

"Not absurd," I said.

"Lisa believes in the dragon," El said to her mom.

"Not *believes*," I said. "Believers are people who haven't seen her. Believers don't dream. I'm one of the dreamers," I said. I told Grandma about Hunter and the Falkland Islands, and all the people we met, the stories, and the wondrous new communities under waterfalls, on cliffs, in trees, on the backs of horses.

"You haven't seen any of those," said El. "We didn't find anything on the Falkland Islands."

"We saw a barge city, an ocean city!" I said. I tried to explain that I'd felt and seen many of the things Fausten told her. Two very different people. A scientist and a teen-ager who never knew each other.

"There is much more, too," Grandma Zu said. "But not now." Then a huge wind shook the cabin again and Grandma Zu exhaled heavily. "We've stayed too long. That's a katabatic, I'm afraid.

We'll have to wait out a storm. But your people will be safe in the cove, and so shall we." She took both of our hands. She whispered, "The simplest things are so unbelievable. What do I do with this?"

Then she got up. She tethered herself to the shack and went outside to check our connection to the sledge that we knew now had been Fausten's. There was one tiny window and she covered it with a thick flap, then came inside where we secured old sheets of canvas against the walls from the ceiling to the floor. Then it was dark and the little cabin shook under the wind, though once the ground seemed to shake, too. Grandma Zu smiled at us. "I've been through much worse inside much less," she said, and she hugged us both.

"I have a letter from Dad," said El. And she gave Grandma Zu the letter from Grandpa Charles.

"I'll save it for a moment of repose," said Grandma Zu. "Let's stay close to each other and get some rest."

We fell asleep there together under Grandma Zu's thick sleeping bag, in her shack, beneath the howling storm. But I awoke in the middle of the short night to the sucking sound of huge lungs. The sides of the shack fell in and out and the air became hot and sweet. I tried to wake El and Grandma Zu but they slept so deeply it was as if they were hibernating. But everything else around me was now alive and breathing with the pulse of a huge heart.

Outside the door the wind was so strong it knocked me off my feet and I quickly grabbed Grandma Zu's tether and tied myself to the cabin. I crawled away from the shack, turning from the wind, trying to see. Then I heard a voice under the wind. It called a name, not mine. It said, "Werther." It was a moan lower than sound, in fact I didn't hear it, not in my ears, but felt it in my cells and my bones. "Werther," it said in a long, drawn-out lowing. It was painful like the cry of the abandoned seal pups, but low, whispery, moaning, "Whoooorrtherr." It filled the blowing air and yet lay under it, too. "Whoooorrtherr." I walked and crawled toward the sound. I don't know how far.

Below the gray clouds, a billowing, purple and scarlet thunderhead formed and a column of fire streaked from its center. The cloud split and unfurled, leaving a narrow bottom like a tail, its top pluming into two humps. Then I saw her at its center, her gigantic wings blasting up and down against the storm wind, her neck arching above the heart of clouds, the snow melting around her fire in buckets of rain. She exhaled flame into the sky and fell as if sliding down a tube of fire. She alighted before me on her hind legs, her forelegs extended and talons arching like scimitars from her fingertips. She was the size of an elephant. I stood before her, her heat so powerful, so fecund, that the storm fell around us as if we were in a shell. I looked away from her so she couldn't take my gaze and I saw that it took her aback. She lowered her forehead and offered me only one, slitted eye.

"Child, who are you?" she said, not in a voice but something deeper, a sensation that I felt in my blood. "I did not call you."

"He's dead," I said to her. "He can't fight you. He's dead."

"My enemy?" she said. "My love. My father." She lowered her head. I felt a sadness deeper than anything I had ever felt before, a despair so shattering it seemed my bones were disintegrating inside me. "You are telling the truth," she said. "I know. But I've waited and waited." She raised her neck and exhaled fire into the sky, the snow hissing above it into steam and then hot rain. "Where is he?" she said.

"Behind the cabin."

She stepped toward Werther Fausten's grave. "I will eat his corpsse," she said.

But I stepped in front of her. Her head lashed out and her breath seared my face. "You are not afraid of me?"

"Will you kill me?" I asked. "Is that why I should be afraid?"

"Yess," she said.

"I'm not afraid of that anymore," I said to her. "Are you immortal?"

"Are you?" she said.

"I don't know."

"Should I know anymore than you?"

"Did I see you in the Falklands?" I asked her.

"The Malvinas? Did you?"

"Did you kill the poets?"

"They wept over trivia."

"My father was one of them."

She tilted her head at me. "I am ssorry for you, not for him."

"Have you killed millions of people?" I said.

"I've killed no one."

"Virgin boys?"

"Well, hardly anyone," she said.

"You took my friend, Hunter."

She raised her head again and this time tried to hold my eyes, but I looked away again. "He *s*saved your boat." She opened her throat to me and sent out flame. "Life is like an object thrown into the air," she said.

"How did you knock out the satellites?" I asked her.

"Child!" she hissed and flame rolled in her mouth. Then she lowered her shoulders and let her wings rest on her back, their tips towering above her neck. "What if the *s*stars are just giant incinerators?"

"Why have you come?" I said to her.

She pulled her neck in and now stood in front of me half of her original size. "I am not *s*supernatural and yet I cannot be explained."

"That's why," I said to her.

She looked at me and I this time, because she'd drawn into herself, I met her gaze. "You dream," she said. "I know you."

"Will you kill everyone?"

"Not the dreamers. The dreamers shall rebuild."

"Not under you."

"Under me there is magic in the world again. And whether your *s*species *s*survives or not means nothing."

"Without us you won't exist."

"And like you, Li*ss*a Piccolo Zu," she said, "I am not afraid." She folded her wings over her legs and feet and retracted her neck until her chin rested on her chest. She looked not much bigger than me then, like an old woman.

"What is *your* name?" I said to her.

"Child, you are the fir*ss*t ever to a*ss*k." I felt her hiss deep inside my heart. "Humanity."

"What do you want?" I said. "Tell me. I've traveled thousands of miles to meet you and find out what you had to say."

She looked at me but shadowed her gaze with her eyelids. "A child," she said. "A girl. I hadn't thought of it."

"I will take you," I said to her. "I will love you."

"Do you dare? After all I have done? And that I might kill you for it?"

"I love you," I said, no longer speaking from my own voice, no longer even me, but something, someone both deep inside me and far, far away, and yet more essential than anything I could ever express. "I've loved you for a thousand lives."

The old woman stood in front of me. "Shield your eyes but do not look away," she said. She lifted one wing and there, in her chest, pulsed a bleeding, fiery heart. In myself, not in my body, but deeper, I trembled with a fire of horror and hopelessness and desire. "If I come to you," she moaned, "I could burn you alive. If I come inside you, it could be worse than death. You might live with all I have done and all I can do."

"I love you," I said. "Come to me."

"We shall *ssee.*"

And the old woman opened her wings. Her chest expanded and her head flew out upon her long neck. Her eyes, golden with black diamond slits, raged at me, and her heart burned, her blood burned, her skin dripped with acid and her scales fell upon the snow. Her wings expanded, blacker than nothingness and from her throat belched fire. I felt hate and sadness and despair. Before me I saw all of death. And I saw the corpse of every child who had died under her wings. Still I cried, "Come to me!" And the dragon spread her wings and stepped forward.

The heat of her breath scorched me. My nerves burned. My brain exploded with a thousand fears. And I became fire. I burned under the storm, the snow. A hot rain fell and boiled the ice at my feet. I felt myself bursting apart and saw the dragon walk into me. I felt her in my chest. I screamed. I was no longer anything but a scream and I screamed, "Humanity! Humanity!" And then it was over and the dragon was gone.

I heard El and Grandma Zu behind me, calling "Lisa! Lisa!" and crawling out to me through the storm on their tethers. They hugged me so hard.

"What are you doing out here?" yelled El.

I laughed and kissed them both as we staggered in the swirling, dark wind. I yelled, "I'm saving the world, of course!"

The Journal of Hestor Zu

Latigo Canyon, Malibu, California

I am Doctor Hestor Zu, the sole surviving member of the International Mars Mission stationed at the Mars Expedition Laboratory, the Amundsen-Scott Base, on the South Pole. It has not quite been five years since the events related here occurred. I have tried to give it all some time. Now it looks like there is plenty of time.

As my granddaughter has related, Captain Evans and his mate Angie, along with my daughter, El Wight, and her daughter, Lisa Piccolo Zu discovered me off the Ross Ice Shelf on the Edward VII Peninsula near Cape Colbek. I was hunting seals. It was late March, 2018.

By the time we reached Dunedin, New Zealand the level of the ocean had already begun to rise. We rested in Dunedin briefly, then Evans arranged passage on a New Zealand clipper for the three of us to, or toward at least, Los Angeles, or what was left of it. He made accommodations for four Chileans for passage to Santiago, as well. He stayed in New Zealand with his crew to wait for spring and attempt the run to the South Pole to rescue Adjoa Neri-Evans. I have never heard from any of them again.

New Zealanders are good sailors. Despite the changing weather and altered ocean currents due to the rising level of the ocean, we made it to the mouth of Latigo Canyon in about six months. The Pacific Coast Highway was under the sea, as was much of Los Angeles, and we made port well up the ascending canyon road. From there we walked home. And there was Charles.

In combination with the greenhouse effect and loss of the ozone layer above Antarctica, there had been a cluster of volcanic eruptions under the west Antarctic ice sheet, of which the eruptions of Erebus and Terror were just a few. The land underneath the shelf, long suppressed by the weight of the ice, now lay below sea level and the lava and gas undoubtedly pushed the already melting ice shelf over the brink. Glaciologists had predicted the possibility since the early greenhouse theory days, so I surmise that when the ice began slipping above, water poured in beneath it at the same time. The ground line eroded and the huge edges of the Ross Ice Shelf began to break off.

The Ross Sea filled with gigantic tabular icebergs and the process accelerated inland. Water rushed in and more bergs broke off and floated out. The western Antarctic ice shelves were gone. Less significantly, I would not have survived there another month. In the six months it took us to arrive home the ocean had risen almost five meters world wide. In the coming year it rose five meters more. Most coastal cities and even some countries like Bangladesh and Holland are under water. Looking back, it seems an inevitability. Anyway, it seems unlikely that we should blame a dragon. Or as Werther Fausten might say, with all his irony intact, thank her.

From everything I can gather, much like the other catastrophes of this century, the crisis produced less chaos than it did cooperation. The ocean rose slowly and the urban fishing coast moved back to the new shore. Community farms, more and more of them organized in concentric circles of villages within a day's walk of each other, much like the system employed over the centuries by the Chinese, came to the aid of the coastal populations, taking in people and giving out food. That's how it's been done here, though Charles, El, Lisa, and I are a bit remote. Still, there is a system of connecting farms that link us to the Concentric Community of Agoura just to the north.

Given that I gave Werther Fausten so much time to tell his story, and placed Lisa's journal here, too, I feel I should have my say. For me it seems obvious that the ecological disasters that have befallen the world can be viewed much like the collapse of the Antarctic Ice Shelves. They were inevitable. Global temperatures had been rising for decades. The ozone was disappearing, as well as the rain forests. Vital species were being rubbed out at a phenomenal rate.

Even before the purported Phenomenon, we could say, looking back, as early as the late Twentieth Century, that there had been increases in violent rain storms off the Pacific coast and in Asia and Europe, draught in Africa and on the Russian steppes, larger and more frequent Atlantic hurricanes, more tornadoes of unmeasurable power in the American South and Midwest.

The now famous updrafts, or quick-storms, sometimes referred to meteorologically as *mesocylcones*, were recorded in the Great Lakes region as early as 1998 and could easily have been confused, as well, with other weather phenomena like tornados and microbursts. Visions inside clouds have been reported for centuries and when not hallucinatory can usually be attributed to a number of optical phenomena due to reflected light: halos, Glory, Subsun, Sun Pillars, Green Flash, and Crepuscular Rays.

As for what remains as the total breakdown in airwave communication, our satellite systems, much like an inbred species, were univocal and fragile. Inexplicably, the sun has moved into a period of constant flaring. This had been known as a potential problem for years, yet no one took the time to diversify our technology or to think about a means to failsafe the system. Right now it seems like we live on a planet where microwaves, radio waves, and all forms of airwave communication have been rubbed out and we have no way to find out what's wrong or fix it because our means of fixing it are based on the things that are broken down. For the time being, we're stuck. But all things change. The solar flare-ups will inevitably end, even if it takes centuries. Likely we shall soon find a way around the problem. I hope we do better next time.

The disruption of communication and power over electric wire systems remains inexplicable. For some reason, after a mile or so, electric currents now break up, even along a wire. I do not understand the problem, though it is certainly not my field. Eventually, we will solve it and start over. Yet despite these ubiquitous disruptions in communication technologies, people were still in possession of cameras and battery-run video cams. Some of these meteorolgical events, which strike me by description as either *mesocyclones* or some sort of Pyrocumulus thunderstorms, should have been recorded.

If there were something besides the weather contained in them, I'd think there would be some recorded visual evidence.

Rumor is more difficult to quell than fact. For those who believe that the destruction which came upon us in the last decade was mainly aimed at destructive technology, or at mosques, temples and churches, I'd speculate that it was wishful thinking on the part of an ecological movement which had expected nature's vengeance religiously for years. In time, it spread by word of mouth into the population and wishful thinking became mass hysteria. In this current world, there is not much travel and no one has seen much of anything, but for my part I've found the destruction of buildings as well as the technological infrastructure rather ubiquitous. Neither do I rule out anti-religious terrorism or eco-terrorism on the part of humans once things got under way.

Some things, like the destruction of armies and navies, and the annihilation of nuclear and petroleum technologies, remain a mystery. Likely some of it, like huge naval vessels and bombers, as well as large nuclear and oil facilities, were the victims of this new kind of Pyrocumulus storm which arose from heat energy the way the more familiar kind arose from forest fires, even as one of Fausten's Nobel peers suggested. Once the chain reaction started, anything that stood out prominently above the ground became a target for lightning. And once the infrastructure began to fall, it fell like dominoes. It will be back, I surmise.

It is true that the human population is significantly diminished and that animal populations have grown like never before. Our coast is filled with whales and sea otters, shore birds and pinnipeds. Our hills flourish with hawks, eagles, deer, elk, and predators. And for the time being there are armies of people to protect them and strictly regulate the taking of game, and forests, even at the cost of human starvation. So deep is our fear now of that unknown thing which protected the animals from annihilation. I rejoice in this. Animals are my field of study and I have long opposed the reductionism which murdered them, experimented on them consciencelessly, treated them as objects, and denied their emotions and subjectivity. But I am a scientist, too. In all my time with Fausten, I never saw his beast. Nor did he. His sojourn over the Ross Ice Shelf seems to have followed the emergency escape routes that ran from the South

Pole to both Ross Island and the Bay of Whales, and between them along the shelf. I doubt he fell upon them by luck. More likely Fausten researched the region, then later, and deeper in his insanity, convinced himself that his protector had laid them in his path.

I do not believe in dragons. But my granddaughter does, even now that she is nineteen. And so did Werther Fausten, a man who once was one of the great geniuses of our day. But I knew Werther Fausten well, in his genius, in his humanity, in his madness. And my granddaughter, who now plays the guitar and draws and paints, though she has shown little interest in social life, particularly boys, is as yet a girl, and a girl whose childhood was robbed by world-wide disaster and an adventure to save my life which would have taxed the bravest of explorers to the edge of sanity. She is permitted her fantasies. In that way, she is no different than the rest of humanity, many of whom harbor some belief about a mythical, vengeful beast who purged the earth.

But this is a story. And if it became partially my story by happenstance, by coincidence, by my foolishness and my consequent survival, then too, it must in the end return to those who began it. In my story, two of the people who saved my life, Werther Fausten and Lisa Piccolo Zu, believed in a dragon.

It is Fausten's story, too, and I place it here because I promised him I would. And it is Lisa's story. I've tried to put it all together in a way that made some kind of sense. I shall give Lisa the last word and then commit this work to oblivion. It is now a world where there are few who publish and almost as few who read. Well, we were heading that way anyway.

For my part, that is fine. I have no commitment to art, nor immortality. I am with Charles Borromeo, my husband and my beloved. I am alive. I live. And what a wonderful thing it is to be born a human being.

Hestor Zu
June 21, 2022

The Dragon Journal of Lisa Piccolo Zu

I want to thank my grandmother for giving me the last word. I've read Werther Fausten's story and also my grandmother's commentary. I've reread my story, too, which was written more or less as the events occurred. If I was only a child then, I was neither foolish nor insane. The world has changed, though how it was before I barely know.

Both the past and future are dreams, if not the rest. I do not know why things happened as they did, but this dream in front of us, this new real world, was created by something deeper than any of us, deeper even than the depths of Werther Fausten. The gods that lie within us are the gods that lie outside as well. May they bless our destiny. May they bless our accident. May we remember that all things are holy. More than holy. They have feelings.

I did not create the dragon, nor did Fausten. He found her and so did I. And whether or not these words are communicated to all human beings or to a few, whether they are committed to all time or to oblivion, know this. The dragon exists. I am the dragon, Humanity. We are not all the dragon. I am the dragon. I am.

About the Author

CHUCK ROSENTHAL is the author of five novels, *Loop's Progress*, *Experiments With Life & Deaf*, *Loop's End*, *Elena of the Stars* and *Jack Kerouac's Avatar Angel*. His fiction has appeared in many journals including *The Santa Monica Review* and *The Denver Quarterly*. He is a full professor of English and Creative Writing at Loyola Marymount University.

He lives with poet Gail Wronsky, and their daughter Marlena in Topanga, California.

JACK KEROUAC'S AVATAR ANGEL

His Last Novel
by CHUCK ROSENTHAL

ISBN 0-9676003-2-4
$23.95 Hardcover

Chuck Rosenthal discovers a lost, unpublished manuscript from the King of the Beats—Jack Kerouac—who returns from the grave to set off one last time, charting chart the experience and conscience of a generation grappling with a changed culture. At once visionary and elegant, restless and incantatory, Rosenthal's writing achieves a rare beauty, his sensitivity to language as great as Kerouac's. In an exuberant novel of great wit and great loss, the emptiness Kerouac encounters in this final journey is palpable and tragic, unforeseen but inevitable, both familiar and foreign to America's most famous mystic traveler.

Hollyridge Press

"You will be dazzled and amazed."
— **David St. John**

THE LOVE-TALKERS
An Erotic Fable
by GAIL WRONSKY

ISBN 0-9676003-3-2
$23.95 Hardcover

The beauty of Gail Wronsky's poetic language has never been better displayed than in *The Love-talkers*. Mexico City, with its parks and cathedrals provides a lush backdrop for the story. A sumptuously rendered book, celebrating passionate imagination with all the sublime joy of physical love, Wronsky's elegiac style summons up the magic of Latin American fiction in this novel of desire which brings us into the depths of erotic charge. From ecstatic awakenings to feverish enactments of appetite, Wronsky's novel reveals what happens when we find our deepest yearnings made true.

"An amazing use of language and clarity
of description compels the reader on."
—**Patricia Gulian**, *Book/Mark*

HUNGER
and Other Stories
by Ian Randall Wilson

ISBN 0-9676003-0-8
$12.95 Paperback

In his first collection of short stories, Ian Randall Wilson's
characters are driven by intense yearnings for the satisfaction of their most basic human desires. All are thwarted by
personal shortcomings, or the shortcomings of others, in
their attempts to fulfill their longing. Here are 14 stories
which "despite their restlessness," former *North American
Review* editor Robley Wilson says, "glitter with persistent
hopes."

"Alexander is an accomplished writer with a deft hand for characterization."
— **Hillary Johnson**, *LA Weekly*

THE FINAL AUDIT
and Other Stories
by Ronald Alexander

ISBN 0-9676003-1-6
$12.95 Paperback

In Ronald Alexander's debut novel, Dexter Giles lives a double life, balancing a straight-jacketed career in the homophobic towers of corporate culture with his secret world as a gay man. Nancy Lamb writes, "The interconnected stories in this novel are serious and unforgettable and told with humor and insight. Alexander displays an intuitive grasp of the complexity of family relationships and the power of long-term friendships."

Hollyridge Press

NEW POETRY ANNUAL
The best in American poetry!

88

A Journal of Contemporary
American Poetry (Issue 1)
Denise L Stevens (editor)

ISBN 0-9676003-4-0
$13.95 Paperback

Issue 1 features an amazing range of poetry:
—The wonderfully comic sensibilities of Amiri Baraka: "I get horrible letters / From Ghosts / Demanding / Money."
—Dean Young writes in an echo of the New York School: "I don't ask for much: a little cleavage, / the honey of deconstruction to go along / with my cereal but something's scorched / my curtsey, one of my eyes's funny."
—Roger Weingarten's poignant narrative poem about fathers: "Into the no man's land / behind the flimsy curtain of my / resolve not to let them / get to me."
—Postmodernism from Gail Wronsky: "She's // greasy as a melancholy rhyme. What / self-esteems are   each day, paradoxically, / dismantled in her beehive?"
Plus essays and reviews. . .

Hollyridge Press

THE BEST IN AMERICAN POETRY!

88

A Journal of Contemporary
American Poetry (Issue 2)
Ian Randall Wilson (editor)

ISBN 0-9676003-6-7
$13.95 Paperback

Including the work of:

Barry Ballard	Jim Barnes	Bill Berkson
Killarney Clary	Patricia Corbus	Stephen Corey
Stuart Dischell	Richard Garcia	Reginald Gibbons
Joy Gladding	Elton Glaser	Rachel Hadas
Jonathan Holden	Mark Jarman	Kate Knapp Johnson
Peter Johnson	Carolyn Lei-lanilau	Gerald Locklin
Fred Moramarco	Elisabeth Murawski	Mary Ruefle
Ron Silliman	Alan Sondheim	Terese Svoboda
James Tate	Elaine Terranova	Susan Wheeler
Charles Harper Webb	Eve Wood	Gail Wronsky

Plus reviews. . .

Praise for *Elena of the Stars*

"Chuck Rosenthal writes courageously, lyrically, about everything in the world that matters most."

—Pam Houston

"One of the great American baroque voices. To read him once is to become an enthusiast."

—Tom Keneally

"A passionate, shimmering fable of man and nature, good and evil, life, death, and achingly transcendent love."

—Carolyn See

"Rosenthal's work is achingly and brutally beautiful."

—*Buzz*

"He is astonishing . . . his plots weave themselves from the fears of the characters, rising like smoke from the fire of old bones and unfinished stories."

—*LA Times*

Praise for the *Loop Trilogy*

"Chuck Rosenthal is bold and brawny, deft and original."
—Boston Globe

"Rosenthal keeps us on the literary ropes, waiting for the knockout."
—Philadelphia Inquirer

"Lovely, turbulent—language like a whitewater rapid that tumbles, disrupts everything in its path, carves out its own unstable geography in which nothing matters but the ceaseless terrible movement of words. And it makes you weep."
—Francois Camoin

"Rosenthal begs to be read aloud."
—LA Times

"Toughly philosophical and memorable."
—Publishers Weekly

"Unwary with the ferocity of his pessimism. Like reading Sterne and Celine."
—Washington Post

"Sucked in, submerged, you may have the feeling that you'll never be able to get out again."
—Salt Lake City Tribune

"Chuck Rosenthal takes aim and always hits."
—New York Times Book Review

www.ingramcontent.com/pod-product-compliance
Lightning Source LLC
Chambersburg PA
CBHW020828260626
47169CB00003B/879